THE PERILS OF POISON AND FORMER HUSBANDS

Also by Rachel Gates

A Brilliant Convergence

THE PERILS OF POISON AND FORMER HUSBANDS

RACHEL GATES

WordCrafts Press

Hardback ISBN: 978-1-967649-24-2
Paperback ISBN: 978-1-967649-25-9

Published by WordCrafts Press
Cody, Wyoming 82414
www.wordcrafts.net

To my husband, who is handsome and charming,
but is certainly not a rogue or a cad.
I love you always.

Christmas Guest List

~ Rupert and Sarah Cunningham, hosts

~ Miss Winifred Osbourne, friend of Sarah

~ Arthur and Mary Cunningham,

Rupert's brother and sister-in-law

~ Lord Belvoir, Marquess, friend of Rupert

~ Mr. Loughty, cousin to Lord Belvoir

~ Miss Loughty, cousin to Lord Belvoir

~ Lord Worthington, Viscount, friend of Rupert

~ Lord Hadleigh, Earl, Lord Worthington's guest

~ Miss Maureen Price, Rupert's elderly aunt

~ Miss Taylor, young debutante and ward of Miss Price

~ Mrs. Emsworth, friend of Sarah

~ Mr. Emsworth, Mrs. Emsworth's son

Chapter 1

December 20th, 1890

Sitting on a divan draped in lambswool by the fire, it was easy to see why my friend Sarah valued the comforts of home and hearth. She sat on the armchair next to me, adjacent to a blazing fire, knitting a small pair of mittens for one of the children sprawled lazily on the rug with a jigsaw puzzle. The occasional newspaper rustle and contemplative murmur across from us told me Sarah's husband, Rupert, hadn't yet begun his customary post-luncheon nap. Snow was falling softly outside, and festive greenery lined the hearth and was twisted into wreaths over each window and door.

All together, it was a picture-perfect advertisement for domestic English life in the countryside. It was enough to warm the heart and bring a tear to the eye of any spinster of twenty-seven—like myself. I, Winifred Osbourne, was only in danger of tears of boredom.

"Winnie, darling, isn't that remarkable?"

"Pardon? I'm afraid I was absorbed in my book," I lied, waving around the third novel I'd started this week. At this rate I was going to read through the Cunninghams' entire library before 12th Night.

I tried to divine which of the two rosy-cheeked children on the floor was responsible for the *remarkable* task. Addie was a bright-eyed six-year-old with as much energy as her rambunctious curls, and Thomas a rather shy lad of eight. They'd given up on their puzzle and were attempting to flip the pieces into an abandoned tea cup on the table.

"They are remarkable, love," I confirmed with a grin.

Sarah giggled.

"Not the children, Winnie! I said isn't it remarkable that we're going to have three Lords at our Christmas house party! And unmarried ones at that. Lord Belvoir I know is a widower, though I do think Lord Worthington might be betrothed." She absently chewed on her lower lip in a way she'd always done when we were studying together at school, her blonde curls spilling out from behind a lace mob cap. "But he's bringing a friend, another Lord something-or-other that has nowhere to go for the holiday, and I daresay he could be single."

I tactfully managed not to roll my eyes.

"Being a Lord, no doubt he has plenty of places he could go, but I'm sure none could hold a candle to your hospitality. Must I remind you they can all be betrothed, as far as it pertains to me. You know I adore you, but I must return to my studies at the *Académie Julian* in January. I'm hardly on the lookout for a husband."

"Winifred is an independent woman, darling," Rupert reminded his wife from behind his newspaper. "She's a talented artist and a traveling woman of the world. And for all we know, she has a dashing Parisian beau to get back to." Lowering his newspaper, he waggled his eyebrows at us, sending his wife into another fit of the giggles.

His defense of my spinsterhood and eccentric career choice warmed my heart. I hadn't seen Sarah since we'd finished our studies at Miss Ellis's School for Girls more than a decade prior. She'd married Rupert after her first season, and I'd moved to the Continent with my grandfather and had lived abroad ever since. Sarah and I had kept in touch via long, monthly letters, and since my arrival nearly a fortnight ago, they'd treated me like part of the family.

"Nothing as exciting as all that, I'm afraid. I've just become accustomed to doing as I please. I've known other women painters in my program who've married, and their husbands forced them to give up their art. I'm afraid most men still don't see it as a legitimate career choice as you do, Rupert."

"Nonsense!" Sarah looked affronted. "No one could see your paintings and expect you to abandon your art, Winnie. You have real talent!"

"So did they," I muttered darkly.

"Well, anyway, three Lords is quite out of the ordinary for our humble home. Even if you don't desire to marry any of them, it shall make for an interesting house party."

There was a topic I could warm to. While the Cunninghams' sprawling estate was far from humble, it was rather quiet. I'd only been in residence for two weeks, and I'd already explored the entire house and grounds, had hours of conversation with Sarah, and read a stack of books that had grown taller than my nightstand. I'd only brought a sketchbook and small case of watercolors with me, so there wasn't much art I could create at the moment, and I wasn't used to being idle. At least the arrival of nearly a dozen guests tomorrow would liven up our little country Christmas celebration.

"Is there anything I can do to help you prepare?" I asked hopefully, looking for a job to occupy my time. "I confess I'm not used to being a lady of leisure."

"Oh no, Mrs. Hudgins has it all in stride I'm sure." Sarah dismissed the notion with a wave of her knitting needles, dashing my hopes of gainful employment. "She and the maids have prepared all the rooms, and will have a cold luncheon laid out in the sitting room for everyone to partake of as they arrive. You only have to be personable and help me welcome the guests."

Despite the talents of Sarah's capable housekeeper, the hostess herself flitted around with excitement the following morning, filling decorative bowls with colorful sweets, leaving her favorite perfumed soaps in guests' rooms, and going over the menus with the cook one last time. She was the perfect hostess, and she shone with anticipation. I was delighted to see my friend so happy, and endeavored to keep myself out of the way by painting watercolors with the children in the nursery.

Thomas proved himself a quick study. I vowed to encourage Rupert to hire the boy a proper art tutor until he began his studies at Eton. Addie, however, quickly abandoned her paints in favor of watching carriages arrive through the large picture window overlooking the front lawn. The snow drifted down in fat, lazy flakes, making the whole scene look like a Christmas card.

"Oh, Auntie Winnie, do come see, I think she might be a princess!" She watched a young lady disembarking in an elaborate traveling costume.

Thomas peered out over his very nice rendition of the nearby forest and huffed.

"If she's a princess, then the lady with her is an old dragon. That's Aunt Maureen."

I watched the sour-faced elderly aunt and her beautiful young companion greet Sarah and Rupert on the snowy steps, then make their way inside. The next carriage to arrive contained a well-dressed gentleman and a stylish older woman, the next a married couple with a young daughter ("cousin Fanny!" the children exclaimed before rushing out of the room and down the stairs to greet her), and the last carriage held two gentlemen and a lady. I wondered if three of the gentlemen that had arrived were the three Lords, or if there were more yet to come.

That evening, I was introduced to all the guests as we waited in the salon for the dinner bell. Apparently the snow had picked up and rendered traveling quite slow, so we were still waiting on two latecomers, but most members of our house party had arrived. Arthur Cunningham, Rupert's younger brother, was just as easy-going and jovial as Rupert. With the same brown eyes and prominent noses, they reminded me of a pair of basset hounds, laughing and joking and chatting animatedly with all the guests. Arthur's wife, Mary, was quiet with wide, doe-like eyes, but she greeted me with a sweet smile and a peck on each cheek in the French fashion, and I liked her immediately. I'd met their daughter, Fanny in the nursery that afternoon, and she was a miniature, six-year-old version of her mother. She was obviously close to Addie and Thomas, and the three children soon had a whole week's worth of adventures planned out.

The other blood relative of the bunch was Miss Maureen Price, Rupert and Arthur's aunt, and I realized within seconds of meeting her why Thomas had called her an old dragon.

"This is Miss Winifred Osbourne, the dear school friend I was telling you about, Aunt Maureen," Sarah said in a loud voice, leaning towards the elderly woman and enunciating carefully. "She's an artist at the prestigious *Académie Julian* in Paris, and is visiting us for the holidays. She is quite talented, and she spent the afternoon teaching the children to paint with watercolors."

Sarah glowed, clearly quite proud of me, the dear, but Miss Price's mouth had pursed severely at the word *artist* and had only gotten more prune-like from there. The wizened woman looked me up and down, making very clear what she thought about my profession when she turned to Sarah instead of speaking a word to me.

"Artists all have loose morals, Sarah, and the French are even worse. You cannot mean to trust her around your children."

She then turned sharply and marched over to where her goddaughter, Miss Taylor, was sitting, nudging the girl over none-too-gently with her cane, and sat down creakily beside her.

I sighed and shrugged at Sarah, whose mouth was clamped shut and face turning an alarming shade of red.

"Don't let her bother you, dearest. It certainly isn't the first time I've been judged morally loose for my profession, and I'm sure it won't be the last."

Sarah was forced to let the matter go as Mr. Emsworth and his mother entered the room. Mr. Emsworth was a slight man that I guessed to be about Rupurt's age, well-dressed, but with thick spectacles and a brown cowlick that looked as if it had been oiled back but had not taken kindly to the endeavor, as it now stuck up like a cockerel's comb. His mother was well past middle age, but still quite beautiful, with thick auburn curls only lightly threaded with silver. Her clothes and jewelry were of the finest taste and quality, and she had a regal bearing about her. Her son smiled kindly at me, and they apparently had no qualms about artists or the French, for the three of us conversed agreeably about her most recent trip to Paris for another quarter of an hour until dinner was served.

In between the hearty—albeit very English—courses, I had the opportunity to talk with the charismatic Lord Belvoir, whom Sarah had seated on my right, and his cousins Mr. and Miss Loughty. When Sarah had said Lord Belvoir was a widower, I'd expected an elderly gentleman, but the man at my side couldn't have been older than forty-five and proved an incorrigible flirt. He spoke fondly of his wife, however, who had passed away two years before, and he possessed enough self-effacing good humor that I knew not to take his flirtations too seriously. Mr. Loughty seemed more reserved, but he was amiable and very attentive to his sister, whom I guessed to be several years his junior and was seated across from me. Miss Loughty was dressed simply but extremely elegantly, and managed to project an air that was at once regal and graceful but also approachable. I liked her immediately, especially after she proclaimed herself an avid reader and asked me for recommendations from the Cunninghams' library. I promised to deliver her all the favorites from my ever-growing book tower later that evening.

I was sitting with Sarah, Miss Loughty, and Mrs. Emsworth in the parlor after dinner, pleased I would have some intelligent companions to converse with over the next fortnight, when a commotion in the hall indicated that the Cunninghams' last two guests had made it through the storm and finally arrived.

"Oh!" Sarah clapped her hands, looking nearly as youthful as the young Miss Taylor sitting across the tea table from us. "Lord

Worthington and his guest must be here! I'm so glad they're not stuck in a snowdrift somewhere."

A man entered the room and was greeted by Rupert and Lord Belvoir.

"That's Lord Worthington," Sarah whispered from behind her tea cup. He was handsome, with light brown hair and a close-cropped beard and mustaches that were fiery red. His mouth crinkled jovially when he smiled at Rupert, and his eyes were kind. He looked like the kind of man Rupert would get along famously with.

Just then, the drawing room door flew open as if blown by the very storm outside, and the final member of our cozy Christmas house party blew in. He was tall and dark, with broad shoulders and chiseled features that would not have been out of place on a Botticelli masterpiece. Crystal blue eyes scanned the room as he began to work his way towards Rupert and Lord Worthington, but he stopped short when he spotted me, frozen in place, my mouth hanging slightly agape.

The newcomer was none other than Lord Hadleigh, the slimiest, vilest blackheart I'd ever met wrapped up in the face of Adonis. This man was a reprobate, a no-good scoundrel, and we'd all be well-warned to quit the room as fast as our legs would carry us.

I was a bit of an expert on the subject.

You see, I'd been his wife.

<h1 style="text-align:center">Chapter 2</h1>

My mouth was as parched as a summer's day in Sicily, and I was vaguely aware that my teacup was about to tremble right off its saucer. I hastily returned it to the table in front of me, clenching my hands in my lap and sitting straight as a ramrod. The ladies sitting around me carried on their conversations, oblivious to the effort it was taking me just to keep breathing.

I was about to make my excuses and escape to my room when the group of gentlemen crossed the room towards us. *Damn.* Well, Winifred Osbourne was not a coward. I steeled myself and mentally calculated how long it had been since I'd seen or spoken to Benjamin Hadleigh. Nearly a decade—not nearly long enough.

"Lord Worthington! So delightful to see you!"

Sarah leapt to her feet and clasped the man's hand in hers. He kissed her hand gallantly and turned to introduce his friend. I wondered if he knew the man was the devil incarnate.

"Mrs. Cunningham, allow me to introduce my dear friend Lord Hadleigh."

"The pleasure is mine," said the reprobate, looking every inch the wealthy Lord. Though understated, his suit jacket spoke of the finest tailoring money could buy, his beard and mustaches were close-cropped and expertly groomed, and his boots shone to perfection despite the conditions outdoors.

"Please, call me Benjamin. I feel as though we are old friends already; Worthington has told me so much about you and Rupert."

Wrongly interpreting my dumbstruck silence, Sarah reached down to grab my arm, pulling me to my feet so I was standing next to her.

"And you must call me Sarah, of course! Please, allow me to introduce my very dear friend Miss Winifred Osbourne." Sarah looked at me with a gleam in her eye. The wretch was enjoying this encounter, though I would forgive Sarah as she had no idea what it was costing me. She couldn't know. She would never know.

I ground my teeth but managed a polite smile for Lord Worthington and a nod to the devil.

"Oh, but Miss Osbourne and I are already acquainted." My former husband was nothing if not smooth, and I tried not to flinch.

Oh yes. How very well acquainted. An image popped into my head, unbidden: the pair of us swimming naked in the moonlit Mediterranean. My cheeks heated, and I forced myself not to look away. At least now I wouldn't look half dead. I cocked my head and waited to see how the silver-tongued serpent would explain this one.

"We were childhood friends, you see, our families' estates bordered on one another. I haven't seen Miss Osbourne in many, many years."

That much was true at least.

"Lord Hadleigh, how very nice to see you after all this time."

That was most certainly not true, but my voice was remarkably steady.

"Oh Winnie, it can't be that Lord Hadleigh is Benji, the childhood friend that you were always running about with on school breaks?"

Sarah looked at me incredulously, but with a twinkle in her eye that didn't bode well for my future peace.

"The one and the same." I tried to smile at her, but it turned into more of a grimace, and Sarah blinked at me, confused. "We lost touch after Grandfather and I moved abroad."

My hand nervously smoothed the dark green brocade of

my evening dress, a dress that was the first order of fashion in Paris. I'd always thought it quite becoming on me, but suddenly I wished I was wearing something drab and plain like my painting smock, something that didn't display quite so much of my bosom or hug my curves to perfection. Benjamin's watchful eye caught me fiddling, and I stilled. I would not give this man a moment of satisfaction by showing any discomfort.

"Winnie is working as an artist in Paris," Sarah was telling the two men, and I was grateful to her for giving me a moment to compose myself. "She is staying with us for the season. It's the first time she's been back to England in a decade, can you imagine that!"

"Well, England is certainly lucky to have you back, Miss Osbourne," Lord Worthington said. "Hadleigh here is a great lover of art himself, perhaps you will show him some of your works. I'm sure you have loads to catch up on."

A shadow flitted across Benjamin's face, telling me he was about as thrilled at that suggestion as I was. He needn't worry, since I was now plotting how quickly I could escape this little house party.

"Sadly, I've left all my art in Paris since I'm only here for a short time."

Very, very short.

We somehow finished the pleasantries and Rupert proceeded to take Lord Worthington and Benjamin around the room to introduce them to the other guests. Mrs. Emsworth asked Sarah a question about the week's festivities, and they happily conversed for a few moments before Sarah turned and noticed my face.

"Winnie dear, are you quite alright? You look alarmingly pale."

"I'm fine, dearest, just a bit of a headache. I think I'll retire a little early tonight."

I made my excuses to the ladies sitting around us and slipped out the door. Once alone in the hall, I'm ashamed to admit I practically ran to my room and didn't stop to breathe until I'd slammed and locked the door behind me. I was as bad as the heroine in a Gothic novel running from imaginary ghosts!

Only my ghost was far from imaginary. He was very real and as dangerous as he was charming.

I lay awake for several hours considering my options. Assuming I could make it through the snow to the train station, I could begin the journey back home to Paris in the morning, missing out on my first English Christmas in ten years. Sarah would be terribly disappointed. But worst of all, Benjamin would likely consider me a coward. I may have been a starry-eyed, green girl of eighteen when I married him, but I was now a confident, worldly woman.

As he had told our friends earlier, we grew up on neighboring estates. Four years my senior, Benjamin was my playmate, my hero from the moment I came to live with my grandfather at age six after my parents died. I adored him and followed him everywhere. When he went off to Eton at thirteen, I cried for a week, but he still made plenty of time to visit me over school holidays. Under my grandfather's watchful and adoring eye, Benjamin taught me to ride and to shoot. And when Grandfather wasn't looking, he taught me to play cards. Benjamin's brother had been eight years his senior, and he'd never made time for Benji as Benji did for me. Thus, I was Benji's best friend in the world, and he mine.

It was no wonder, then, that I fell headlong in love with him as a girl of fourteen. He'd come back from Eton for a summer before going up to Oxford.

"C'mon, Freddie, race you to the other side," he'd said like always, running towards the lake and peeling off his shirt. I stood there on the bank and looked at his broadening shoulders and stubbled jaw as though seeing him for the first time. From then on there was no doubt in my mind who I was going to marry. If only I'd known then what it would cost me.

Benjamin had seemed just as surprised to see me this evening as I was to see him. Since Paris was my home now, and I had no family left in England, a snowy house party in York was a rather unlikely place to run into me. But considering we grew up together and moved in the same circles for the first two decades of our lives, our paths had been bound to cross again someday. I had just planned on that someday being much farther in the future. After everything that had happened, I could not—would not—give him the satisfaction of running me off from my friend's home—a friend he hadn't even met until this evening.

I would have to stay through Christmas at least, and attempt to avoid the guttersnipe. That was only four days away. There were plenty of other pleasant people in the house to talk to, and when I needed to, I could escape to the nursery under the pretense of continuing the children's art education. And there were always the novels. I sighed and rolled over, glancing at the stack of books looming in the darkness like a phantom beside my bed. I had completely forgotten to bring a few to Miss Loughty. Well, sleep didn't appear to be within my grasp anytime soon, so there was no time like the present.

It was well past midnight now, and most of the household had surely retired, but I could leave the books outside her door in case she found herself unable to sleep as I was and in need of something to read. I lit the oil lamp next to my bed and crossed to the desk, scribbled a hasty note to Miss Loughty, and picked two mysteries, a volume of poetry, and a reasonably interesting biography out of the stack.

Donning my dressing gown, I padded quietly across the hall and down two doors to where I knew Sarah had placed Miss Loughty for the week. The curse of my excellent visual memory was that even mundane details like the guest bedroom chart Sarah had asked me to assist her with lived rent-free in my head for all eternity. I didn't bother bringing the lamp with me, for my eyes quickly adjusted back to the dark. Setting the books gently on the thick carpet, I slipped the note under her door, hoping that if she were awake, she would see the note and retrieve the books I'd promised. If not, she'd simply find them in the morning and have them at her disposal. I heard no stirring within the room, so I turned to return to my own room—and stifled a gasp.

At the other end of the long landing that separated our two hallways, Benjamin slipped quietly out of a room. I could see him clearly in the glow from his candlestick, while I remained still and unseen in the darkness. I held my breath and watched as he came closer to the landing, then stilled and looked straight ahead as if he sensed someone watching him. There was no way the light of his candle could reach me this far down, so I remained silent, and after a few tense moments he turned away and entered his own room. When the door clicked shut behind him, I raced back to my room, shutting the door as quietly as possible.

Sleep, however, still eluded me for quite some time.

Chapter 3

The next morning dawned clear and cold, and I squinted at the sun reflecting off the snow below my window as the maid, Betsy, started my fire and opened the curtains.

"Goodness, what time is it?"

I blinked the sleep out of my eyes and struggled to sit up.

"Nearly time for breakfast, miss. The missus said not to wake you until the last minute, since you'd had the headache last night."

I let the girl help me dress in a warm, rich emerald velvet day dress, but I barely heard her cheerful chatter as I pondered what Benjamin could have been doing out of his room last night. He'd been fully dressed, but shoeless, as though he were trying to creep along the hallway as quietly as possible. His midnight assignations were hardly any of my business, but unless his proclivities had changed a great deal over the last nine years, it seemed unlikely he was having an amorous rendezvous in the bachelor's wing. If my memory served me correctly, and it usually did, he'd been leaving Mr. Emsworth's room. Had the other gentlemen been inside? Or were there more late-night revelers still downstairs?

I was the last guest down to breakfast, and I tried to slip in unnoticed as everyone chatted over cups of tea and coffee. Most of the gentlemen had apparently already departed for some morning activity, so I was spared the torture of having to converse politely with Benjamin at the moment. In fact, the only gentleman still present was Mr. Emsworth. He was seated across from his mother and reading a newspaper, or at least attempting to read a newspaper in between answering Mrs. Emsworth's constant chatter with polite nods and "mmm…hmmm, of course, Mother." After filling my plate at the sideboard, I was about to head over to where Sarah and Miss Loughty were having a cozy chat, when I thought better of it, and slid in next to Mr. and Mrs. Emsworth instead.

"Is this seat taken?" I smiled cheerfully when Mr. Emsworth looked up in surprise, his mother matching my smile brightly.

"Of course not, dear!" She looked genuinely delighted for the company. Mr. Emsworth was likely hopeful that I would come distract his mother for a spell, so he could read in peace. I gave him a sympathetic smile, but he wasn't about to get off the hook that easily.

"I'm afraid I nearly missed breakfast this morning." I tapped gently at a soft-boiled egg and scooped it onto my toast, amazed I could manage such an appetite knowing my scapegrace former husband was somewhere on the Cunninghams' estate. "It took me ages to fall asleep last night due to my headache. Did the rest of the party stay up late, Mr. Emsworth?"

If Mr. Emsworth was startled that I directed my question at him, he didn't show it. I suspected the man had the patience of a saint. He lowered his newspaper for a moment, pushed his spectacles up his nose, and answered me with a shy smile.

"The ladies retired before midnight, I believe, but many of the gentlemen stayed up until at least one in the morning playing cards." Mr. Emsworth spoke slowly and deliberately, but whether he was prevaricating or this was how he always conversed, I couldn't say. I suspected the latter. "I have no taste for poker, myself, and attempted to start a new historical account I've been eager to read."

He began to raise the newspaper, but I wasn't finished.

"I imagine Lord Worthington and Lord Hadleigh were eager to get to bed early after their harrowing journey through the snow."

"Lord Hadleigh was, I believe, as he made his excuses and went up to bed shortly after the ladies retired. Lord Worthington, however, seemed rather interested in the book I was reading, as he kept peppering me with questions."

Mr. Emsworth sighed, as if all he wanted in the world was for someone to leave him alone to read in peace.

"Eventually, I suggested he find his own historical account from the Cunninghams' library, and he finally retired as well. I confess at that point, my heart wasn't in it, and I retired shortly after. I believe the rest of the gentlemen played cards for a while more. It's a wonder they were able to rouse themselves for an excursion so early. They were all out before I made it down to breakfast this morning."

Mr. Emsworth looked as if that were perfectly fine with him, and raised his newspaper with another sigh. Taking some pity upon the beleaguered gentleman, I turned to his mother, who had been watching our exchange somewhat curiously.

"And where did the gentlemen run off to so early?"

I schooled my features into something like polite curiosity. I had originally assumed they were out riding, but judging from the depth of the snow I could now see out the breakfast room window, that would have been a rather difficult endeavor. I needed to know what the devil was up to and when he would return.

"I believe Mr. Cunningham mentioned hiking up the road in snowshoes to cut up a tree that has fallen over the main village road. They left quite early so traffic back and forth to the village could be restored. I imagine they'll be back before long."

I then asked Mrs. Emsworth about her favorite Paris modistes, and spent the next quarter of an hour nodding politely as she waxed on about this season's styles. I offered a few of my preferred dressmakers, but my mind was entirely fixed on what Benjamin Hadleigh had been up to last night. Mr. Emsworth had not been in his room when I'd seen Benjamin exiting, for which I was strangely relieved, but it also meant Benjamin had been in his room without his knowledge or permission.

Images of Benjamin's father and older brother, Augustus,

flashed across my mind. The crusty old Earl had been a consummate liar and philanderer, while Augustus had been a drunkard and a gambler. When the Earl had died suddenly and Augustus inherited the title at the young age of twenty-six, we'd all hoped that he would take the chance to grow up and change his wastrel ways. Overwhelmed with his new duties, however, he leaned into his bad habits and began to slowly drink himself to death. His one saving grace, if you could call it that, was that he refused to marry and failed to saddle a wife with the burden of his vices. Perhaps he'd seen enough pain caused by the Earl's infidelities, perhaps he just couldn't be bothered to expend the extra energy. Instead, he ran the estate and completed his parliamentary duties during the day, and drank himself into a stupor every evening, pinning all his hopes for the family lineage and future Earldom on Benjamin.

How foolish I'd been to think that Benjamin would be any different. Petty theft did seem rather beneath him, however, as he surely had more funds than any one man could spend in his lifetime, despite Augustus' excesses. What, then, did he stand to gain by sneaking about in other guests' rooms? I'd watched Benjamin and Lord Worthington as they had been introduced to Mr. Emsworth last night. There'd been no flicker of recognition on Mr. Emsworth's face, so they didn't seem to be prior acquaintances.

After a few more moments of inconsequential chatter with Mrs. Emsworth, she was beginning to get a familiar gleam in her eye. I'd seen it many times before when a mother was having trouble marrying off her son and decided that a personable, decent-looking spinster of twenty-seven like myself was exactly what she needed to get the job done. Not wanting to give her false hope, I pushed aside my now-empty breakfast plate and stood.

"Thank you so much for the lovely breakfast conversation Mrs. Emsworth, Mr. Emsworth. I'm afraid I told Sarah I'd help her plan the ladies' Christmas activities as soon as I was up this morning, and I'd better not keep her waiting any longer."

Nodding to them both, I scurried over to where Sarah and

Miss Loughty were still nursing cups of tea, though they had unfortunately been joined by the formidable Miss Price. I was not to be deterred, however, and sat down with a bright smile on my face.

"Winnie! Good morning, dearest! How was your conversation with the Emsworths?" Sarah offered me a fresh cup of tea from the table in front of her, and I took it gratefully.

"Mrs. Emsworth looked lonely with only her son and his newspaper for company." I gave Sarah a wry smile. "We mostly chatted about her favorite Parisian dressmakers. How are you all this morning?"

"I was just telling Aunt Maureen and Miss Loughty about the Christmas crafts we've planned for the ladies today. First, we're going to arrange some greenery to put in vases around the house, and then Mary is going to teach us how to craft these adorable angel paper chains she and Fanny make every year."

Miss Price sniffed. "Now there's a respectable creative pursuit."

She looked down her nose at me through her spectacles in a way that reminded me of Miss Ellis, the founder and strict headmistress of Miss Ellis' School for Girls. For a brief moment, I was fifteen again and desperate to become a proper lady and make Lady Hadleigh proud of me—to make myself a respectable candidate for wife of an Earl's second son. I shivered and sat up a little straighter.

Sarah must have also seen the resemblance to Miss Ellis, because she attempted to stifle a giggle behind her teacup and sloshed a few drops onto her pale pink morning dress. While she dabbed at the damp spot with a napkin, I simply nodded at Miss Price, as if she'd said something very wise, and turned to Miss Loughty.

"Did you find the stack of books I left you last night?"

"I did! You are too kind. I hardly expected you to haul books over to my room when you retired with a headache. I'm sure I could have fended for myself for one night."

Miss Loughty smiled at me, and I thought that perhaps we

could be kindred spirits. She was pretty, with light brown hair and a charming smile, and her eyes sparkled with intelligence. I judged her to be somewhere between the adorable, button-nosed Miss Taylor (just out of the schoolroom) and myself in age.

"Well, it took me ages to fall asleep, so I thought that I might as well bring you a few to get you started. The biography was a bit slow, but it was the perfect thing to get me to sleep each night. The mysteries were quite entertaining, though."

"Perhaps then you should have kept the biography last night to lull you into sleep. I also retired somewhat early; I'm always so tired after a day of travel. The maid brought the books to me this morning when she came in to stoke the fire."

"A true lady only reads works that will improve her moral character or instruct her to be a dutiful wife." Miss Price nodded sagely at Miss Loughty and I as if we'd asked her opinion. "I can recommend several volumes of sermons in the estate's library. My late brother, Rupert, and Arthur's father, made sure the library was well-stocked with religious texts. None of these horrid novels that are all the rage among ladies these days."

Miss Price glared at me as though I were personally responsible for the corruption of young women everywhere. Thankfully for the rest of us, Rupert and Sarah had supplemented the library with plenty of *horrid novels* and modern works of fiction as well. I imagined winter in the country could become tedious without the ability to get lost in a good book.

"Mary, darling!"

Sarah waved to her sister-in-law as she entered the breakfast room, and I was grateful for a distraction. As if staying in the same house with Benjamin wasn't enough, I'd somehow made an enemy of Miss Price and wasn't sure I could continue the current conversation without giving her a piece of my mind.

Mary Cunningham smiled at us as she approached, her apple cheeks rosy and her eyes sparkling.

"I've just come in from checking on the children. They are

building an army of snowmen and are so delighted to have snow at Christmas!" She winked at Sarah. "I may have helped to build a couple myself."

Miss Price looked down at the damp hem of Mary's heavy velvet day dress and made a noise that I could only imagine signaled her disapproval, but Sarah chimed in before she could begin another lecture.

"Since you're here, Mary darling, I have the perfect job for you."

She jumped up out of her chair, pulled me to my feet, and steered me and Mary away from Miss Price's disapproving gaze. I felt oddly relieved that it was not just me the old woman was judging.

"I need you and Winnie to go fetch all of the Christmas vases from the attic. I had the maids pull them out and dust them this week, so they should all be in a crate at the top of the stairs."

"You have vases especially for Christmas?" I was intrigued.

"These are very… unique vases." Her back to Miss Price, Sarah grimaced. "You'll see."

As she led me through the house to the attic stairs, Mary told me the story of the Christmas vases.

"Arthur and Rupurt's mother, the previous Lady Cunningham, was a bit eccentric. She liked to collect hobbies. She would latch onto one for a few months until she got bored and moved onto something else. One of her pet projects was pottery, and she actually stuck with that one for nearly a year. She was quite prolific, though I'm afraid she never mastered the art. Her pièce de résistance, as it were, was a set of Christmas vases. Arthur and Rupurt are the kindest souls, you see, and they have many cherished memories of their mother decorating the estate during Advent, so Sarah cannot bring herself to disappoint them. It's become a bit of a tradition: we gather greenery from around the estate and place the vases throughout the house."

"That sounds really sweet. I'm sure the vases are lovely, if a bit rustic."

"Oh, rustic is too kind a word for them."

Mary gave a long-suffering sigh, and now I was quite intrigued to see these infamous works of art. We passed through the servants' hallway on the third floor, then reached the narrow wooden stairs that led up to the attic storage rooms. I nearly sprinted up the stairs in my eagerness to solve the mystery, Mary chuckling behind me at my enthusiasm. When I reached the small landing, I looked back at Mary's grin and ran straight into something hard and unyielding.

I would have fallen backwards, but strong arms reached out and caught me by the elbows to steady me. Dread filled my chest, seeping around all my organs and pushing the air out of my lungs— or perhaps the impact had knocked the wind out of me—but I stood frozen on the spot, unable to lift my head, and look up into the face I knew would be a mere six inches above my own.

The devil had caught up with me.

Chapter 4

"Lord Hadleigh! We didn't see you there." Mary caught up to me and put her hand gently between my shoulder blades as if she was afraid I would still topple down the stairs. "Are you okay, Winifred?"

Mary's presence calmed me a bit, and I took in a few slow breaths.

"Quite alright. I'm afraid I just had the wind knocked out of me. Thank you for your concern." I did not thank Benjamin for catching me, since it had been his fault I nearly tumbled down the stairs in the first place. I narrowed my eyes. "I didn't realize the gentlemen were back from their excursion yet, Lord Hadleigh. Whatever were you doing in the attic?"

"I came back a little early." Benjamin smiled at me and Mary in the charming way that had always left women of all ages swooning at his feet. Mary smiled back, but I was pleased to see she looked more curious than overcome. "I believe my valet accidentally left something in my trunk when he was unpacking last night, so I just popped up to the storage rooms to take a peek."

"Do you always do your valet's job for him, my Lord?"

"Only when it's a sentimental item I want to make sure to recover."

He gave another dashing smile to Mary, who was looking back and forth between us thoughtfully.

"I don't recall you ever being sentimental when we were young.

22

In fact, I think you once left something very important behind without thinking twice."

I flinched even as the words flew out of my mouth, unbidden, but I was unable to stop them. There was no flicker of emotion in Benjamin's eyes, but his jaw firmed as if he was gritting his teeth. After a moment of silence, Mary came to my rescue.

"Sarah has sent us to fetch a crate of Christmas vases. Did you see anything like that at the top of the stairs, my Lord?"

"As a matter of fact…" Benjamin turned and took the remaining stairs to the attic two at a time, likely grateful to break the tension that had surrounded us with my outburst. At the top, he bent and lifted a large wooden crate as though it weighed nothing. My curiosity got the better of me, and I scurried up after him to peer into the crate.

"Oh!" I quickly backed away, then put a hand over my mouth. "Mary, I see just what you mean."

Attempting to ignore the cad holding the crate—I sincerely hoped it was as heavy as it looked—I peeked back at the painted clay vases carefully packed in straw. The vases were obviously made to be angels, with wings spreading out from the sides and painted golden halos around each rim, their mouths open in what was likely supposed to be a holy song—but looked more like screams of terror. Their misshapen faces and glossy, unseeing eyes only added to the macabre effect.

"They are—unique—to be sure." Benjamin grinned at us, his charm on full display once more, and I scolded my heart for giving a little leap. My head knew what a reprobate this man was, but apparently the rest of my body still struggled to catch up. "Shall I carry this down for you ladies?"

"Yes, please, my Lord," Mary said politely, just as I nearly shouted, "No! We can do it."

I gave Mary a little shrug, remembering that the crate was likely quite heavy. I tried to inject a note of nonchalance into my voice as I began descending the attic stairs.

"You may leave it on the table in the sitting room, Lord Hadleigh, thank you."

Once I was out of sight, I raced back downstairs without waiting for Mary.

I spent a few minutes composing myself and tucking stray hairs back into their pins in my bedroom. By the time I joined the other ladies in the sitting room, two long work tables had been set up in the center of the room, and Sarah and all her female guests were gathered around them. Large branches of greenery were already piled in the middle of the tables, and each guest was trimming bits of evergreen and holly and arranging them in an attractive fashion in the screaming angel vases. I pulled up a chair in between Sarah and Miss Loughty, determined not to let my literal run-in with Benjamin spoil a fun day of holiday merrimaking. Thankfully, he was nowhere to be seen, though several ladies in the group were still discussing the reprobate.

"Did you see the way he carried that heavy crate as if it were a feather?" Miss Taylor tittered happily. "How thoughtful he was to carry it for Mrs. Cunningham. What a true gentleman."

"And not at all proud for an Earl," Miss Price added with something close to charitableness.

Mary looked at me thoughtfully.

"This morning before breakfast, I saw Lord Hadleigh on the landing outside of the nursery. He said he was dropping off a picture book he and Lord Worthington had brought for the children."

While I noticed Mary's emphasis on the word *said*, everyone else seemed to take her statement as more praise for Benjamin's character.

"How kind of him. He seems the very picture of amiability," Mrs. Emsworth gushed. "Lord Worthington, too. They both conversed with my son at length last night in the drawing room, and I know how hard the poor dear is to draw out of his shell. He struggles to make friends, so to have two members of the aristocracy attempt to get to know him speaks highly of their character."

I liked Mrs. Emsworth, but I doubted her son would appreciate her talking so freely about his social struggles. Even though he wasn't present to hear her, I felt some empathy for the man and changed the subject.

"How did all this greenery appear so quickly?" I picked up a few sprigs of cedar and a pair of gardening shears and began to trim the ends so they would sit nicely in a vase.

"Oh, I had Rupurt and the other gentlemen cut some for us on the way home from taking care of that downed tree," Sarah offered. "Since they were all bundled up and carrying saws anyways, it was the perfect time."

We spent an amiable morning filling the vases with greenery and chatting with the other ladies. Occasionally one of the gentlemen would wander in to say hello and check on our progress, but since Benjamin was not among them, I was able to relax a bit and enjoy our creative pursuit for a few moments. There was something about creating that always calmed my mind and quieted the turmoil in my head.

When I was a child and had first come to live with Grandfather after my parents died in a carriage accident, Lady Hadleigh seemed to understand that I needed to keep my hands busy in order to keep the emotions at bay. She'd first taught me how to embroider, but when I proved to have more vision than patience, she wisely switched mediums and taught me to paint. She was a moderately-accomplished painter herself, but when my talents quickly outpaced her, she hired an art tutor to teach the both of us. We spent many an afternoon in her light-filled conservatory, drinking tea and giggling to ourselves when a painting technique went terribly wrong. We'd never ventured into pottery, but I suspected Lady Hadleigh would have enjoyed laughing with me over the hideous Christmas vases. She'd been gone for eight years now, but the loss still stung nearly as much as the more recent loss of my grandfather.

I gathered a few branches of holly in one hand and turned away from the group as though I was studying my arrangement in the light of the window while I discreetly wiped at my eyes. I was able to keep the melancholia at bay at home in Paris, where there were art lessons, commissions to be completed, and a magical city to explore. But when I was quiet and still, it was too easy to dwell on all that I'd lost. Thankfully, a welcome distraction came in the cheerful person of Lord Belvoir, who whisked into the room carrying a large, ornately carved wooden box. Though he was hardly in his salad days, he moved with the energy and enthusiasm of a much younger man, and there was something roguish and likable about him.

"Good morning, ladies!" Lord Belvoir smoothly inserted himself between myself and Miss Loughty, brushing our piles of greenery to the side with the edge of the box as he slid it onto the table. She glared at him, hands on her hips, then laughed, and I remembered the two were cousins. "Miss Osbourne told me last night at dinner that it was her first English Christmas in a decade, and I thought this required a bit of celebration."

He opened the lid of the box, setting it down on the sofa behind us, and began assembling the apparatus inside.

"Now, Miss Osbourne, I know you're quite the sophisticate, living in Paris and all, but have you ever had the good fortune to hear a phonograph?"

I couldn't help but smile at his infectious enthusiasm.

"I saw an early prototype demonstrated last year at the World's Fair, but I confess it looked quite different. Is this a trumpet?"

At Lord Belvoir's encouraging nod, I ran my fingers gently over the bell-shaped brass attachment that was now reaching up and out of the box.

"Very like that, I assure you. It's going to magnify the sounds that are made when the needles read the patterns etched in the wax cylinder. It's a smaller unit, suitable for traveling, so the range of sounds is not as broad, but it's still quite entertaining."

He adjusted a few things on the phonograph, cranked a small handle on the side, and music began to fill the room.

"Why, it's a Christmas carol!" I clapped my hands appreciatively. "It's lovely."

"If you ladies are going to be slaving away in here for the sake of our yuletide cheer, you might as well have a little entertainment."

The rest of the ladies all clapped as well, even Miss Price, and Lord Belvoir gave a sweeping bow to the room. He then pushed me to the side gently with one shoulder while reaching across the table to grab a still-empty vase.

"Miss Osbourne and dear Cousin Helen, teach me the art of arranging greenery, I beg you. I shall be terrible at it, I'm sure, but the company can't be improved upon."

Miss Loughty shrugged and smiled, and together we began to instruct Lord Belvoir how to arrange the tallest pieces of greenery in the middle of the vase, with shorter pieces spilling out around the edges. Several of the ladies sang along with the Christmas carols while we worked. The rest of the gentlemen remained in other parts of the house until luncheon, and while I had no more encounters with Benjamin, I couldn't help but glance towards the open sitting room door and even out the window a few times. Perhaps I'd forgotten what it felt like to be around a large group of friends, or perhaps my mind couldn't rest easy knowing my rakehell former husband was in the same house—but I couldn't shake the feeling that I was being watched.

Chapter 5

I managed to shake off my paranoia and even enjoy myself for the rest of the day. Sarah had a light luncheon spread out on the side board in the sitting room, and we helped ourselves to plates of meats, cheeses, minced pies, and steaming mugs of cider. To my relief, Benjamin must have been among the stragglers eating sandwiches in the billiards room as the gentlemen continued a lengthy tournament. Mr. Loughty joined his sister and cousin and I around our table, and I spent an enjoyable meal listening to them reminisce about their adventures on the Belvoir estate as children. As morning stretched into afternoon and amiable conversation continued, the gentlemen began to wander back to the billiards tournament, and several ladies excused themselves to retire to their rooms for a rest or to catch up on correspondence. When Miss Loughty yawned and proclaimed herself in need of a nap after their long travel day yesterday, Mr. Loughty stood and offered her his hand.

"Come, sister. I'll walk you upstairs. I have some estate business to attend to, I'm afraid. Can't let the place go to ruin while we're gone, can we Felix?"

He winked at Lord Belvoir, who chuckled.

"You know I would be lost without you, Teddy."

Mr. Loughty sighed, but smiled at me and continued in a stage whisper.

"He knows I detest being called Teddy. My name is Theodore,

but he christened me Teddy when I was still in leading strings, and I'm afraid it stuck."

"Do you also live on Lord Belvoir's estate?" I asked, smiling up at Mr. Loughty.

"Next door. Our fathers were twins you see, and since Felix's father was born first, he inherited the title and the estate. My grandfather thought that didn't sound fair, since they were born on the same day, so he purchased the land adjoining his and built a grand manor house there for my father. It's nothing so impressive as the Marquisate property, obviously, but it's a lovely place to call home. Since we're so close, we share a steward, and I assist him in his duties in taking care of both of our estates, just as my father did. He took great pride in the land and was an avid gardener and nature-lover. I'm only trying to do justice to his memory by maintaining all that he worked so hard for."

Lord Belvoir clapped his cousin on the back.

"Teddy is too modest. He's a shrewd businessman, and has increased our yield tenfold since he took over. I've no head for numbers myself, and since I'm unlikely to marry again, I'm grateful I have such a talented cousin for an heir."

Lord Belvoir grinned at Mr. Loughty, whose cheeks pinked. Looking embarrassed by all the attention, he bobbed his head meekly.

"Thank you, cousin. You're too kind, really. Miss Osbourne, it's been a pleasure, but I must get a bit of work done."

He gestured at the door through which Miss Loughty was already disappearing, gave me a little bow, and headed off after her. I turned to Lord Belvoir just as Sarah appeared with fresh cider for each of us.

"Your cousins seem lovely, Lord Belvoir. I always wished that I had cousins growing up. It was just me and my grandfather."

We took the proffered ciders and settled into overstuffed chairs by the roaring fire. Sarah and her staff had thought of every comfort. The room was cozy and the atmosphere convivial even as the sunlight began to wane outdoors. Darkness came early in England this time of year.

"My cousins have always been great companions, and they have been such a comfort to me during trying times."

"I was very sorry to hear about the passing of your wife a few years ago, my Lord." Sarah sipped on a cider of her own and pulled her chair a little closer to the fireplace. "I'd only met her once, but she seemed to be a darling creature."

Lord Belvoir's face took on an uncharacteristically serious expression.

"She was loveliness itself. I confess I'd never planned to marry. I was quite the rake in my youth, Miss Osbourne, and abhorred the idea of matrimony. I didn't meet Katherine until I was almost forty. But there was just something about her that I could not resist, and my bachelor days were numbered. I knew she wasn't in the best of health when we'd married, but I expected to have many more years with her than I did. She declined much quicker than the doctors predicted. We were only married for two years when she passed of consumption."

He rubbed a hand over his face, and for a moment I thought I glimpsed a broken man behind the cheerful facade.

"She loved Christmas and always made it special." He smiled sadly, looking over at the phonograph. It required cranking and had ceased to play, but none of us wanted to move quite yet. "Christmas carols were Katherine's favorite, so when I saw that invention, I knew I had to get it to honor her. She would have loved it."

For a moment, I knew the grief in my eyes mirrored the grief in his own, and I quickly blinked and looked away. While it was by betrayal and not death, I'd lost my spouse as well. As much as I tried to pretend it hadn't devastated me, the wound hurt deeply just the same. Lord Belvoir must have sensed the pain in my eyes, for he looked at me with some concern.

"Are you alright, Miss Osbourne? I'm afraid I've ruined the mood by becoming a bit maudlin."

"I'm quite all right, thank you—please don't apologize. My grandfather, the man who raised me, died just after Christmas last, and sometimes the realization catches up with me."

Sarah reached out and grabbed my hand, and I was grateful for her support, though she didn't know the full story. I was suddenly struck with the idea that if she were ever to learn the full wretched tale of my marriage and abandonment, she would be my staunchest defender, and my heart warmed at the thought.

"I'm grateful you're able to be here among friends, then," Lord Belvoir said kindly. I didn't detect any pity in his tone, just genuine sympathy. "Personally, I was delighted to receive Arthur's invitation. Christmas preparations for just three people seem a lot of effort to put my staff to, and I haven't had the heart to host any guests since Katherine passed. But I've talked enough for today. Tell me, Miss Osbourne, what is it like being an artist in Paris? Is it as scandalous as it sounds?"

Lord Belvoir leaned forward and rubbed his hands together like an old woman waiting for some juicy gossip, and my sentimental mood lifted instantly.

"I'm afraid you'll be disappointed, Lord Belvoir," I teased. "My life is quite proper. I am privileged to learn from the best artists in Europe at *Académie Julian,* but Madame Beaury-Saurel, Monsieur Julian's wife, carefully oversees and chaperones all aspects of our education.

"When I'm not in classes," I continued, "I take painting and drawing commissions and have worked on a number of interesting projects—everything from drawing headache tinctures for a local doctor, painting a commissioned portrait of a Vicomte's hunting dogs, and doing some rather macabre illustrations for a book on poisons and their effects on the body."

I grimaced, and Sarah squeezed my hand again in sympathy. I'd told her how difficult the research for that project had been for me, and how I couldn't sleep for weeks afterwards.

"But," I added brightly, trying not to relive those images again at the moment, "nothing scandalous. My grandfather even pur-chased me my own apartment in a very respectable arrondissement, so I don't board with any of the other female artists in Montmartre."

No, the scandalous part of my story went much further back, but I wasn't about to share my role as a jilted and abandoned wife with anyone. Setting my now-empty cider cup on the side table, I stood and stretched.

"Sarah, my love, I'm afraid I can't sit still any longer. Where are Mary and those paper angels Miss Price was so keen on us putting our hand to? We have hours before dinner yet, and I slept too late this morning to be in need of a nap."

"Mary was just reading a story to the children, and she'll be down to join us in a few minutes. I'll fetch the extra butcher paper Mrs. Hudgins picked up from the market the other day."

"No, you sit! You've been running around like a headless chicken all day, and I need to stretch my legs. I'll pop down to Mrs. Hudgins' office and be right back."

I thanked Lord Belvoir for his company and decided I needed more exercise than a quick run downstairs. I donned my coat and went out the front door, taking the long way around the house to the staff entrances in the back. The snow was deep and would have been nearly up to my knee had it lain untouched, but the paths around the house had been shoveled and salted, and the way was easy. I took my time making my way around the house, walking slowly and taking in great lungfuls of the cold air. The sky had cleared, and a beautiful winter sunset was just visible over the tops of the trees behind the house. By the time I was wiping my feet at the servants entrance, I felt more refreshed than I would have if I'd retired to my room for a nap. Paris may be cold and gray in the winter, but we rarely saw snow, and I found it invigorating.

Unbuttoning my coat and slinging it over my arm, I made my way through the bustling kitchen. I nodded a quick hello to the staff, most of whom seemed to be getting used to my odd wanderings and barely blinked an eye at the lady invading their space. I was raising a hand to knock on the housekeeper's office door, when the door opened and Mrs. Emsworth stepped out, nearly running into me.

"Mrs. Emsworth!" I raised a hand to steady her in case she were to repeat my encounter with Benjamin on the steps this morning, but she was quite steady. She looked surprised to see me for a moment, but then smiled brightly.

"Hello, Miss Osbourne. I was just going to check in with the housekeeper to make sure she remembers *ma petite allergie d'au-mande* as she's preparing the menus, but she doesn't seem to be in right now. I scribbled a little reminder on her desk instead. You can do the same if you need to speak with her about something."

"Just fetching some butcher paper for our angel garlands. Mrs. Hudgins has some set aside for us, but I'm afraid I wouldn't know where to begin to search. I'll just run back to the kitchen and see if one of the maids might know where to find it."

"Very well, my dear. My hands aren't quite fit enough for paper crafting, I'm afraid. A touch of arthritis." She flexed her fingers for me, and I smiled sympathetically. "But I'll see you at dinner. Perhaps you and my son can speak more. He went on and on this afternoon about how much he enjoyed chatting with you at breakfast."

She smiled warmly at me, and I nodded uncommittingly. I was sure her son had said nothing of the sort, and I was afraid I'd already been too chatty today. I liked Mrs. Emsworth and her son, but I knew a matchmaking mama when I saw one, and I was going to have to tread carefully for a few days.

"Well, Sarah's waiting, so I'd better finish my little errand. I'll see you at dinner."

Once the butcher paper was located by a kitchen maid, Sarah, Mary, Miss Taylor, and I spent a half-hour crafting paper angel garlands under the watchful eye of Miss Price, whose presence put a damper on what should have been an enjoyable activity. She spent the time lecturing an overwhelmed-looking Miss Taylor on how to best comport herself to catch the eye of one of the three lords present. I wanted to shout at the girl to avoid Benjamin Hadleigh at all cost, but the poor chit looked nauseous at the thought of even speaking to a peer of a realm, so I decided there wasn't too much danger there. But I vowed to keep an eye on her this week just in case.

When the urge to add my own opinions on matrimony to Miss Price's lecture became too strong, I promised to help Mary finish the garlands the following afternoon and excused myself to get ready for dinner. I took a long, leisurely bath, letting the warm water soak away some of the tension that had been present since Benjamin had arrived the previous evening.

Betsy had just finished buttoning me into a crimson silk evening dress with tiny, fluttering sleeves when the dinner gong sounded. While the sleeves were the height of fashion in Paris at the moment, they didn't offer much in the way of warmth, so my modiste had made me a pair of long velvet gloves in a matching shade of crimson. I'd spent too long deciding what to wear, and there was no time left to do my hair, so Betsy quickly wrapped it into a low, loose chignon at the nape of my neck, leaving a few loose curls to spill out artfully. Not wanting to inspire any more lectures from Miss Price, I resisted the urge to dab a bit of rouge on my lips, thanked Betsy for her assistance, and practically ran down the stairs so as to not keep everyone waiting.

I blamed Benjamin for making me dither on my clothing choices. It wasn't that I wanted to impress him; I just didn't want to give him any reason to find fault in me. I wanted to show him that I was doing just fine in my life without him. I may not be an Earl's wife, but I was a proper, sophisticated Parisienne with a promising career ahead of me. As I rounded the second flight of stairs I slowed to a ladylike walk and took a few deep breaths.

Assuming I was the last to assemble in the drawing room, I slipped up to Sarah and kissed her on the cheek.

"So sorry to keep you waiting, dearest."

"Oh, no, Winnie, it's no trouble. Mr. and Miss Loughty just arrived, as well." Sarah gave a little wave to Miss Loughty, who smiled at us from across the room, wearing a lovely sapphire blue evening dress with a daring neckline. "Ah, and there's Lord Hadleigh. Lovely, we're all here."

I looked up in surprise as Benjamin slipped through a door at the opposite side of the room—not at all from the direction of the guests' wing. This was the fourth time that Benjamin had been spotted in or coming from a part of the house where he should not have been. What was that reprobate up to? As I watched his charming face ooze confidence and self-satisfaction while he greeted Arthur, a lead weight settled in my stomach. No one else here seemed to know this man's true nature, so it was up to me to get to the bottom of his strange behavior. I refused to let him ruin my friends' Christmas. Although I had decided to stay far away from him this week, it appeared I was going to have to confront him the first chance I got. The thought quickly chased away any appetite I may have had.

I managed a polite facade during dinner, picking at my food and discreetly watching Benjamin for any clues as to why he was sneaking about the Cunninghams' house. Sarah planned on switching up the seating arrangements each night for dinner so we could each have a chance to converse with someone new. Tonight, I was seated between Rupurt and Miss Loughty, with Lord Worthington directly across from me and Lord Belvoir next to him. Lord Worthington and Rupurt had attended Cambridge together, and regaled the rest of us with tales of their antics as young men. Miss Loughty was engaged in conversation with Mrs. Emsworth to her left, so other than asking her a few questions about what books she'd enjoyed reading lately, I was free to appear to be entertained by the men's conversation while my thoughts were elsewhere.

A few stolen glances to the other end of the table told me that Benjamin was as charming and confident as ever. Except… the way he worked his jaw when he thought no one was looking.

He was troubled about something. Hearing Lord Worthington thank Rupert again for the invitation to join us for Christmas, I found myself suddenly interested in the conversation taking place around me. I smiled my most winning smile at Lord Worthington, who blinked at the sudden attention being directed his way.

"How kind of you to pass the invitation on to Lord Hadleigh as well, my Lord."

"Yes, well, Hadleigh doesn't have any family left, and we'd been planning on spending the season at my estate, but. . ." Lord Worthington paused, wiping his fiery red moustaches with his napkin. "I couldn't pass up the opportunity to spend time with Rupert and Sarah. Hadleigh thankfully agreed to go along with the change in plans, and here we are."

He glanced quickly at Benjamin, smiled at me, and dug into his roasted quail with gusto, but I couldn't help but feel I was missing part of the story.

When it was time for the men to have their port and cigars, the ladies adjourned to the drawing room for tea and sherry. I excused myself for a quick stop at the ladies' room, then wandered back towards the drawing room, my thoughts somewhere between the distant past and the devil I was somehow sharing an intimate house party with.

As if I had conjured him out of thin air, I rounded the corner just in time to see Benjamin crack open the Cunninghams' library door and peek inside. He was still wearing his shoes this time, but something in his posture told me he was trying to remain unseen. I ducked behind an ornately carved sideboard just as Benjamin looked up and down the hall and slipped through the door.

This was my opportunity! A chance to confront him, to save my friends possible grief. My feet, however, failed to receive the command, and I stood rooted to the spot, staring at the library door. I was being as ridiculous as a silly schoolgirl. As much of a cad as this man was, he wouldn't hurt me—at least not physically. I just needed to find out what he was up to, send him on his way, and I could once more look forward to my English Christmas. It was quite simple, really.

I put my shoulders back, took a deep breath, and slipped quietly inside the lion's den.

Chapter 6

Like the rest of the house, the Cunninghams' library was a cozy, welcoming place, with lots of little nooks set up for reading amongst the bookshelves, and deep, upholstered window seats with sweeping views of the back gardens. It was an excellent place for hiding away on a dreary day, but now that darkness had fallen, the long shadows cast around the room by the fire and flickering wall sconces seemed ominous, almost sinister.

I did not want to be alone with this man in such a place.

Still treading softly, I closed the door as quietly as I could behind me, glancing into the shadows around the room to see where Benjamin had gone. He'd spotted me, as I'd known he would, and stood straight as a general next to a row of bookcases, arms crossed over his chest.

For a moment we both stood there, silent. I'd imagined this moment in my mind a thousand times. What I would say to my former husband if we ever found ourselves face to face again without an audience. My mind whirled, and my stomach clenched. For a moment, I thought I was going to be sick all over the ornate Persian rug. I decided it was best to get right to the heart of the matter.

"Why are you sneaking around the Cunninghams' house?"

Benjamin looked completely unruffled, bored even, but I saw his left eyebrow twitch just a hair. Whatever he was expecting me to say to him after all these years, that was not it. When he said nothing, I continued.

"I saw you, leaving Mr. Emsworth's room last night. You were snooping around the attic this morning, and when we assembled before dinner you arrived from the wrong direction—from a door that happens to be directly across from Rupert's office. And Mary! Mary saw you outside the nursery before breakfast, with some outlandish tail about dropping off a picture book. You also seem to be mysteriously absent whenever the other gentlemen have joined us—not that I'm complaining, mind you, but it is still suspicious."

Warming to my theme, I began pacing slightly in the middle of the room.

"Since you're as rich as Croesus, and no one's reported anything missing, I doubt you're a petty thief. If you'd been leaving one of the women's rooms, I'd have suspected you to be following in your father and brother's amorous footsteps." I tugged the tops of my gloves, as if to cover myself a little bit further, but still Benjamin just stared at me with those cool blue eyes. "I used to know your face better than my own. But as it is, I can't get a read on you. The Cunninghams are my friends, and I won't let you hurt them. So what is it? Are you searching for something? Having an amorous rendezvous with one of the staff? Cataloguing all of the guests' jewels to steal later? Attempting to blackmail someone?"

Benjamin's mouth twitched at the corner just slightly. I'd been throwing out more and more outlandish things to disarm him into telling me what he was really up to.

"It is blackmail, actually."

I stared at him, dumbfounded, as he spoke for the first time since I'd entered the room. I knew he was a rubbish heap of a human, but what need would he have to blackmail someone? He must have correctly read the dumbfounded look on my face, for he groaned, wiping a hand across his face and looking suddenly tired.

"Freddie, do you really believe that ill of me?"

I flinched at the use of my childhood nickname. He was the only one who had ever called me Freddie. I'd hated it as a girl of twelve, but whispered into my ear under soft Italian moonlight, it had been my favorite sound in the world.

"You haven't given me a reason to think any better of you in the last nine years."

Benjamin sighed, looking somehow older and more worn than he had when I'd entered the room, though he was barely thirty-one. Gone was the erect military-like bearing, and he motioned towards a settee tucked between two bookshelves.

"C'mon. I can see you're not going to let me rest until you know the truth. Glad to see you haven't lost your tenacity."

I shook my head. That alcove was far too dark. Far too close. I jerked my head towards a pair of leather armchairs near the fire instead.

"I haven't lost anything except 190 pounds of dead weight masquerading as a husband."

Ignoring my jab, Benjamin lowered himself to the armchair, which creaked beneath his weight. I'd hoped he'd turn to fat and get less attractive with age, but whatever he had been doing for the last nine years had sculpted his figure to perfection. Those disturbingly clear eyes stared into the fire, then back at me.

"Freddie, you're like a dog with a bone when you latch onto something. Can I simply tell you that I'm here for my work on behalf of the government, and you leave it be?"

"Are we drafting parliamentary laws at Christmas house parties now, then?"

"That's not all I do for the government. I…" Benjamin broke off, running a hand carefully over his perfectly-styled hair. "My brother certainly had his faults."

I blinked. This was the last direction I expected this conversation to go.

"What does Augustus have to do with any of this?"

"He wasn't the villain you believed him to be, Freddie."

"He demanded you abandon your wife, Benji. That sounds pretty villainous to me."

Benjamin rubbed his hand through his hair again in agitation, this time leaving a few strands in disarray.

"This was not something I planned to get into here."

"And I wasn't planning on ever seeing you again, but here we are."

He sighed and shifted in his chair as if he were settling in for a long story. I kept my back ramrod straight and sat on the edge of my chair.

"My brother was a drunkard, yes, but underneath all that… Augustus worked for the Home Office, protecting state secrets."

For a moment, I could only blink at him.

"I'm sorry, are you saying that your brother was a spy? I find that even harder to fathom than you as a petty thief."

"Augustus was a hard man to truly know. Before my father passed, he worked abroad for the Home Office. He shouldn't have, being the first in line for the Earldom, but Augustus seldom did what was expected of him. And that's what made him a valuable government asset. He was good at his job—too good. When father died and Augustus became the Earl of Hadleigh, he never adapted back to the life of a gentleman. He drank to forget things that he'd seen—things that he'd done. His work was quite dangerous. That is one reason he never married. He'd built up a vast network of connections in his years in the service, however, and he needed someone to pass them onto when he became the Earl. He had just recruited me to work with him when… well, when I ran off to Italy and married you."

"Hold on a minute." I peered at him warily, wondering if anything he was telling me was true. "Are you trying to tell me that not only was your wretched, drunkard brother a spy for Queen and country, but now you are too? Honestly Benjamin, you've told a lot of lies over the years, but that one takes the cake."

"Freddie, I have never, ever lied to you."

"What about *till death do us part?*"

Benjamin flinched as if I'd slapped him, but I didn't regret a word.

"Why are you here, Benji? Did you follow me? It seems pretty coincidental that I return to England for the first time in nearly ten years and you just happen to be at my best friend's home."

Benjamin held up both his hands wearily.

"I swear I didn't know the connection between you and the Cunninghams. I had no idea you would be here or I would have… sent someone else."

"Someone else to do what?"

"Find the blackmailer."

"And who is being blackmailed, exactly?"

"A close relative of the Queen." He held up a hand to stop my next question. "I'm not at liberty to say which one. But we knew the suspected blackmailer would be here, at this house party."

"How did you know that? Surely you don't suspect Rupert or Sarah!"

"The Cunninghams are not suspects, no. But one of their guests is. We've been following this person for a long time. The blackmail letters the Queen's relative received were all mailed by one of our suspect's servants at a post office in Mayfair. The servant has been loyal to this suspect for more than a decade, has no criminal record, and doesn't have the sort of connections that would allow him the information the blackmailer had. When the servant was questioned discreetly, he had no idea that anything that he had mailed was anything other than the usual household correspondence, so the master of the house must be the blackmailer. We had that person's residence and club searched as soon as they departed London for the Cunninghams, but could not find the evidence we were looking for. I assumed they must have taken it with them for safe keeping, so we went to plan B, and I came with Worthington, who had previously secured an invitation for me for that very purpose."

"So you think this blackmailer brought the evidence he holds against the Queen's relative here to the Cunningham's house. Who is it?"

"I can't divulge that information, Freddie. I've told you far too much already as it is. Once I find the evidence I'm looking for, I'll make some excuse and be out of your hair again. For good. The blackmailer will be arrested once they return to London, and no one else in this little house party will have to know."

I sat there, dumbfounded, the wheels in my mind spinning rapidly. In all of the possibilities of what Benjamin was doing here, working as a government operative to find a blackmailer would not have seemed a likely one.

"Is Lord Worthington also a spy?"

I wasn't sure exactly where that question had come from, but it was the first one that popped into my head.

"No, just a good friend who knew the Cunninghams wouldn't mind an extra guest. He knows my purpose here, but he is not involved."

A thought occurred to me, and I blinked rapidly, staring into the fire.

"It's Mr. Emsworth, isn't it? The suspected blackmailer. Mrs. Emsworth was just gushing on about how you and Lord Worthington had befriended him. And Mr. Emsworth himself told me Lord Worthington kept asking him questions while he was trying to read. I'll bet he was keeping Mr. Emsworth busy while you searched his rooms for your evidence."

"You're bright, Freddie, I'll give you that. But this secret of the royal family—it's a very sensitive, very damaging secret. Only a fool would leave something that valuable in his own room. That's why I have to search the whole house."

Benjamin hadn't said that it wasn't Mr. Emsworth. I sincerely hoped it wasn't. Matchmaking mother aside, he seemed a decent fellow.

"So, now that I know what you're doing, I'm supposed to just let you finish your work and disappear again off into the night?"

"That was the plan. Isn't that what you want me to do?"

Chapter 7

I hesitated. There was still so much I wanted to ask him about the last nine years, so much that remained unsaid. But I couldn't let a few minutes of an unusual and intriguing conversation lure me back under this man's spell. I couldn't afford to be fooled again.

"Yes, yes that's exactly what I want you to do."

After returning to the drawing room and making a half-hearted attempt at conversation with the other ladies before I gave up and retired for the evening, I spent another night fighting for sleep. This time my brain alternated between trying to decide which member of our house party was daring enough to blackmail a member of the royal family and reminding myself why I wanted Benjamin to stay as far away from me as possible.

Ours had been a fairytale courtship, and I should have realized much earlier that it was too good to be true. Lady Hadleigh and Grandfather were both well-traveled intellectuals, and struck up a plan for us to spend the summer together in Italy the year I turned eighteen. Lady Hadleigh was relieved to get away from the drinking, gambling, and debauchery of Augustus, and Benji and I reveled in the wonders of the world: moonlight swims in the Mediterranean, hot summer days running through vineyards, wandering quiet cobblestone streets hand in hand. After only a month abroad together, Benjamin proposed.

I should have known better. Grandfather should have known better, but his judgment was clouded by his love for me and for

Benji. He had wanted me to wait to marry until I was older and had achieved my dream of studying art abroad, but Benjamin and I both begged for a quick wedding, and Grandfather came around easily. We were his children, and he wanted us to be happy, and if we were happy together, even better.

We married in Tuscany under the shade of a laurel tree, Grandfather and Lady Hadleigh by our sides. Lady Hadleigh had written to Augustus about the wedding, but he did not deign to answer, a fact in which none of us were disappointed. We feasted on fresh fruits and olives on a picnic blanket for our wedding meal. I had not been so happy since my parents had been alive, and everything seemed to sparkle with an effervescent joy.

We spent the rest of that dreamy summer on our honeymoon, traveling the coast of Italy and staying in delightfully run-down pensiones and inns. I was as brown as a walnut in weeks, my hair hanging in wild curls down my back, any pins no match for the sea wind. We were young and naïve, but what we lacked in experience we made up for in enthusiasm. One particular nona was so worried about our health after we hadn't left our room for a few days that she took it upon herself to supply us with regular meals lowered down in a bucket from her flat above ours.

As with all fairy tales, the magic didn't last.

We'd been married just shy of two months, staying in the tiny fishing village of Vernazza, when a very upset Grandfather and Lady Hadleigh arrived to warn us that Augustus was hot on their heels. He'd just learned about the wedding, and was furious, coming to drag Benjamin home in a fit of rage. Considering what Benjamin had just revealed in the library, Augustus had likely just realized his plans to recruit Benjamin into service for the Home Office had a significant kink in them—me. Late one evening, Augustus burst into our tiny pensione on the Mediterranean, fire burning in his eyes, railing at Benji for defying his wishes and marrying a nobody like myself. Until that moment, I thought Augustus had barely known I existed, but apparently he'd been warning Benji away from me for years. He had an illustrious match planned for Benjamin, one that would further his career in parliament and political connections. I was not nearly well-connected or wealthy enough to be a suitable match.

I would never forget that night—the night Benjamin abandoned me.

The two brothers were nearly to blows when Lady Hadleigh collapsed. Her health had been declining for years, and we'd hoped the warm Mediterranean climate would be healing for her. But watching her two sons at war with each other proved too much for her fragile heart.

Augustus decided she should begin the journey home the next day, and Benjamin agreed. Lady Hadleigh thought if we all gave Augustus a little time to cool off, he'd realize our marriage wasn't the disaster he'd first believed, and all would be well. I was due to start an art residency in Florence in the fall—the reason we'd planned our summer in Italy to begin with—so we arranged for Benji and Augustus to accompany their mother home. Grandfather and I would join them in a few months after my residency was complete. Benjamin and I were loath to be parted, but thought we could handle a short time away, knowing we'd soon be together again in England once more.

How shocked I was, a few weeks later, to receive an official document from Augustus' lawyer, stating that mine and Benjamin's marriage had been annulled by the authority of the Queen of England. Most devastatingly of all, Benjamin's signature was right on the bottom, sealing my fate in terrifying, bold ink. Apparently since I was only a woman, my signature had not been required.

Our fairy tale was over.

I tossed and turned the rest of the night, somewhere between sleep and dreams. When the sky began to lighten with a faint, pre-dawn glow, I gave up on sleep and dressed myself quietly in a soft blue skirt and velvet-trimmed blouse. Despite the cold ashes in the fire grate and the frost gathering on the inside of my windowpane, the walls of my bedchamber were starting to feel stifling. I needed space to think. I grabbed my sketchbook and pencils and tiptoed down the stairs. The rest of the household was still fast asleep, with the exception of a lone kitchen maid beginning preparations for the day's meals belowstairs. Buttoning my coat, I slipped out the servants' entrance with a sleepy nod in her direction and began my chilly walk through the back garden, looking for inspiration in the early morning shadows.

The garden walkways had been shoveled and salted again the evening before, so I had no problem making my way through the hedgerows of holly, my breath leaving great clouds of fog around me. I walked briskly, sketchpad and pencils tucked securely in my coat pocket, attempting to calm my nerves and clear the cobwebs from my sleep-deprived brain. Thoughts of blackmailers and spies swirled with memories of those long months of confusion after I'd been informed of our annulment. Grandfather had wanted to return to England right away and fix matters, but I'd convinced him to stay for the length of my Florentine residency, letting Augustus' ire cool and Lady Hadleigh's health recover. Meanwhile, I wrote Benjamin daily long letters, pouring out my heart and soul into the pages. I was still convinced that he'd signed the annulment under distress, that surely he would continue to fight tooth and nail for me, as I would have for him. As week after week went by with no reply, I sank further and further into despair. Did his brother truly convince him that I was unworthy of the Hadleigh name? Was I that easy to forget?

A lone tear slid down my cheek, and I cursed myself for being so sentimental now, as a grown woman. A woman who now knew that her husband had been a manipulative, selfish rake who thought nothing about using a young girl and then abandoning her. He was the worst kind of human.

But the hard part was that last night, in the library, he didn't seem like the worst kind of human, like the vile villain who still featured in my nightmares regularly. He seemed like… Benji. My best friend and playmate, ever rushing off to get embroiled in an adventure and eager to play the rescuer. Lost in self-pity, I wondered if there was just something terribly unlovable about me, after all.

I didn't see the body until I almost fell over it.

Chapter 8

I stared, dumbstruck, at the dead man on the walkway in front of me. His stockinged feet twisted away from the body at an odd angle, an open dressing gown splayed around him like a snow angel. I glanced up to the still-open window. The scullery maid must not have made it to the bachelor's wing to stoke the fires yet, as the bedroom above was still dark and quiet. No sounds of distress rang through the still morning air.

There was no need to check and see if the man was dead: his eyes were open and unseeing, mouth agape in a silent scream. A pair of spectacles lay in pieces on the ground next to him.

Poor Mr. Emsworth.

I supposed I should scream, or run and alert someone to the man's tragic fall, but something stopped me. I was certainly no medical expert, but after falling from such a great height, shouldn't there be a great deal of blood around the body? Taking a few tentative steps closer, I edged around Mr. Emsworth to take a closer look, holding my skirts back with one hand so they didn't disturb the body. His pupils were tiny dots within the huge whites of his eyes, and faint stains around his mouth and on his nightshirt told me he may have been sick during the night. Was he ill, and fell out of the window in his weakened state? Why would he even have a window open on a cold night in the middle of December?

On an impulse, I bent and sniffed around the poor man's mouth and nose. Thanks to my work on *A Physician's Illustrated*

Guide to Poisons, I was more versed than most in popular poisons and their symptoms. Illustrating the poisonous plants and substances had been enjoyable, as deadly substances are often some of the most beautiful, but the author had insisted on some rather gruesome depictions of their effects on the body as well. I'd fought hard for that commission, as the academy of medicine had originally balked at hiring a female artist. Still, they needed someone proficient in minute detail work, and the leaders of *Académie Julian* were able to help convince them I was the right artist for the job. I wasn't about to turn squeamish, then, when Monsieur Carbonneau, the author, insisted I accompany him to the coroners' office to document the more obvious poisoning cases.

The man at my feet was the first corpse that I'd known when it was a living being, however, and that was part of the reason I felt compelled to linger. Something about Mr. Emsworth's fall seemed off to me. I just wasn't sure what it was yet, but I had a feeling it was related to my work on *Poisons*. I sighed. I knew where I had to go next, and the fact that I would rather stay out in the freezing cold with a dead man than knock on Benjamin Hadleigh's door was rather telling.

Well, if I could handle seeing Mr. Emsworth dead on the cold cobblestones, I could handle a conversation with my ex-husband. Decision made, I turned and made my way briskly back to the servants' entrance. There were two kitchen maids now, tending a roaring fire and stirring a large pot of hot chocolate, a sure sign that the rest of the household would begin awakening soon. Not wanting to alarm them, I simply told them that a guest had had an accident in the back garden, and if one of them could go fetch the butler and the housekeeper and have them meet me back in the kitchen in ten minutes, I would be most appreciative.

Not bothering to remove my coat, I strode up the stairs two at a time, and knocked as quietly as I dared on Benjamin's bedroom door. I wanted him to see the body before anyone else could disturb it. I was just debating whether I should knock again, when the door flew open and Benji glared out at me. His striped wool pajama shirt hung open to the waist, a pair of matching pants mercifully covering his lower half.

"Freddie, what in God's name possessed you to wake me before the fires are even lit? And why…" he trailed off, looking suddenly concerned. "Why do you look like you've seen a ghost?"

I took a deep breath but was appalled at myself when not a sound could come out. It had to be from the shock of finding Mr. Emsworth, and not the awareness of Benjamin's state of undress. I cleared my throat and tried again, grateful when my voice managed a small croak.

"Mr. Emsworth. Dead." Seeing the unfortunate man in my mind's eye helped me to focus. "Benji, I think he was murdered."

It was to Benjamin's credit that he didn't question me or my state of mind. He glanced up and down the hall, then quickly pulled me inside and eased the door shut.

"Sit," he commanded, pointing me towards a chinois armchair next to a small occasional table. Without waiting to see if I obeyed, he stalked to the other side of the room to the dressing room, pulling his pajama shirt off as he went. Averting my gaze, I peered out the window behind me, but could not see the back garden from this side of the house.

"Talk, Freddie," Benjamin all but growled from the dressing room. "What did you see? Who else knows?"

I let out a shaky breath.

"I … think I'm the only one. I couldn't sleep, so I went outside to find a spot to sketch. He's in the back garden. It looks like he fell out of his window."

"And because you suspected him of blackmail, you think he was pushed?"

"No! I don't suspect him, I mean…"

I was failing miserably here. I had to collect myself. I stood and started pacing back and forth in front of the large windows.

"Something was off about the body. To start with, there was very little blood around it for such a great fall."

"And you're an expert on corpses, now, is it?"

I refused to let this man bait me. Mr. Emsworth deserved justice.

"More than you would think, actually. But that's not it. His pupils were contracted, and there were stains around his mouth and on his clothes. I think he'd been sick. In fact…"

It suddenly hit me.

"I think he was dead before someone pushed him out the window. I think he was poisoned."

"And you know that because?"

"I illustrated a book on poisons a few years back and had to do some very… hands on research." I couldn't repress a shudder and was glad Benjamin was still in the dressing room and unable to see me. "There's something about Mr. Emsworth that reminds me of some of those cases, but there are many poisons that can induce vomiting and affect the pupils." I would not mention that I'd spent the better part of a year attempting to block those images out of my mind just so I could sleep.

Properly dressed now in a shirt, waistcoat, jacket, and trousers, Benjamin strode out of the dressing room, grabbing my arm without even slowing. When we reached the door, he glanced out to make sure the hallway was clear, then pulled me out behind him. It was as if he suspected I would break down if I didn't keep moving, which was not altogether an unlikely assumption. We stopped briefly at the door next to Benjamin's where he knocked softly. Still he didn't speak to me, so I simply waited, grateful for a moment to collect myself.

Thankfully, Lord Worthington must also be an early riser, as he was fully dressed when he opened the door.

"Emsworth is dead." Benjamin spoke softly, mincing no words. If Lord Worthington was surprised to see me, he didn't show it, but gave Benji his full attention. "He's in the back garden. I need you to accompany us there, then handle the magistrate."

Lord Worthington paled, stifled a curse, and straightened an already perfect mustache. "Hadleigh, I'd been rather hoping you were wrong about him being… well, you know."

So it had been Emsworth they suspected. Worthington darted a quick glance at me. Benjamin just shook his head.

"I'm seldom wrong."

I'd recovered from my shock enough to roll my eyes. Lord Worthington caught me, and his eyes twinkled.

"Are you sure this is a sight for a young lady?" he asked Benjamin, with an apologetic smile at me.

"She'll manage. She found the body, and I need to know if it's exactly the same by the time we get down there. Freddie can succumb to hysterics later if she wishes."

I saw Lord Worthington's brows raise at the use of my nickname, and I thought Benjamin must be more shaken than he let on to display such an intimacy around his friend. Or perhaps they were very close friends, and Lord Worthington was privy to our secret. I certainly hoped not.

"I will not be succumbing to any hysterics, Lord Hadleigh," I said haughtily, "and the more time we spend here talking, the higher the chance someone else will disturb the body. I asked a maid to summon the housekeeper and butler, so they should be waiting for me in the kitchen by now. We must hurry."

If Mr. Emsworth had been murdered, every second counted.

Chapter 9

I led the way down the servants staircase to the kitchen. The fewer people who encountered us out and about this early, the better. Mrs. Hudgins, the housekeeper, and Jackson, the butler, were waiting for us by the large staff table. Both looked appropriately concerned for having been summoned, but not hysterical, so I assumed they had not yet seen the body.

"Mrs. Hudgins," I began. I assumed this should come from me since she was familiar with me and my habit of roaming the estate—and since I found the body. "I took an early morning walk and discovered that one of the guests has…" Benjamin stiffened, likely realizing he'd forgotten to coach me on what to say to the staff. He needn't worry. Even I knew that running around shouting murder at this juncture was foolish. It was best to make Mr. Emsworth's fall seem like a terrible accident. "Mr. Emsworth fell from his window sometime overnight and has unfortunately passed away. He is lying on the path in the back garden."

Mrs. Hudgins gasped, covering her mouth with both hands, and Jackson's solemn face somehow managed to become even more serious. I turned to Benjamin, letting him step in and direct the staff as he saw fit. After all, his blackmail investigation may have just become a murder investigation.

"I am Lord Hadleigh, and I have some experience with terrible accidents like these. Could you send a footman to summon the doctor and the magistrate? My friend Lord Worthington is

going to assist me in making sure no one disturbs the body until
the authorities get here. We also want to avoid alarming the staff
and the other guests."

"Oh! Rupert and Sarah will need to be informed as well," I
added to Mrs. Hudgins. "As well as poor Mrs. Emsworth."

My heart constricted at the thought of the pain the kind
woman was going to feel. Had Mr. Emsworth been her only child?
I realized I hadn't asked her if she had other children. I sincerely
hoped her son's untimely death was not about to leave her destitute.

Mrs. Hudgins curtsied, and Jackson bowed gravely, and the
two hurried off to see to their duties. Lord Worthington motioned
that I should lead the way to the back garden.

The sun's first welcoming rays were just peeking over the trees,
promising a lovely, if chilly, day ahead. I walked quickly to the spot
where Mr. Emsworth's body lay, grateful to see he appeared undis-
turbed. Crouching down to examine the body, Benjamin used the
handle of a fountain pen to gingerly lift the man's dressing gown
and check his pockets. Now that I was here, in the growing light
of day with the two men, I began to doubt my earlier suspicions.
Perhaps it really was just a terrible accident?

"I... I could see some slight staining on his nightshirt and
around his mouth, but nothing extreme," I began cautiously. "His
room could be searched for evidence he was sick during the night.
If he'd been very ill, though, why didn't he summon a doctor?"

"Perhaps he didn't have the time. Perhaps he didn't realize
that he had anything other than a passing illness." Still Benjamin
worked quickly and quietly. I assumed he was examining the body
for any other kinds of marks or signs of struggle.

"As far as I know, he was well when everyone retired for the
evening," offered Lord Worthington. "When we finished our conversation and parted ways at the top of the stairs, he didn't seem
ill as far as I could tell."

"He could have opened the window for some fresh air if he'd
been feeling ill, then tripped and fallen," I offered.

Benjamin straighted, his voice gruff.

"He could have. But you told me he was murdered. Why?"

"Well… I could be wrong but… the pupils, the stains, and lack of blood around the body. It seems to me that he was dead before he fell out the window."

"I agree."

I blinked. For some reason I hadn't expected Benjamin to agree with me. I was hoping he'd tell me I was mistaken, that Mr. Emsworth had just had a terrible accident, and that was that.

"If he was poisoned," I said slowly, "I don't think it was arsenic, or cyanide. Poisonings from those substances can be quite violent. I think someone would have heard him during the night, and there would be more evidence on his person. Also, I detected no lingering odor, such as the burnt almond smell left by arsenic."

"Then what could it have been, Miss Photographic Memory? Put that unnerving brain to good use. You know it's in there."

I shuddered again, only this time I couldn't hide it from Benjamin's notice. Turning away, I gritted my teeth, allowing all of those disturbing images to flood my mind for a few seconds.

"I remember!" I blurted out, resisting the urge to sink onto the cobblestones beside Mr. Emsworth. I put my shoulders back and lifted my chin instead. "But I'll only tell you if you let me help you figure out who killed him. Mrs. Emsworth and her son were kind to me, and she deserves to know the truth about what happened."

"Absolutely not!" Benjamin's eyes flashed angrily. "If you think I'm going to let you go poking around a murder investigation— with a murderer who's more than likely in the house at this very moment—"

"Let me? You have absolutely no claim over me, remember? You have no right to tell me what I can do in my friend's house."

"I have every right to decide who meddles in my investigation. I will not have your death on my conscience, too."

I almost bit back a retort about how ruining my life hadn't been a problem for his conscience, but I remembered we had an audience. Lord Worthington's eyes were bouncing back and forth between me and Benji like we were in a thrilling tennis match.

"Very well, I don't have to know exactly what poison killed him to continue this investigation. It's enough to know he was likely dead before he fell out the window."

"But you're going to need to know what to look for. If someone has a particular substance in their room or with their belongings, it's a pretty good chance that they're the one who killed him, isn't it?"

"Freddie, I mean it, you are not getting involved! I've told you far too much already."

Benjamin turned around, facing the woods for a moment, and ran his hands over his face in exasperation.

"Might I offer a suggestion?" Lord Worthington smiled at us both diplomatically, as if we were sitting over tea in the drawing room, and I had a feeling he was very good at his job in parliament. "Am I correct, Hadleigh, in assuming you want everyone to believe Emsworth's death was an accident, so the house party continues on as usual while you hunt for both the blackmail evidence and the killer?"

"You are correct. I'll encourage the doctor to rule death by fall. I'll bribe the magistrate if necessary. He's hardly going to argue with an Earl. Assuming the cold weather holds, it will take at least a couple more days until the roads are passable by carriage. That should give us enough time for a thorough search of the entire house."

"And if it starts to thaw earlier and someone decides to leave early?" Lord Worthington asked.

"I'll figure out a way to detain them."

"Which could be difficult without probable cause. It occurs to me that it is in the best interest of your case to have as many hands searching the house as possible. Miss Osbourne could be helpful in searching the women's rooms, as she would be much less conspicuous than you or me in that wing. And having some idea of what sort of poison we're looking for would certainly speed things up. Perhaps she could be useful without putting her in any dangerous situations? Well, any more dangerous than it is for all of us, staying at a house party where one of our members or servants could be a murderer. If Emsworth was indeed your blackmailer, he was likely killed by an accomplice or by someone with a secret they'd also like to keep hidden. I suspect as long as Miss Osbourne doesn't try to blackmail anyone, she—along with the rest of us—will be fine."

Benjamin stood silent for a moment, his back still to us. Turning slowly, he looked resigned, and I knew I'd won. For a split second, his eyes locked with mine, and I felt a frisson of something electric crackle from my scalp to my toes.

"You can help search," he conceded, "but only in the women's areas, and you should try to stay with the Cunninghams, me, or Worthington at all times."

"Except when I'm in my bedroom of course. At night."

This was hardly the time to goad him, but I couldn't help myself.

"Of course," he ground out. "Doors locked."

"Very well, you have yourself a deal."

I held out my hand, and after a few beats Benjamin shook it, a little harder than necessary.

Chapter 10

"I believe Mr. Emsworth was poisoned by foxglove, otherwise known as digitalis," I said quietly as I poured tea for Lord Worthington, Benjamin, and myself in the breakfast room. I glanced around once more to make sure no one had yet joined us, and continued.

"It has a cluster of purple or white bell-shaped flowers, and is commonly used in extremely small doses in heart medications. But larger amounts can cause nausea, vomiting, contracted pupils, confusion, weakness, and heart failure."

"It sounds plausible." Benjamin added cream and several scoops of sugar to his tea, and we all occupied ourselves with buttering hot scones as a footman entered to deposit a warming pan of sausages on the sideboard.

"Have you heard of it? Foxglove that is?" I asked when the footman had left again.

"You don't last long in my profession without at least being aware of the ways that someone could be trying to kill you," Benjamin admitted. "I've heard of foxglove, but I was unaware of its symptoms."

I wished he was being dramatic, but I doubted it. While I would easily claim the scapegrace as my mortal enemy, the idea of him being in such a dangerous line of work left me uneasy.

The doctor had arrived moments after Benjamin had agreed to let me help them with their search, as he only lived down the lane and was easy to track down. He was a wizened, elderly fellow with bright white moustaches and twinkling eyes. The magistrate stumbled in a half hour later, out of breath and covered in snow up to his knees. I'd told them both my story about searching for a place to sketch in the early morning light and stumbling across the body, leaving out the pertinent details about the suspected poisoning. As it was early, and the magistrate had a house full of relatives for the holiday, he was all too eager to wrap things up with a Christmas bow and be on his way. Benjamin didn't even need to bribe him or coerce the doctor into declaring the death an accident. Under any other circumstances, I would have been concerned at both men's lack of attention, but in this case it suited our purposes nicely. Two burly footmen were called to carry Mr. Emsworth's body to a gardening shed, where the cold temperatures would preserve it until it could be transported back to London for a funeral. The doctor, who was currently meeting with the Cunninghams and Mrs. Emsworth in the parlor to inform them of Mr. Emsworth's tragic demise—I was grateful the task had not fallen to me—kindly refusing my offer of sustenance in favor of his own breakfast awaiting him at home after the gruesome news had been delivered. I suspected we had little time before Sarah rushed into the breakfast room to see how I was handling the discovery.

"So what do we do next?" I asked.

"We have to expand our search," Benjamin said as he polished off another scone. "Now we're looking for evidence of blackmail *and* murder. No one has left the estate, so if someone is in possession of foxglove, it would be easy enough to locate."

"Or it could be growing somewhere on the estate," I offered. "Perhaps in the conservatory?"

"It's unlikely, but possible. We should check."

"It would also be useful if you told me what sort of blackmail evidence you're looking for. I could look right at it while searching and not know what I'm seeing."

"There are two letters that we know of."

Lord Worthington, who'd been silent during the whole exchange, cleared his throat and looked meaningfully at Benjamin.

"And two, erm, photographs."

Benjamin looked decidedly uncomfortable, and if a man hadn't just been murdered, I might have laughed out loud.

"I take it the photographs are of a somewhat salacious nature?"

Benjamin looked at me sharply.

"For heaven's sake, Benjamin, I work with artists. I'm hardly a prude."

"Let's just say you'll know it if you see it."

I sighed. Benjamin may have agreed to let me assist in the search, but he wasn't exactly being forthcoming.

"I believe Sarah has more Christmas crafts planned for the ladies today, but I can tell her I've had a shock and would like some time alone. I'll inspect the conservatory first, since I know what foxglove looks like—"

"Not alone, Freddie. Take Sarah or Mary with you."

"I take it, then, that Arthur and Mary Cunningham aren't on your list of suspects either?"

"They don't seem to have any connection with my suspect, but we cannot rule anyone out completely. Anyone here could be an unwitting accomplice if compromising materials were hidden in their rooms."

"What then shall I tell them I'm looking for? I know you don't want me to tell them I'm searching for a substance that may have been used to poison Mr. Emsworth. I love Sarah, dearly, but the entire house would be alerted within minutes. She's never been able to keep a secret."

Which was precisely the reason I'd waited to write to her about my marriage to Benjamin all those years ago, preferring to keep the news quiet until we'd returned home from our travels and could tell our friends in person. This minor hesitation had saved my reputation amongst our social set—a fact I was grateful for to this day.

"Perhaps you're heading to the conservatory to look for artistic inspiration among the winter plants," suggested Lord Worthington with a smile. "My sister used to paint and draw to relax. It's only natural that you would want to do some sketching after such a stressful morning."

"Perfect. After I search the conservatory—"

The footman returned with a warming pan filled with coddled eggs.

"—for the perfect winter flower. I hear the Cunninghams have a beautiful collection of poinsettias that I would love to paint," I improvised. As the footman again retreated, I added softly, "I'll begin on the ladies' bedchambers afterwards, once everyone has come down to breakfast. We should also find out if anyone present takes heart medication. It would take a large amount of medication to kill someone, but not so much that you wouldn't be able to dissolve it in some type of food or drink. Perhaps Miss Price? She is quite elderly, and the elderly often have heart problems. She seemed quite taken with you yesterday; you should ask her, Benjamin."

He barked a laugh. "You just don't want to talk to her yourself."

"Of course I don't! The woman hates me. She'd hardly be forthright about her health routine. Though, I can't say I'd be surprised if she had it in her to murder someone. She's a calloused, prejudiced old bird."

I grimaced, suddenly aware I was not being at all ladylike. I seemed to revert back to my wild teenage years in Benjamin's presence.

"I'm so sorry, Lord Worthington. I'm afraid this morning has put me out of sorts."

"Completely understandable, Miss Osbourne." Lord Worthington finished off a scone and went to the sideboard to fill his plate, his eyes twinkling as he looked between me and Benjamin. "Anyone would under the circumstances."

"There's one more thing I'm confused about, however." I sipped my now-lukewarm tea absent-mindedly. "We're searching for evidence of blackmail, but doesn't Mr. Emsworth's death suggest that *he* was the blackmailer? If that's the case, wouldn't the queen's relative now be safe?"

"It's possible, but since the evidence wasn't in his home, bank, or club in London, it's likely he brought it with him and it's here on the Cunninghams' estate. I'd rather not have information that sensitive fall into anyone else's hands. All it takes is one clever servant who stumbles upon the letters or photograph and sees an opportunity to make some extra cash, and we're right back where we started."

Lord Worthington came back to the table with his plate piled high, and Benjamin took his place at the sideboard, still speaking softly in case any other guests decided to join us for breakfast.

"There's one other thing we should keep in mind."

My heart gave a little leap at being included in the *we* of this investigative team.

"Emsworth could have been working with a partner. Perhaps they disagreed on how to proceed next, and the partner killed him. He could still blackmail the royal family."

"So it's in our best interests to hurry."

"We must catch the killer before Christmas."

Chapter 11

The rest of the guests started filing in to breakfast soon after, and from the hushed whispers around me, I gathered word of Mr. Emsworth's fall had spread quickly. Benjamin and Lord Worthington said their polite but appropriately-reserved good mornings to the other guests and bowed out of the room quickly to begin their search. I decided to remain a few minutes longer and watch the guests for any signs of guilt. Filling my teacup, I helped myself to another scone and took both to an armchair by the window where I could observe without being forced to make polite small talk to recount how I found the body. I had a strong constitution, but I still wasn't ready to relive it again quite yet.

Miss Taylor and Miss Price sat at one of the breakfast tables, Miss Taylor a rather alarming shade of green, and Miss Price bemoaning the loss of such an eligible bachelor on the marriage mart. I also overheard her wondering if Mr. Emsworth's younger brother would be coming to assist his mother home, and was comforted to know that Mrs. Emsworth had another son to care for her in her time of need.

After Lord Belvoir and his cousins filled their plates, the Marquess approached me with a sympathetic smile and took my hand in his.

"I can see, dearest Miss Osbourne, that you'd like to be alone for a few moments, and I don't blame you a feather. But if I can serve you in any capacity, or you need someone to talk to, please don't hesitate to come find me this morning."

I couldn't help but smile back at his heartfelt demeanor. I promised him I would, indeed, come to him if I needed anything, but the entire time I was looking at Lord Belvoir, I wondered: *Could this kind man be a murderer?* Someone in this house had to be.

Mr. Loughty nodded and waved at me from the sideboard while they were filling their plates, and Miss Loughty motioned for her cousin to join them and leave me alone, mouthing, "Sorry!" with a polite smile from across the room. After the cousins were settled, Arthur and Mary came in and began filling their plates at the sideboard, but as soon as Mary spotted me, she abandoned her breakfast, ran over to my corner by the window, and plopped on the floor at my feet in a billowing cloud of skirts and petticoats.

"Oh, Winifred, I am so so sorry you had to make such a gruesome discovery this morning! Are you quite all right? May I bring you some breakfast?"

I stood, gently grabbing her hands and pulling her up with me.

"I am quite unharmed. I feel terrible for the Emsworth family, of course, but I'm hardly a swooning debutante. And I had quite a large breakfast already. I just needed a moment to collect myself, but I'm about to leave to find Sarah."

"She is worried sick for you," Mary admitted, "but Mrs. Emsworth fainted upon hearing the news of her son's accident and had to be carried up to her bedroom. Sarah is looking in on her now."

"Oh, the poor woman. I'll check in on them both and see if there's anything I can do."

"If you need anything today, please don't hesitate to ask me," Mary offered. "I suspect the house party will go on as planned, since no one can travel just yet because of the snow, but it's so hard to feel festive when a man has just died."

I squeezed Mary's hands.

"I confess I do need a few moments alone this morning, but if you don't mind, do what you can to keep the spirits of the others up. I'll rejoin you shortly, and we'll see if we keep everyone's minds off things." *And keep everyone at the Cunninghams' long enough for Benjamin to find a murderer.*

A few moments later, I was standing outside Mrs. Emsworth's bedroom door. I tapped lightly, and Sarah's soft voice called for me to enter. Mrs. Emsworth was lying on her side in the bed, eyes closed and breathing deeply. She was fully clothed, but her hair had come out of its pins and was spilling down around her pillow. She looked pale, and suddenly much older than the vibrant matron she'd been just the day before. Grief has a way of making one feel old and worn down long before their time. I suspected Mrs. Emsworth had some long, hard days ahead of her, and I was glad she was resting.

"She's sleeping now," Sarah whispered. "The doctor left us a tonic to help her rest, and I'm grateful he did. What a terrible thing, to lose a son right before Christmas." Sarah's eyes filled with tears, and I bent down to give her a hug.

"I'm grateful she has such a kind hostess to look after her. Has anyone sent word to her other son yet?"

"Apparently he's in Bavaria, spending time with his wife's family for the holiday. They are often traveling back and forth, which was why Mrs. Emsworth lived exclusively with her elder son. It might be some time before word can reach the younger Mr. Emsworth and he can make his way back. I've offered for Mrs. Emsworth to stay here until he does, so she doesn't have to go back to London alone."

"That's very generous of you, dearest. I'm sure she's grateful to be among friends."

"Oh, it's the least we can do. But how are you, Winnie? Finding the poor man must have been—" Sarah broke off, the tears spilling down her cheeks as she wiped at them with a dainty handkerchief. "It must have been quite a shock. Why were you outdoors so early? It's freezing out there!"

"I hadn't been able to sleep, so I was searching for something to sketch," I told her. "It's probably a good thing that it was I who stumbled across Mr. Emsworth and not one of the kitchen maids. I've seen my share of dead bodies and am not prone to hysterics." Sarah grimaced, having heard all about my commission on *Poisons*, though I'd spared her the more gruesome details. "While I'm heartbroken for his family of course, I will be just fine." *As long as we located Mr. Emsworth's killer.*

I couldn't bear the thought of something happening to the Cunninghams, and was reminded that we needed to work quickly. I wasn't about to pull Sarah from Mrs. Emsworth's side, and Mary was busy keeping the spirits of the other guests up, so I needed to go ahead and make the trip out to the conservatory and then start searching the ladies' rooms.

"I'm going to go wander your conservatory, dearest, to look for something to sketch and get my mind off things. Is it locked? Should I have one of the gardeners let me in?"

"No, we have a small winter garden in there, and the kitchen maids are always going back and forth. It's always open."

I leaned down and gave my friend another hug.

"What's that for?" Sarah asked, her eyes still glittering with tears.

"For being the kindest, most considerate hostess, even in a very unfortunate circumstance such as this one. Don't stay in here too long; Mrs. Emsworth's lady's maid can watch over her while she rests."

"Sommers, her lady's maid, has been fluttering about like a mother hen," Sarah admitted. "I finally sent her down to the kitchen to fetch something for Mrs. Emsworth to eat when she awakes, just to get Sommers out of the room for a moment and let the poor woman sleep. I'm sure she'll be back soon, and I'll go check on the other guests."

"Don't forget to take care of yourself, too," I ordered. "Have you eaten yet?"

Sarah waved a hand dismissively.

"I couldn't bear the thought of food yet, but I'll go down and have some breakfast after Sommers returns. Now go, find something beautiful to draw, and I'll see you at luncheon."

On my way back down the stairs, I briefly thought about stopping to ask Mary to accompany me to the conservatory, but I'd already told her I needed a few minutes alone, and she was more useful keeping the guests calm and diverted until Sarah could get away from Mrs. Emsworth. I'd stopped by my room to grab my coat, my sketchpad and pencil still tucked in the pocket. I supposed I should sketch a few things while I was outside, just to avoid suspicion. I'd told Benjamin I'd take Sarah or Mary with me, but even if the foxglove had been procured in the Cunninghams' conservatory, the killer was hardly going to return now, so I could be in no danger if no one knew my true intentions.

I nodded to the kitchen staff on my way out the back door once again, and walked carefully to the conservatory, avoiding a few icy patches on the cobblestones. I noticed the path to the conservatory had been carefully treated like the rest of the back garden, so anyone could have made their way out here without leaving tracks in the snow. Opening the heavy glass and metal doors, I stepped into the unnaturally quiet space. Even the winter birdsong had ceased, muffled by thick panes of glass. The only sound was the soft crunch of my footsteps on the gravel walkway, and I found it unnerving, the hairs on the back of my neck prickling in apprehension.

Out here, I was utterly alone.

Chapter 12

Taking a deep breath, I looked around me and tried to relax. The conservatory was a modern, intricately-designed building, with carefully-carved metal work that reminded me of all the grand structures currently being built all over Paris. The roof curved up to a pointed arch filled with more scrolling metalwork and tiny, intricate panes of glass. I knew the Cunninghams had the conservatory built only a few years earlier, but it had been so well-designed and bountifully-planted, that I had the illusion of walking into an ancient, hidden fairy garden. It wasn't an overly-large structure, maybe thrice the size of the Cunninghams' sitting room. Two long planters ran down the center of the room, each spilling over with small fruit trees, flowers, palms, and exotic plants. I knew that Rupert was a bit of a novice gardener, and liked pottering about in here during the warmer months. Could he have cultivated foxglove without knowing its deadly properties?

It was going to take me longer than I'd thought to look carefully through all the plants here. In addition to the two planters down the center of the room, a metal bench ran around its perimeter, and was covered with more plants of all shapes and sizes. The section closest to the door was obviously the kitchen garden; I spotted thyme, sage, and tarragon, and even a rosemary plant. Running my fingers across its needle-like leaves, I inhaled the heavenly scent and was instantly transported back to Italy.

A few deeper troughs were filled with cabbages, carrots,

and other root vegetables. A good conservatory was not only an ornamental delight, but served a very practical purpose for an estate by allowing food to be grown even in the coldest months. Scanning the kitchen garden quickly, I moved towards the middle of the conservatory, gently pushing aside the fronds of a large fern on a decorative stand. This section contained more ornamental varieties, shrubs, and small trees in pots being sheltered from the winter cold. Towards the back of the conservatory, I could see English roses mingling with exotic orchids and many other species of flowers I couldn't name. My knowledge of poisonous plants may have been excellent, but my expertise on botany ended there. Still, the conservatory was a marvelous place, and I could see that I'd been remiss in neglecting it so far on my explorations of the estate. I would have to sit and sketch in here in truth when this murder business was taken care of and Benjamin was out of my life once more.

The thought caused a knot in my stomach I didn't care to evaluate at the moment. Picking up a discarded trowel from one of the potting benches, I used the pointed edge to gently move trailing greenery around, careful not to miss any plants that could be hiding under the dense foliage. After a quarter of an hour, I was starting to sweat in the warmth of the conservatory, so I took off my coat and hung it on a series of pegs conveniently located by the door then continued my search. I was almost confident in my ability to declare the conservatory a foxglove-free location, when I heard the doorknob rattling at the other end of the structure. Surely it was just one of the gardeners or kitchen staff, but I remembered Benjamin's warning to keep someone with me at all times, and I groaned. I'd never hear the end of it if the killer caught me here alone—assuming I survived the encounter.

Clutching the trowel, I glanced quickly around me, but the back wall of the conservatory held no door, only several metal storage cabinets which ran from ceiling to floor and were painted a dark green to match the rest of the structure. I opened the largest, which held more gardening tools on hooks along the back wall. I considered grabbing one of the long, sturdy shovels, but I doubted I would be able to swing it hard enough to do any damage if someone tried to attack me, so I kept hold of the small trowel and retreated back behind a large potted palm towards the end of one row. The door creaked open, and almost instantly I regretted my choice of hiding place, as I couldn't see the path from the door without revealing myself. There was nothing to be done but wait and see if I was discovered.

The door closed with the soft click of iron on iron. I heard footsteps, a man's most likely, but he was walking lightly over the colorful pavers as if trying not to be heard. *Could this be our killer?* My heart thudded in rhythm with the man's steps. I was being ridiculous, wasn't I? Even if the killer had found foxglove in the conservatory, there would be no reason to come back, would there? Unless they wanted to keep me from finding the source of their poison, and came back to remove it. I took a few deep breaths to calm my nerves. I should have waited until Sarah was finished sitting with Mrs. Emsworth and asked her to come with me. The footsteps were only a few steps away from me now, and I decided I should go on the offensive before the person reached me. I would at least have the element of surprise in my favor. Bringing the trowel up in my hand to wield it like a dagger, I jumped out right before the man reached my potted palm.

"Arrrrrrrg!"

It took me a few moments to realize it was my voice that was yelling as Benjamin deftly deflected my blow with one arm, then gripped my wrist and turned me around with the other. I'd hardly had a chance to blink, and I was facing the potted palm I'd just been hiding behind. The arm holding the trowel was twisted around my back, Benjamin close behind me in a mockery of an embrace, so close I could feel his breath on the back of my neck.

I stood there, frozen for half a moment, then I opened my hand and dropped the trowel on his foot, wrenching my arm away and turning so I was facing him. I then took a step backwards to put some distance between us once more.

I was annoyed that I was breathing heavily, as though I'd just run here from the house, while Benjamin appeared to be at his leisure, not a hair out of place. The only sign that something was amiss was the thundering expression on his face.

"Bloody hell, Freddie! What were you thinking? Are you trying to kill me?"

"You're obviously more than a match for a small woman with a garden trowel." I rolled my eyes at him. "And what was I thinking? Why in God's name did you sneak up on me like that? I thought you were the murderer! You could have identified yourself and saved me an apoplexy."

"Because I didn't want to alert all and sundry who might be standing nearby that we were in here."

"Well, between my screaming and us arguing like schoolchildren, I'm sure we've already done so. Why did you come looking for me?"

Benjamin sighed, looking marginally less furious as he picked up the garden trowel and inspected the top of his boot for scuff marks.

"I was examining Emsworth's room, and I saw you out the window."

"What did you find?"

"It was as you suspected," Benjamin admitted. "He'd been ill but not violently so. The poison could have been in his cup of warm milk. I talked to the housemaids, and they said he sent for one each night before bed. He liked to have it while he was reading."

My heart squeezed. The man had just wanted to read his books in peace and drink warm milk before bed. Surely such a person would not resort to something as banal as blackmail?

"I'll return to Emsworth's room in a moment and check once more for any letters or photographs. He could have moved evidence around since my first night here. But dash it all, Freddie! You promised you would take Sarah or Mary with you. What if I

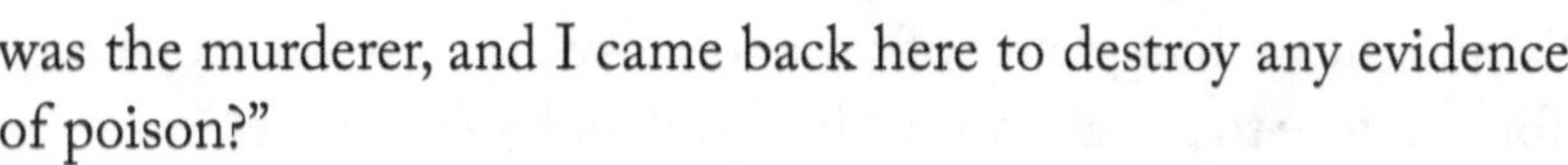

was the murderer, and I came back here to destroy any evidence of poison?"

Benjamin's eyes flashed, but I refused to cower.

"I did think of that, but I don't think there's any evidence here to destroy. I've searched nearly the entire conservatory, and there's no sign of foxglove anywhere. Nor anything else poisonous that I recognize."

Reaching over, I took the trowel from him, then returned to the planter box where I had left off and began to push aside ferns and trailing vines once more.

"Help me search these last few benches. You're looking for white or purple flowers that are bell shaped, all stacked up on top of one another on a single stem."

With a sigh, Benjamin walked around to the second path and began checking the planters on that row.

We worked in silence for a few moments.

"Thank you, anyway, for being concerned about my welfare, but I am quite able to take care of myself."

"So I noticed," Benjamin said dryly, "at least so long as your enemies are members of the plant kingdom."

"I can't help that you're a government operative who seems to haul bricks or heavy lumber in his spare time. I think I would have been quite capable against a real Earl."

"You know as well as anyone that my title is quite genuine."

"I meant an *ordinary* Earl. One whose concerns of state are limited to those of Parliament."

An uncomfortable silence settled around us as we rifled our way through the greenery. The strain of the day must have been getting to me. It's the only reason I could think of for what I blurted out next.

"You took her away from me, too, you know."

I didn't have to tell him who I meant. Being in this conservatory together without her must be eating at him, too.

"I know." He spoke quietly, never looking up from the planters.

"I thought we had plenty of time to make amends, plenty of time for you to—to say goodbye. Until suddenly—we didn't."

"Why didn't you at least write to me and Grandfather about the funeral? It broke Grandfather's heart not to be there."

It had broken my heart too. We'd found out about Lady Hadleigh's death barely two months after I'd received the annulment papers. After the funeral was over and it was too late to return to pay our respects. It had felt like the final nail in the coffin of our family, and I'd grieved the loss as I hadn't even grieved the loss of my own parents. Benjamin had to know how much that had hurt me.

"I can't tell you why, Freddie. Just know that it was too dangerous for you to come home at that point."

"Dangerous? How could it be dangerous? What are you not telling me?"

Benjamin had stilled across the conservatory. He was facing away from me, arms at his sides, but I could see the tension running through him. After several long moments, I sighed and went back to my work. I had dirt under my fingernails, and my hands were scratched where thorns had torn at them, but I was proud that they didn't shake. I was never going to receive an explanation from this man, and the sooner I could accept it and move on, the better for my pitiful, damaged heart. Some wounds were better off not reopened.

We worked in silence for a few more minutes, and I'd just inspected the last of my row when Benjamin froze and held up a hand for me to be silent.

I, too, could hear the crunch of footsteps on the gravel leading up to the conservatory.

Chapter 13

Before I could speak or even move, Benjamin had crossed the narrow rows of plants, grabbed my arm, and shoved me into the largest of the cabinets lining the back wall of the conservatory. I was about to protest when his hand covered my mouth, and he climbed into the cabinet after me, shooting daggers the whole time as if daring me to open my mouth. The cabinets were narrow, built for tools not people, and I thought for a moment there wouldn't be room to close the door on Benjamin's muscular frame. Somehow he managed to shut the door with one arm, while pushing me deeper into the cabinet with the other, and we were plunged into darkness.

I wanted to protest, to tell him it was likely Sarah or Mary coming to check on me, but what did I know? The last two days had completely turned my world upside down. I'd seen an acquaintance dead on the cobblestones only a few hours earlier, and here I was, locked in a dark closet with the man I hated more than anyone in the world, and who, until two days ago, I thought I'd never have to see again. A man who—I was beginning to realize—we were far more dependent on than I wanted to be, at least until we knew if there was a murderer loose in the house.

So I kept quiet, inching further back into the cabinet. About the width of a carriage seat and slightly longer, it was dark and smelled of earth and metal, with only a faint hint of the heady aroma of orchids from the exotic flowers planted nearby. I saw a scrolling design of light breaking through the darkness and illuminating my feet and realized there was intricate ventwork at the bottom of the cabinet that could give us a view of what was happening in the conservatory. I tried to turn sideways, but the cabinet was too narrow to accommodate my hips and full skirts, so I bent my knees and tried to slide down the best I could. Benjamin stood, tense and straight, holding the door of the cabinet shut from the inside, and I imagined him rolling his eyes at me, though I couldn't see him in the darkness. I tried to motion to the scrollwork so he would understand what I was trying to do, but it was unlikely he could see me either.

I was dying to know what was happening outside in the conservatory. I couldn't hear footsteps, but perhaps someone had entered while we were hiding away in the cabinet? What if we were discovered? The impropriety of being discovered in such close quarters with a man I was not related to would ruin me. It's not like we could tell all and sundry that it didn't matter because this man had once been my husband. Polite society would never recover from the scandal.

I thought that perhaps I heard a slight scraping sound. Noises were distorted inside the cabinet, so it was hard to tell. I needed to look out of those vents. I slid down more until my knees touched the front side of the cabinet, my back against the other. If I could just get my arm down on the floor, I could lower myself to the ground and see out. I leaned sideways, and my fingers had just brushed cold tiles when my left foot slipped out from under me, sending me to the ground and causing me to kick a large shovel off its hook on the way. Thankfully, I caught myself on an elbow and lowered myself to the ground without making too much noise, but I watched in horror as the shovel teetered and began to fall, the heavy metal blade coming right towards my head.

I could just make out the shape of Benjamin lunging at the shovel in the darkness. But somehow, he didn't stop, and was moving towards me at an alarming rate. Good lord, he was falling on top of me! I raised the arm that wasn't currently underneath me to cover my head, but he caught himself with one arm, hand planted firmly on the tile floor. He hovered inches above me, the other hand still holding the shovel between us where it pressed roughly into my hip. I hardly dared to breathe. *Did whoever was in the conservatory hear us fall?*

After a few seconds of tense silence, I felt Benjamin's arm shaking from the effort of keeping him suspended above me with one hand. Feeling for the shovel, I managed to grab it with my free hand, pushing it down towards my feet so it wedged between my leg and the wall and was no longer between us. Not wanting to even whisper lest we be discovered, I grabbed Benjamin's other hand and placed it on the floor on the other side of my waist, then tugged the front of his waistcoat and pulled him down so his forearms were on the floor. His shoulders were wedged into either side of the cabinet so that one was at least six inches higher than the other, but at least he wasn't holding all of his weight on one arm anymore.

I held my breath and tried not to think of how close we were, his legs straddling one of mine and his face inches from my own. For one wild moment I had the insane urge to grab the back of his neck and pull him in for a kiss, but I wrenched my thoughts away from that dangerous precipice and motioned towards the scrolling ventwork with my head. We were close enough to see each other in the dark now, or perhaps our eyes had simply adjusted, but Benjamin nodded.

Inching my head in that direction, I peered through the delicate design into the conservatory. All I could see were colorful floor tiles and the legs of the planters and potting benches. I angled closer, which had the unfortunate effect of pushing my body closer to Benjamin's, and I could hear his breath hitch softly. At least this horrible situation seemed to be affecting him as much as it was affecting me. If I had to suffer, then so did he.

Finally, a pair of men's topboots came into view. They were of the highest quality and blackened to a brilliant shine, so it was a gentleman, not a servant. But which gentleman? The feet turned towards our cabinet, and I stifled a gasp. Were we about to be discovered? Instinctually, I held a hand against Benjamin's mouth to indicate he should be quiet, but I doubted I needed to. He knew what was at stake here as clearly as I did. Being discovered by a killer could prove deadly. But being discovered by anyone else would be nearly as bad; Benjamin would be forced to marry me yet again or leave my reputation in tatters for the rest of my life. Both prospects were equally chilling.

After a few moments, the topboots turned away again, and gradually I could make out the entire man's silhouette as he walked back towards the door of the conservatory. My stomach dropped, but I needed to see his face to confirm. As if on cue, he turned back and scanned the conservatory once more, and even from here I could tell that his handsome brow was wrinkled in thought. He left the conservatory then, the faint crunching of boots on gravel fading as he walked back towards the house.

After a few more tense moments, I felt safe enough to whisper.

"It was Lord Belvoir. Do you think he is involved in all of this?"

"It's possible. Perhaps he had a secret Mr. Emsworth threatened to expose." Benjamin pushed himself up off of me, and using the cabinet walls, somehow managed to bring himself back to a standing position. Grabbing my arm, he pulled me roughly to my feet, but caught my waist to steady me when I nearly fell back over.

"Sorry. My leg fell asleep. You're heavier than you used to be."

"I could say the same about you." Benjamin's lip twitched as he held me a second longer than necessary. Was this wretched man holding back a smile? My figure had certainly filled out since I'd seen him last, but I was far from overweight.

"Yes, well, neither of us are children anymore, are we?" I huffed, somewhat indignantly, opening the cabinet and stepping cautiously outside. "And Lord Belvoir didn't seem interested in the plants at all. Perhaps he heard I came out here to draw, and he was looking for me."

"Ah, fancy becoming the next Lady Belvoir, do you?" Benjamin followed me into the conservatory, straightening his jacket and brushing dirt off of his rumpled trousers. Heaven knew what I looked like. I would have to find a mirror before I could return to the house. I couldn't stop the unladylike snort that burst out at his comment.

"Heavens, no. Matrimony is not a mistake I plan to repeat ever again." After brushing out my skirts, I tried to remove the dust and cobwebs from my blouse, but gave up when I saw a small tear in the fabric. I would just have to hide it with my coat until I could slip back up to my room to change. My coat!

"Damnation! My coat is on the hook by the door. Lord Belvoir probably saw it. He'll know I was in here."

"There's nothing we can do about it now. Come here, you have cobwebs in your hair. You can claim you left your coat behind and had already returned to the house, but you hardly want to look like we were rolling around on the floor together, hmm?"

"Hilarious, Benji." I stood still and allowed him to remove the cobwebs from my hair. His touch was almost gentle as he swept the loose strands up off my neck and pinned them back into place. I shivered involuntarily, but if Benjamin noticed, he had the grace not to comment on it.

"I'm no lady's maid, but I think it will do. Next time, if you have to go off alone, let me know, will you?"

"Eager for another conservatory tryst?" I'd meant to tease him, to show him how little his presence affected me, but the words caught thickly in my throat.

Benjamin glared at me in response.

"Just try not to get yourself killed. I haven't yet lost a civilian in the line of duty, and I'm hardly about to let you be the first."

He turned and stalked to the door of the conservatory without looking back.

"Don't forget to sketch something while you're here," he barked out on his way out the door. "You wouldn't want to disappoint Lord Belvoir."

Retrieving the notebook and pencil from my coat pocket, I sketched a few of the orchids and a particularly attractive palm tree, taking my time and allowing my rapid breathing to return to normal. When I was satisfied I had enough work to show any of the guests who may ask what I'd been up to, I slipped out of the conservatory, making sure to leave my coat on the hook just in case Lord Belvoir enquired about it later. I slipped back in through the servants' entrance and made my way up to my room via the servants' stairs, managing not to see anyone on the way.

The encounter with Benjamin in the conservatory had shaken me more than I cared to admit. I didn't dare call the lady's maid, but unbuttoned my blouse with trembling fingers and swapped it for a festive red blouse trimmed in navy to match my skirt, which was made of a sturdy fabric and thankfully was none the worse for wear after its foray on the conservatory floor. My hair was harder to tackle on my own, however, so I hoped Benjamin had done a decent job of repinning it in the back.

When I felt presentable, I walked down and joined the rest of the guests in the sitting room, my sketchbook and pencil in hand. Everyone but Miss Price expressed delight in my return and fussed over my welfare, and no one seemed to notice my change of attire or slightly disordered hairstyle. Sarah had a warm cider in my hand and a blanket tucked around me within seconds of my sitting down, and I allowed myself to relax for a few moments before I considered my next steps.

Though somewhat more subdued than yesterday's merriment, the women chatted pleasantly about fashion predictions for the upcoming spring as they sat in comfortable chairs around the fire and cut out more paper angel garlands. I sat in silence, content to half-listen to the conversations around me. *This is what our Christmas holidays should have been like,* I thought wryly. *Crafts and conversation by the fire, with no murders, and no troubling ex-husbands that stirred up long-buried, unwelcome feelings.*

Chapter 14

Benjamin remained absent the rest of the morning, no doubt continuing his search in the gentlemens' wing, but Lord Worthington joined the rest of us in the sitting room shortly before luncheon. He chatted pleasantly with Mary and Miss Loughty until the meal was served at the sideboard, then took the seat next to me while the others headed over to fill their plates.

"I trust you are faring well after your ordeal this morning, Miss Osbourne?"

"Yes, I'm quite well."

Somehow, my encounter with Benjamin in the conservatory had left me more shaken than finding Mr. Emsworth's body, but I wasn't about to tell Lord Worthington that.

Lord Worthington lowered his voice so that only I could hear him.

"If you're still willing to assist me and Benjamin in our search, I could accompany you in going through the ladies' rooms before they retire for afternoon rest."

I nodded. I'd been plied with cider and cakes and dried fruit for the last hour, so I was hardly hungry for luncheon anyway.

"I think Sarah has a card tournament planned for this afternoon, so I will tell her I need to rest beforehand."

We arranged to meet in fifteen minutes outside my room, and Lord Worthington made a show of building two plates to take to eat with Benjamin, who was "dealing with some pressing estate business," then cheerfully made his excuses to Sarah and left the rest of the guests to their luncheon. After I told Sarah I was going up to rest, I overheard her telling Miss Price that Mrs. Emsworth was still resting and was going to take a tray in her room, so Lord Worthington and I would be sure to avoid that room.

In fact, we'd better be careful to avoid being seen entirely. I doubt Lord Worthington's fiancée, whoever she was, would appreciate our being alone together, even for a pursuit as noble as catching a murderer. I'd known of multiple couples who'd been forced to marry for something as harmless as being caught in a room alone together at the wrong time. As amiable as Lord Worthington was, I had no desire to be at the mercy of any man for the rest of my life. I'd certainly learned that lesson the hard way.

A few minutes later, I answered the small scratch at my bedroom door and nodded to Lord Worthington, indicating with a wave of my head that we should start in Miss Loughty's room. We worked as silently as possible. Her desk seemed as logical a place as any to store any incriminating letters or photographs, and I thumbed through a small collection of correspondence tied up in a pretty coral ribbon. It contained all the usual kind of letters a young woman would receive from her friends and family members, recounts of balls and celebrations, marriages and illnesses. Nothing seemed out of the ordinary.

As I checked all the drawers in her desk, nightstand, and dresser, Lord Worthington looked under the mattress and flipped the armchairs and side table over to make sure nothing had been tacked up underneath. I was grateful for his thoroughness, because I wasn't sure I would have thought of it. Perhaps he'd done this kind of thing before.

A brief examination of Miss Loughty's wardrobe revealed many day ensembles and evening dresses in the latest styles. I felt a twinge of guilt for going through another young woman's things, a woman who I might become friends with if given the opportunity. But I was also becoming fascinated by what I could learn just by looking at someone's things. For one thing, Miss Loughty seemed to embody the height of fashion and privilege. For someone who seemingly enjoyed participating in society events, wore up-to-date styles from the best modistes, possessed a head for reading and pleasant conversation, and had the distinction of being a cousin to a Marquess, I found myself somewhat surprised Miss Loughty was in her mid-twenties and not yet married. I was hardly one to encourage matrimony as a rule, but she seemed the sort of girl that would have followed the conventional path in society. With her beauty and station in life, she'd likely already attracted a number of suitors. Perhaps she enjoyed being mistress of her brother's house, and as such was in no hurry to set up her own—though he had to be at least in his early thirties and could marry eventually. I saw the four books I'd lent her from the Cunninghams' library on her nightstand and smiled. Perhaps, like me, she was keen to pursue a passion rather than settle down and have children. I'd have to ask her what her favorite pursuits were other than reading.

Lord Worthington blushed scarlet and turned away as I gently went through Miss Loughty's more personal garments. They were of the finest quality, and I made a mental note of several pretty details to have my modiste in Paris incorporate into my next order. Even if my lady's maid and I were the only people that were going to be seeing them, it wasn't an area in which I was willing to cut corners. Most Parisiennes felt the same, and it appeared Miss Loughty did too.

After a few more moments, we went on to search Miss Price's room, which proved to be no more enlightening than our endeavors so far. The novelty of voyeurism started to lose its shine, and I began to develop a keen respect for the Bow Street Runners. I wasn't sure I'd have the patience for investigating matters like this as a career. It was incredibly tedious work.

If Miss Price did take digitalis for a heart condition like many older people did, there was no evidence of it in her room. Just more of the same stiff, black bombazine dresses of a bygone era, a half-written letter on her desk that made me feel sorry for her unfortunate relatives (it appeared that I wasn't the only person on the receiving end of her scorn), and a miniature of Alfred and Rupert's father, his name printed carefully on the back in Miss Price's precise handwriting. If he had been as unpleasant as he looked in the photograph—and as his sister was—then Alfred and Rupert must have inherited their jovial charm from their mother, the eccentric hobbyist.

From there, we went to Miss Taylor's room. When we first entered, I'd stifled a gasp, believing that someone else had beaten us to the search. After a few moments, however, I realized that Miss Taylor was just an exceedingly untidy young lady.

Lord Worthington chuckled softly.

"Looks like someone's not as prim and tidy as she appears," he whispered with a wry smile.

There was no need for me to go through Miss Taylor's unmentionables drawer, as the garments were already strewn about the room. It appeared the maids hadn't made it into this room to tidy yet today. Last night's dinner dress was laying in a crumpled heap on the floor, and I cringed at the wrinkles that had set in the soft, pink satin. A collection of letters were strewn haphazardly across her desk, splatters from the ink pot marring the otherwise well-polished wood. I thumbed through them, this time gasping out loud as I read the contents. Miss Taylor and her friends apparently were advising each other how best to entrap high-ranking gentlemen into marriage. Several letters included flirtation techniques, how to appear in need of rescue, and tips for what to do once they were fortunate enough to find themselves alone with their victim. I felt my cheeks redden, and hurriedly arranged the letters back on the desk as I had found them.

"Miss Taylor is not quite the innocent she appears," I whispered softly to Lord Worthington, when he looked towards me quizzically from where he was searching the mantlepiece. "You would do well to avoid being alone with her. She seems to be on the hunt for a titled husband and is willing to resort to entrapment."

He raised a brow thoughtfully.

"Perhaps her hunt for a husband led her to be compromised, and Emsworth found out and demanded she pay for his silence? She is an heiress after all."

"I have a hard time seeing Emsworth desperate enough to blackmail a chit barely out of the schoolroom," I said quietly. "But, it's not like we knew him well. I suppose it's certainly possible. And poison is often a woman's weapon of choice, so we shouldn't rule her out just yet."

Worthington rubbed his hands together excitedly, walking over to my side of the room, but continued in the same low tone.

"Or, perhaps he was blackmailing Miss Taylor, but Miss Price found out and murdered Emsworth to save the reputation of her charge."

"I could more readily believe Miss Price a murderer than Miss Taylor. And she'd be the most likely person here to take digitalis medicinally, even though we didn't find it in her room. Perhaps she keeps some on her person in case she needs to take it suddenly for a heart episode. It would be easy to slip a couple of extra pills into Emsworth's food or drink when no one was paying attention. I hope Benjamin has been able to talk with her."

"He does have a way of charming a lady." Lord Worthington's eyes sparkled, and I could tell he was teasing me. I shooed him back towards his side of the room without further comment.

We fell into silence again as we finished searching Miss Taylor's room. As I worked, I thought about Mr. Emsworth. I know Benjamin had some compelling evidence to suspect him of blackmail, but what if he was wrong? What if Emsworth had stumbled across the actual blackmailer and had been killed for it? Or what if he was merely an accomplice, and his partner had turned on him? He didn't seem like a malicious man; he could have developed a conscience and decided he was no longer comfortable with the arrangement.

The problem was that, if he was a blackmailer or an accomplice, anyone in the house could have had a reason to kill him. Secrets are powerful, and everyone has at least something they wish to hide. I knew that better than most.

I hoped my deepest, darkest secret was currently asking Miss Price whether she took any heart medications, because murderer or not, I wanted to interact with her as little as possible.

After checking to make sure no one was in the hallway, I motioned for Lord Worthington to exit Miss Taylor's room, and after tipping a non-existent hat my way, he quietly made his way back to the bachelor's wing. He was a curious gentleman, all sparkling eyes and good humor, but with an intelligent side that hinted at a depth of character that not everyone got to see. I could see why Benjamin considered him a good friend.

He and Benjamin were headed to search all of the Cunninghams' rooms in the family wing. I shuddered at the thought. Just a few days ago, I would have trusted that family more than anyone else on earth. But now, with my ex-husband perhaps not quite as much of a villain as I'd thought him to be, and a gentleman I'd have thought unable to hurt a fly a possible blackmailer, I wasn't sure what to think. I liked to think my judgment was more sound as a grown woman than it had been when I married Benjamin at eighteen, but what if it wasn't?

I shook my head as I entered my room and sat on my bed, staring out the window at the snowy landscape. The sky was blue, and bright sunshine was beginning to melt some of the snow on the roads and walkways. No, there was no way any of the Cunninghams could be our culprit. But someone in the house was, most assuredly, a murderer. And we were running out of time.

Chapter 15

I had one more thing that I wanted to do before I rejoined the ladies for the afternoon card tournament, so I slipped down the back stairs to the kitchens and knocked on Mrs. Hudgins' door. She answered, her face a bit anxious, but she smiled at me just the same and motioned for me to join her.

"Is everything okay, Miss? Have you quite recovered from finding that poor gentleman this morning?"

I sat in the comfortable chintz armchair opposite her desk and returned her smile.

"I'm quite well, thank you. I feel terrible for the man and his family of course. I did have a couple questions to ask you on Sarah's behalf, as she has her hands full keeping the guests busy today."

"Anything that would be helpful, Miss Osbourne."

I'd thought carefully about how to phrase my request on the walk down. As far as everyone else knew, Mr. Emsworth died when he accidentally fell out of his window. We needed to talk to the servants, but discreetly.

"We're trying to figure out, for Mrs. Emsworth's sake of course, what her son did in the last few hours before his accident. Do you know if he ate or drank anything after retiring from the sitting room with the other guests?"

"He did, yes. Mr. Emsworth was in the habit of drinking a cup of warm milk before bed each night. He had his usual service on a tray shortly after eleven, I think."

"And he didn't complain of being ill, or request a doctor?"

Mrs. Hudgins looked at me carefully.

"No, Miss. It was Rosie, the undermaid, that brought him the tea tray. Would you like me to ask her if he mentioned anything about it?"

"Yes, please, that would be most helpful." Sensing the housekeeper's curiosity, I continued cautiously. "Mrs. Emsworth was just wondering if her son had felt ill, since that would explain his need to open a window on a cold, December night. It's also possible an illness could have caused him to lose his balance and fall."

Mrs. Hudgins sighed. "Poor man. So young, too. Let me call Rosie in here and see what she says."

Mrs. Hudgins disappeared, and I looked around her office while I waited. It was homey and cozy, and smelled of vanilla and spices, much like the woman herself. The desk in front of me was tidy, while the shelves behind me were filled with neat rows of preserves, baskets of perfumed soap, stacks of fresh linens, and crates of candles. Unused baskets were arranged artistically on hooks on the wall, and braids of dried herbs and wildflowers hung from the ceiling above. These things should have caused the housekeeper's office to feel more like a cramped storeroom, but somehow it just added to the cozy cottage ambiance. A side table next to me held a stack of books and a spare cup and saucer. Maybe Mrs. Hudgins would let me hide away in here for a while when I needed to escape Benjamin.

After a few moments, Mrs. Hudgins returned with Rosie. I stood and smiled at the girl, who nodded at me timidly. She was petite and pretty, with reddish-blond curls sticking out haphazardly from her maid's cap.

"Rosie, did you bring Mr. Emsworth his tea last night before bed?"

"Yes, Missus."

"Did he say anything when you brought it, or indicate he was ill in any way?"

"No, Missus. I knocked on the door, and 'e 'ollered from inside the room that I should leave the tray outside the door, just as 'e did the night afore that. I reckoned 'e was gettin' into 'is night clothes or somethin'." The girl's cheeks pinked. "So I left it right outside like 'e'd asked and went back to my duties, I did. Sounded normal, 'e did, not sick or nothin.' But I don't reckon I rightly know what a sick person sounds like, an' I never did 'ave a look at 'im."

"So you did not see him retrieve the tea tray?"

"No, Missus. More 'n likely 'e did that after I'd already come back downstairs. We was cleanin' up the tea sets 'n glasses from the parlor, and gettin' ready fer bed. But I know that 'e drunk it, 'e did, because this mornin' the dirty things was all on the tray, and the milk was gone."

"And when did you retrieve the tray? Was it after Mr. Emsworth was found this morning?"

"Yes, Missus. We 'adn't made it to the bachelor's wing to start the fires 'n pick up last night's dishes yet when that poor bloke was found, 'e was. Went back up to fetch 'em just a little while ago. They was back outside the door, all empty-like."

Hopefully Benjamin had had a chance to examine them for evidence this morning before Rosie had retrieved them. Any residue of poison would be long gone by now, washed away in the soapy water with the rest of the breakfast dishes.

"Thank you Rosie, you've been most helpful. I'll let you return to your duties now."

Mrs. Hudgins opened the door and let Rosie out, but the girl hesitated, looking at me.

"Is there anything else you remember that might be helpful, Rosie?"

"I was just thinkin' that if 'e was a gettin' into 'is nightclothes, 'is valet was like as not helpin' 'im. In fact, the valet coulda been the last person to see the poor bloke alive, as it were."

I nodded.

"Excellent point, Rosie, thank you. We will be certain to talk to Mr. Emsworth's valet to see if he noticed anything as well."

As Mrs. Hudgins let the girl out, I sat back in the chair, lost in thought. Anyone could have walked by and slipped something into Mr. Emsworth's tea in the minutes between when Rosie left it on the floor and Emsworth retrieved it, if that was indeed how he was poisoned. It seemed as likely a method as any. And we definitely needed to talk to Mr. Emsworth's valet.

I turned to find the housekeeper watching me carefully. She was no fool, and she had to have guessed that there were at least some suspicions around Mr. Emsworth's death after the questions I'd just asked Rosie. I knew she wasn't the type to gossip, however, and I felt that I could trust her with at least a shred of the truth.

"Thank you so much, Mrs. Hudgins. Lord Hadleigh wants to tie up some loose ends regarding the accident, and has asked me for my assistance. Do you know if any other staff members had interactions with Mr. Emsworth at any point yesterday evening or last night, apart from Rosie and the valet?"

"I don't think so, Miss. In fact, I asked around this morning, just to make sure, you see. Jackson and Jeb, one of the footmen, saw him while serving dinner, and of course Jackson brought the tea tray when everyone was assembled in the parlor after dinner last night."

"And no one else saw Mr. Emsworth after that?"

"Not that anyone admits to, at least. But since the valet isn't a member of my staff, but an employee of one of the guests, I haven't talked to him yet."

Mrs. Hudgins was a very shrewd woman. She seemed well in tune to the movements of her staff, but a guest's valet or lady's maid was not part of the Cunningham household, but rather traveled with their employer. They were often considered a step above the other servants of a household in class, and as such didn't tend to share meals or operate on the same schedule as the other servants. It would be wise for us to talk to all of the lady's maids and valets currently residing at the Cunninghams' estate, not just Mr. Emsworth's. At this point anyone in the house could have killed the poor man, including the other guests and the servants. I was beginning to get a headache just thinking about all the possibilities.

"Thank you, Mrs. Hudgins, your help has been invaluable. Will you tell me if you hear anything else that you think might be relevant?"

She quickly agreed, but as I was turning to go, I was struck with one more thought.

"Mrs. Hudgins, could I come sit down here sometimes, when you're not working, just to get away from … everyone?"

The housekeeper was used to my eccentric habits, but asking to use her personal space when there was a whole manor at my disposal—well, it was an audacious request. But the older woman smiled, a true smile that lit up her eyes and took years off her countenance, and I almost breathed a sigh of relief.

"You're more than welcome to hide out down here anytime, Miss Osbourne. I seldom lock the door, since we don't store any-thing terribly valuable in here. And I promise, I won't tell a soul where to find you."

For the remainder of the afternoon, I played whist, hearts, and a few rounds of a very demure form of poker, betting with Christ-mas sweets instead of money. I was normally a fairly talented card player, as I had a habit of remembering which cards had already been played, but that afternoon I lost more than I won as I paid more attention to the conversations around me than to the game.

Now that I had been through several of my fellow players' rooms, it was hard not to look at them in a different light. Old Miss Price was as crotchety as ever. Would she have killed to protect her charge's reputation from a blackmailer? But with her strict morality, I got the feeling that she was unaware of her young ward's proclivities. If she knew what Miss Taylor was willing to resort to to land a titled and wealthy husband, she might renounce her, ward or no. I watched the two women carefully, hoping to glean any bits of information I could, but they talked of acquaintances in London, Miss Taylor's school friends, and last Christmas's Yule

Ball at a Lord Stefferingham's house, which apparently put all other holiday festivities to shame. Through it all, Miss Taylor gave no indication that she was anything but the proper, polite young lady she seemed. Either she was not as ruthless as her correspondence had suggested and just went along with her friends' schemes as a diverting pastime, or she was a very good actor.

I quickly grew bored of those two, and switched tables to join a game of hearts, so I could chat with Miss Loughty. There wasn't much mystery to puzzle out from her room. Perhaps she was simply a woman who preferred the company of women and decided to remain unmarried. I knew a few women of that inclination in Paris, though most had married anyway for financial security rather than love. Miss Loughty's brother was wealthy enough, however, that she would likely not have to resort to a marriage of convenience. We chatted at length about an Oscar Wilde serial that we had both recently read in *Lippencott's* and enjoyed, shocking Sarah, who hadn't yet read it, into giggles with the more scandalous details.

At long last it was time to adjourn to rest and dress for dinner. I sat in the parlor, ostensibly perusing yesterday's newspaper, and waited until all the other ladies were safely up the stairs before I went in search of Benjamin or Lord Worthington.

I found Benjamin alone in the billiard room, standing over a plate of sandwiches resting on an ornately carved, heavy sideboard.

"Sandwiches? And an hour before dinner! Cook must really love you." I'd been regretting skipping luncheon for the last two hours, and my stomach growled loudly at the sight of food. Benjamin held the plate out to me without a word, and I gratefully took a small triangle of soft bread stuffed with thinly sliced ham.

"Worthington was informing me of your rather disappointing search of the ladies' wing, but Rupert Cunningham has just summoned him to the stables to offer his expert opinion on a recently-acquired horse."

"I'm sure there wasn't much to fill you in on. Other than the revelation that you both should avoid being left alone with Miss

Taylor unless you fancy a hasty marriage, I'm afraid we learned nothing of interest. And we couldn't find any evidence of Miss Price taking digitalis, though she could still have some on her person."

"I spoke with her, and she claimed not to need it. I did confirm the fact with her lady's maid."

I took the time to chew slowly, mulling the situation over.

"How did you charm that information out of her?"

"The lady's maid was eager to help. I simply asked nicely."

I snorted, brushing a stray crumb from my bodice. "I'm sure she was quite taken with you."

"As for Miss Price, it took some time and multiple cups of tea with her and Miss Taylor."

"She is likely hoping you'll make a match of it with her young protégé. It's a wonder you didn't send Lord Worthington in your stead."

"Apparently he tried to charm her this morning while we were in the conservatory, but wasn't able to get anywhere with her due to his, erm, ineligibility. He *is* engaged to be married."

"She must be serious in her quest to see Miss Taylor well-settled. It's a wonder she hasn't yet brow-beaten some poor fop into marrying her charge. From what we read in their correspondence, Miss Price is as terrifying as she seems, and Miss Taylor is no less determined to make a brilliant match." I rolled my eyes and reached for another sandwich. I was aware dinner was in an hour, but I was famished. Apparently investigating a murder gave me an appetite.

"So far, she hasn't tried anything with me. And believe me, I'm always on my guard any time there's a marriage-minded young lady around. I've had carriages carrying young ladies mysteriously break down right outside my gate, women swooning into my arms on the sidewalk just as I happen to pass by, even one enterprising young lady that managed to break a doorknob after tricking me into walking into a room alone with her."

I tried to stifle a laugh and choked on a bit of bread. Benjamin pounded me between the shoulder blades as I coughed and sputtered. When I could breathe again, I made what I hoped was a straight face and continued.

"I'm surprised that none of these determined debutants have yet managed to drag you to the altar. You are quite the catch on the marriage mart, you know—"

Benjamin looked up at me, startled, as if surprised that I'd said something nice about him for once.

"—seeing as how you're one of the only Earls this side of fifty and still possessing all of his teeth."

"A rarity to be sure."

The wry look on his face was suddenly replaced with something much more serious.

"You know, Freddie, I had no intention of marrying ever, much less marrying you."

Chapter 16

"Well, then," I huffed indignantly, "I apologize for dragging you to the altar against your will."

Benjamin sighed, setting his half-eaten sandwich back on the plate as if he'd lost his appetite.

"Will you just let me finish, for once in our lives, Freddie? When we went to Italy, it was only supposed to be a family holiday. I'd already signed the contract for the Home Office. I was committed to begin working for them when we came home from our summer abroad." He shook his head, staring at the billiards table instead of looking me in the eyes. He looked far away, no doubt revisiting that ill-fated summer as I had so many times in the last nine years.

"What happened?"

"You happened."

I raised an eyebrow, impatiently waiting for Benjamin to explain.

"You were my best friend, but I never dreamed that you would become more. I was ready for a life of service to Queen and country."

Benjamin stepped closer, mere inches separating us now, and looked at me with so much intensity that my hands went slack. The last bite of my sandwich dropped to the ground, crumbs scattering around our feet. I felt my cheeks redden against my will, but I couldn't look away from that startling blue gaze.

"You know how we'd hoped Mother's health would turn

around in the warm climate. We were going for her. But instead, Italy changed me. You changed me. After just a week of travel, it was like something clicked inside me. Suddenly, you were glowing—this magnificent creature of light and life. I realized you were the most beautiful woman I'd ever seen, and that it wasn't Italy at all—you'd always been glowing. I don't know why it took me all those years to realize it. I should have married you years before… before everything."

Blood roaring in my ears, I almost fainted right then and there, but I forced myself to keep listening, forced myself not to take a step back.

"You could have hardly married me before that—we were mere children."

I tried to sound flippant, irreverent, as if what he was saying was of no importance to me at all. Holding my breath, I waited, not entirely sure if I wanted him to continue. A big part of me wanted to keep hating him, to keep holding onto all the wrong that he'd done to me. But a tiny part, a small sliver around the hard shell that had encased my heart for so long—that part had a tiny crack. Oblivious to my inner turmoil, Benjamin kept going as if he'd been bottling up all these revelations for years, and once he'd started, he couldn't stop.

"Two weeks into the trip, you told me you'd loved me since you were fourteen, and it seemed like we were living in a dream. It was a dream. I know my mother and your grandfather had always hoped we'd make a match of it. There among the olive groves, the sea air—well, I was intoxicated, and it just seemed right. I was so young and naïve, and I figured it was easier to marry you as quickly as possible, and I'd sort out the consequences with the Home Office once I got back to England."

I'd often wondered why Benjamin had seemed so eager to marry right there in Italy rather than waiting until we got home. I'd been in love with him for so long that I never stopped to question it at the time.

"I never dreamed they would force us to annul the marriage. I was supposed to remain unattached. It was important to the job: no one could have a greater claim on me than the Crown. Then when my time of service was over, I'd be free to marry. I just thought if I came home and we were already married, there would be nothing they could do about it."

"So what, when you got home, you just sat by and watched Augustus and his Home Office cronies force you to annul the marriage?"

"No. At first, I refused. I told them that what was done was done, and if they didn't like it, they could tear up my contract and I'd be on my way and live my life with my new wife. Augustus would have come around eventually. But then…"

I was so intent on Benjamin's words that I'd edged a step closer, our bodies nearly touching now. Part of me still wanted to slap him, but a very real part of me wanted to take his face in my hands and kiss him senseless. He must have sensed the conflicting emotions on my face, for his gaze softened, and his eyes dropped briefly to my lips before searching the rest of my face.

"Freddie, you have to know," he purred, voice low, "I've never—"

But what he was going to say, I never found out, for he stiffened suddenly, turned and whisked the plate of sandwiches off the sideboard, holding it between us like a shield, while simultaneously kicking the discarded bit of sandwich that I had dropped under the sideboard. His movements were so swift, that I was left blinking at the tray of sandwiches in front of me, unsure of what had just happened, when Lord Belvoir strolled in through the open billiard room door.

He was already dressed for dinner, and his handsome face broke into a grin when he saw us.

"Ah, there you are, Hadleigh. Miss Osbourne, a pleasure as always."

He bowed low, taking my hand and pressing a kiss on the back of it. I hoped I didn't have any sandwich grease on my fingers.

"Miss Osbourne missed lunch," Benjamin was explaining, "so I was sharing my boon from the kitchen before she headed up to dress for dinner. It appears Cook likes me more than the other guests; apparently it's devilishly hard to get food this close to dinnertime."

He winked at Lord Belvoir, which was some sort of code, I supposed, though I didn't know what for. Was he implying that he'd been flirting with the cook, or that we weren't merely sharing sandwiches?

As Lord Belvoir helped himself to one of the proffered sandwiches, I turned to go.

"Thank you, Lord Hadleigh, for sharing." I hoped he knew I meant more than the food. "I really must run up to dress for dinner, or I'll be late."

"Please allow me to walk you into dinner tonight, Miss Osbourne," Lord Belvoir implored. "I haven't seen nearly enough of you today."

He waggled an eyebrow at me and grinned rakishly.

I couldn't help but smile at his antics and bowed my head in acknowledgement.

"Very well. I'll see you all in the drawing room in a few moments."

I turned and hurried out of the room. It wasn't until I reached the top of the stairs that I realized I'd forgotten to ask Benjamin if he'd spoken with Mr. Emsworth's valet.

Chapter 17

Lord Belvoir was about to see more of me than I was comfortable with, but I had no choice if I was going to make it down to dinner in time. I pulled out the only evening dress I'd brought that I could get on by myself, knowing there was no time to ring Betsy to help me dress. Fingers shaking, I could barely hold the skirts still enough to step into as I thought about what Benjamin had just revealed in the billiards room. What could have possibly happened to cause him to abandon our marriage, when he'd been so sure he could just charm his superiors into accepting it, or quit? I knew from experience that Benjamin was doggedly determined when he set his mind to something and incredibly apt at getting his way. What could they have possibly said or done to convince him?

Even more disturbing, had he been about to kiss me before Lord Belvoir walked in? Had I been about to kiss him?

Mind whirling, I finally got the soft, gold velvet dress up over my hips and onto my shoulders. Long, fitted sleeves stretched to my wrists, with large, jet black ruffles at the shoulders. The reason the dress was so easy to get on was that rather than buttoning down the back, it had a deeply plunging neckline that fastened in the front. The bodice was held together and kept from indecency by thick, black velvet ribbons that one tied into bows from neck to sternum, leaving teasing glimpses of décollaté underneath. It had felt mildly daring in Paris, but here in the country, it felt almost scandalous. Or perhaps it was just me, now keenly aware that at least once upon a time, years ago, Benjamin had thought me the most beautiful creature he'd ever seen.

The dinner gong rang just as I was slipping my feet into black satin slippers. I glanced in the mirror, tucked a few stray curls in with extra hairpins, and fastened dangling earrings made of jet on my ears. Hopefully they would distract from the messy hair. And the plunging neckline.

I slipped into the drawing room with seconds to spare.

"Winnie, how gorgeous you look!" Sarah, who was closest to the door, embraced me, then held me out at arm's length to look me over. She must have sensed my self-consciousness, for she linked my arm through hers and said in a voice just loud enough to carry, "You must let me come visit your Parisian modiste soon. I simply must have some of these stunning dresses of yours made for myself."

As she turned around and led me into the room, the sound of shattering glass interrupted the conversations around us. All eyes turned towards the sideboard, where several of the gentlemen were standing with drinks. Benjamin was bending down on one knee, picking up shards of what had likely been his glass.

He gave the room his most charming self-deprecating grin.

"I may have gotten started a bit too early this evening," he admitted, and the other gentlemen laughed as the buzz of conversation returned around us.

I could tell from across the room he wasn't the least bit drunk, and I was about to walk over and ask him what was really going on when I spotted Mrs. Emsworth on the settee.

"Mrs. Emsworth!" I quickly made my way over to her and clasped her hand. "It is good to see you up and about. Can I get you anything?"

Her face was pale and drawn, and she looked far older than she had just the day before, but her back was straight, and she didn't look to be at risk of fainting away. Mentally, I applauded her courage for even being out of bed.

"No, dear, you're too kind. I will be quite alright, it's just the shock, you know. Such a terrible thing."

Her voice wavered a bit, and I sat down next to her and took her hand. She didn't even know her poor son had likely been murdered. I was certainly not going to add to her pain by telling her, at least not until we had caught the culprit.

"I am so, so sorry for your loss. Mr. Emsworth seemed to be a kind man."

"I'm heartbroken, of course, but I can't say that I'm surprised."

I stiffened, looking at her carefully. Did she know something that we didn't?

"Why do you say that?" I asked slowly, careful to keep any suspicion out of my voice.

"You may have noticed that Harold is—*was*—a bit different. He was always so absent-minded, in another world half the time. When he was a boy, he would wander off into the street or into the woods without any regard for his own welfare. He even fell out an open window once as a youth, because he was sitting next to it reading a book and not paying attention. Thankfully, it wasn't a high window, and he was unharmed. So you can see why, Miss Osbourne, it's not out of the question that he would open the window for some air, and forget all about it and fall out."

She brought a handkerchief up to dry her eyes, and I squeezed her hand, thinking. *Had I gotten it wrong then? Perhaps it truly was an accident.* But then I remembered the lack of blood, the stains on Mr. Emsworth's nightshirt, the contracted pupils. No. I didn't think I was wrong about the poisoning. But could such a kind, absent-minded man really be a blackmailer?

"Mrs. Emsworth, please allow me to express my sincere condolences on your loss," said Lord Belvoir as he appeared next to us, grasping Mrs. Emsworth's free hand and bowing over it.

"If there's anything at all I can do for you, please don't hesitate to ask."

"Thank you, my Lord. Your offer is much appreciated. Indeed, everyone here has been so gracious to me today."

Just then, the butler appeared to announce that dinner was ready, and Arthur Cunningham approached us, offering Mrs. Emsworth his arm with a kind smile.

"Mrs. Emsworth, would you accompany me to dinner?"

She took his arm with a grateful smile, and I turned back to Lord Belvoir, who lowered his voice to a whisper.

"Not to be indelicate during this difficult time for Mrs. Emsworth, but Miss Osbourne, you look ravishing tonight."

Standing, I thanked him, and took his outstretched arm to head into the dining room. I noticed that Benjamin was taking in Miss Taylor, and far from looking intimidated as the girl had before, she was looking quite as pleased as the cat in the cream pot. I hoped he could subtly interrogate her while they talked.

"Are you all right, Miss Osbourne?"

Lord Belvoir followed my gaze, and I quickly turned my attention back to him with my most charming smile.

"I'm afraid I'm a bit frazzled. I didn't leave myself enough time to get ready and had to wrestle myself into this dress on my own."

Suddenly aware of the image that admission must have conveyed, I felt my cheeks flare and looked down at my slippers in embarrassment. Gratefully, Lord Belvoir didn't remark on my inappropriate comment, but his eyes twinkled merrily.

"And what a stunning dress it is," he said smoothly. "Tell me, are you always this well-dressed in Paris?"

His eyes didn't so much as glance at my décolleté, and I was able to shake off my nerves a bit as we walked towards the dining room.

"When I'm painting, which is much of the time, I am a veritable mess," I chuckled. "But I confess that when I'm not working and I'm out in town with friends, I do love to follow the latest fashions. I think it's a bit of balance, really, for wearing baggy painting smocks most of the time."

Lord Belvoir continued flirting smoothly as we were seated and began our first course at the dinner table, but I didn't mind. His compliments were always respectful, and he never made me feel ogled or leered at, just appreciated. In fact, it was nice to take my mind off of the murder investigation for a few moments and just enjoy the conversation.

"Tell me, how is it that some dashing young Frenchman hasn't snatched you up yet?"

I'd gotten used to the question over the years. Despite the somewhat looser societal expectations of those of us who ran in artists circles, there were still plenty of matchmaking mamans who tried to figure out what was *wrong with me* as I painted their portraits or danced with their sons at a ball. I always gave the same answer, but with the rawness of seeing my ex-husband for the first time in years, the lie flowed less easily than it usually did.

"I've just never found someone I liked enough to give up my freedom for."

"Ah, perhaps you've never truly been in love then."

Lord Belvoir looked at me with what I guessed was supposed to be a searing glance, but I caught the tinges of sadness around the edges. He may be a practiced flirt, but it was clear to me he was still grieving his late wife. I covered his hand with mine briefly, and a look of understanding passed between us. I suspected that all the flirting was a front, a way to dull the pain he still carried. I was a safe person to flirt with, as he was unlikely to raise any expectations he couldn't fulfill. I smiled at him gently.

"Perhaps I've never been as lucky to be in love as you and Lady Belvoir were. A love like that, however brief, will change us, will it not?"

Feeling my eyes growing misty, I quickly looked around the table, searching for a new topic of conversation. My breath caught in my throat, and my eyes dried instantly as they fell on Benjamin, who was staring at me with such a murderous look on his face, you would have thought he really was the devil incarnate. My jaw dropped, and my heart beat wildly for a moment. What had I done to earn such scorn, when we had seemed to be getting along so well this afternoon? And then another thought hit me, even icier than before. *What if I'd gotten this all wrong? What if Benjamin had been the one to murder Mr. Emsworth, and this whole investigation was a sham to distract me?*

Chapter 18

My heart thundering wildly in my chest, I clutched my salad fork in a death grip. As I withered under his icy stare, I thought back quickly over the day's events. Had Benjamin been stringing me along all this time, letting me believe we were looking for a murderer, while he himself was the culprit? After all, I'd been the one to discover the body and cry poison. Perhaps if I hadn't interfered, Mr. Emsworth's death would have been deemed a tragic accident, and no one would have been any the wiser.

Thankfully oblivious to my sudden inner turmoil, Lord Belvoir changed the topic of conversation and began chatting about the theater, of which he was an ardent supporter and patron. Benjamin had quickly ceased glaring at me and resumed his conversation with Miss Taylor, and I was left blinking and nodding at Lord Belvoir, wondering if I'd imagined the whole thing—or if I needed to be very, very careful indeed.

When the third course was served, I turned as was custom to talk to Mr. Loughty, who was on my left. My brain was only half-aware of the conversation as he extolled the virtues of his extensive orchards and gardens, which joined together with Lord Belvoir's estate and sounded magnificent indeed. I kept what I hoped was a rapt expression on my face, and pondered my dilemma.

I only had Benjamin's word that he worked for the Home Office, though the presence and support of Lord Worthington did seem to corroborate his claim. The two men seemed close, and Lord Worthington appeared to be trustworthy. He was good friends with Rupurt, and I trusted Rupurt's judgment. But when it came to Benjamin, I knew my own judgment wasn't sound. He'd deceived me before and very nearly ruined my life. If I hadn't had Grandfather and his wealth to get me back on my feet and introduce me into Parisian society—if my status as a jilted wife had gotten out—I could have been ruined when Benjamin left me.

Or perhaps Benjamin really had been sent here by the Home Office, but to kill Mr. Emsworth for some highly secret matter of state. This whole claim of blackmail could just be a diversion. We'd searched nearly the entire house and had found no evidence thus far, and we only had Benjamin's claim that the proof had to be somewhere in the house. Could it all be a ruse?

My mind spun, and I was grateful when dinner was over and the ladies withdrew to the drawing room for tea and card games. I sat next to Mrs. Emsworth on the sofa and let her rattle on about her younger son's children. She was still pale, but the tea and conversation seemed to soothe her. She excused herself to retire just as the gentlemen rejoined us.

"The poor dear," Sarah murmured at my side, as the gentlemen wandered in and helped themselves to eggnog and brandy. "I told her she didn't need to dream of coming down to dinner tonight, but she seemed to be in need of the company. Apparently her son was rather accident-prone, and she feels terrible for dragging him out of his familiar surroundings at Christmas time."

I sat for a moment, sipping my tea thoughtfully.

"Why did they come here? I mean, who invited them?"

"Why I did, of course. I met Mrs. Emsworth a few years ago at a society event, and we hit it off. She's a very social creature and seems to thrive around company, so when I learned her younger son was abroad for the season, I invited her and Mr. Emsworth to join us. He was the kindest creature, but came only to please his mother as far as I know. He preferred to keep to himself."

Once again, I thought about how unlikely a blackmailer Mr. Emsworth seemed to be. What if Benjamin were lying?

"Sarah, can I ask you a question?"

"Of course, darling. How can I help?"

"How well do you all know Lord Worthington?"

Sarah blinked in surprise.

"Oh, Winnie, you have not set your cap at him, have you? You know he's the one Lord here that's engaged. Besides, I thought you and Lord Belvoir were getting along famously at dinner tonight."

I had to smile at the hopeful look in her eyes.

"I admit Lord Belvoir is a delightful conversationalist, and I would be honored to call him my friend, but that's all. I suspect that he's still hopelessly in love with his late wife. I think he finds flirting with me a diverting pastime, but his attentions are hardly serious. But back to Lord Worthington—how well does Rupurt know him? Is he trustworthy?"

A little line appeared between Sarah's eyes as she pondered the implications of my questions.

"He and Rupurt have been thick as thieves since Cambridge. I believe Rupurt would trust him with his life. He is an honorable man."

I lowered my voice so that I was speaking barely above a whisper.

"What about his friend, Lord Hadleigh?"

Now Sarah's pretty face looked even more confused.

"But didn't you know each other as children?" Sarah lowered her own voice to match mine. "I thought he was your Benji, your best friend and playmate? For a long time when we were at school, I thought that you must have had a *tendre* for him, for as often as you talked about him. It was always *Benji this* and *Benji that*, but once we left school and you left for Italy and then France, you never once mentioned him in your letters. I thought you must have lost touch as childhood friends often do. Winnie, darling, I'm confused. Don't you know him better than any of us?"

"Well, we did know each other as children, and we were quite close, but that was a long time ago. I haven't had so much as a letter from him in the last decade, and people can change. Let's just say that I've heard some things that might bring his character into question, and I'm wondering if we should be wary of him."

She looked thoughtful, but Sarah did not ask me what rumors I had supposedly heard, for which I was grateful.

"Lord Worthington seems to trust Lord Hadleigh, and he's been nothing short of a gentleman since he arrived."

Sarah glanced discreetly over to where Benjamin and Arthur were standing with cups of eggnog, laughing.

"He seems to be a very charming but very proper Earl. Rupert said that he consults for the government from time to time, and is even known to be an intimate friend of the Queen."

Well, that part was true at least. If he was known in diplomatic circles, it was likely that Benjamin really did work for the Home Office. Sarah looked back at me with a curious look on her face.

"Why do you ask? Could you… Winnie, do you like him?"

A broad smile broke out across her face as I felt the heat rush to mine, inwardly cursing my untrustworthy complexion.

"No! Not in the way you're hoping, darling. I've just—I've seen him acting strangely, that's all—skulking about. I'm wondering if he could be up to something."

"Well, it's not every day a house guest falls to their death." Sarah's eyes quickly lost their sparkle, and I squeezed her hand. "Lord Hadleigh is probably just being thorough. He told us that he's handled accidents like Mr. Emsworth's before. With his connections to the government, it makes sense that he would take care of—things."

From the other side of the room, Rupert and Arthur were gathering all the guests together for a game of charades.

"Perhaps I'll retire for the night," I said, thinking that I might be able to use the chance to search Benjamin's room while he was occupied.

"Nonsense. I know it's been a dreadful day, but I must insist you stay for at least a few minutes and try to have some fun." Sarah stood and grabbed my hand, pulling me to my feet and towards the group. "I'll even help you keep an eye on your Lord Hadleigh."

"He's not my—" I began, but my words were drowned out as Rupert began to explain the rules of the game. We were to play on teams of two, each team receiving a word that must be acted out in two parts, while the rest of the players would try to guess.

I stood on the edge of the group as Arthur began pairing the participants into teams, and Rupert scribbled out our word assignments on little scraps of paper. My stomach lurched at the impropriety of playing charades as a member of our party was laid out cold in the garden shed, likely murdered by someone in this very room. But then, other than the murderer, no one other than myself, Benjamin, and Lord Worthington knew that Mr. Emsworth's death was anything but an accident. I started, glancing around the room quickly, realizing the importance of what I'd just thought. No one other than the murderer knew that anything was amiss. Perhaps I should stay and play, but watch the others for signs of guilt. Hit by sudden inspiration, I walked over to where Rupert was starting to hand out word assignments. While everyone's attention was fixed on him and Arthur, I discreetly grabbed the pencil and one of the extra slips of paper and jotted down a word. Then, turning towards the group, I bent down and *retrieved* the paper off the floor.

"Rupert, you dropped one." I tapped him on the shoulder and offered the little folded piece of paper with a smile.

"Jolly good, Winnie, love. You know Sarah says I'd forget my head if it wasn't attached. Have a partner, yet, do you?"

"No, not yet."

"Would you be Mr. Loughty's partner, then?"

"I'd be delighted to."

I turned to Mr. Loughty with a smile, noting that his sister and cousin had paired up for the game and were standing on his other side.

"I'm afraid, Miss Osbourne, that I'm not all that talented at charades," Mr. Loughty said with a self-deprecating smile. He looked down at me kindly, and I realized then how tall he was, even taller than Benjamin, and strongly built compared to his cousin's leaner, lankier frame. Their family was certainly blessed with good looks, though it seemed to me that the soft-spoken Mr. Loughty wasn't nearly as much of a rake as his cousin. "My sister and cousin always team up, and they always beat me soundly."

"Well, I can't say I have any particular talent for this game, either, but perhaps we will surprise ourselves. Just engaging in such a lighthearted activity after the day's sorrow is sure to lift our spirits, don't you think?"

"You're quite right. Such a terrible tragedy to lose a member of our party in such a way. And one so young, too."

"I've been worried about Frederick," Mr. Loughty added, nodding to his cousin. "I'm sure the death of one so young has brought back memories of his dear Katherine's death only two years ago."

"That was rather expected, though, was it not? Lord Belvoir mentioned that she'd been ill for some time."

"Yes, of course. Katherine was sickly most of her life, I believe. Still, it's never possible to know exactly when one will succumb, I suppose, and Frederick was so besotted with her that he likely didn't even notice her rapid decline there at the end as did the rest of us."

"It's all so terribly sad. Your cousin is lucky he has you and your sister for support."

"We've been very close since we were children, and it's been hard to watch him go through such an ordeal."

I watched as Benjamin acted out a scene for his partner, Miss Price, whom he had apparently charmed into joining the game with the others. He must have come to the same conclusion as I had, that the game would be an opportunity to watch the others for signs of guilt. I'd half-expected him to make his excuses and sneak off to search the house some more. Unless the searching was in fact, a ruse, and Benjamin himself was indeed the murderer. Involuntarily, I put a hand to my aching temple. How was I ever to find justice for Mr. Emsworth if my brain kept running circles around Benjamin? I needed to find a way to strike him off my suspects list.

"Are you quite well, Miss Osbourne?" Mr. Loughty asked, pulling up a nearby straight backed chair for me to sit in as we waited for our turn. I sat and adjusted my skirts, mentally giving him points for gentlemanly behavior both for procuring the chair and for not glancing at my décollaté even once despite his now advantageous vantage point above me.

"I am fine, thank you. Just a bit tired after the events of the day."

Mr. Loughty's face turned instantly sympathetic.

"I did hear that you were the one to find Emsworth's body this morning. I'm so very sorry, that must have been terribly upsetting for someone with your delicate constitution."

I wasn't sure I'd been delicate a day in my life, but Mr. Loughty, like most men, likely thought all of us females fragile and incapable.

"It was a shock, to be sure."

Everyone broke out in polite applause when Miss Price correctly guessed the word *forfeit* that Benjamin had been acting out for her, and the old dragon actually smiled at him! I couldn't help but chuckle.

"Looks like Lord Hadleigh has managed to charm the formidable Miss Price."

Mr. Loughty gave me a conspiratorial smile.

"Better him than I. I confess I've been keeping my distance from her."

Arthur and Rupert were up next, with Rupert hilariously acting out the word *coxcomb*, first strutting around the room as a rooster, then meticulously styling his hair with an imaginary comb. Finally, it was our turn. Mr. Loughty flailed around a bit before I figured out he was attempting to portray getting caught in a rainstorm. The second half of the word came a bit easier, as he only had to execute a credible bow, and I correctly guessed our word was *rainbow*.

We went around the circle a few more times, Mr. Loughty indeed correct that his sister and cousin were well-matched in the game. They guessed each of their words in a matter of seconds, and Miss Loughty began to take on a glow that I hadn't noticed since we'd arrived. It was wild speculation on my part, but I wondered if she perhaps held a bit of a *tendre* for her cousin. He certainly was handsome and charming. He seemed to treat her with avuncular affection, but many successful marriages had been built on far less. It had no bearing on our investigation into Mr. Emsworth's death, obviously, but I was curious just the same.

As the game wore on, I became increasingly aware that no one had yet to draw the paper I'd slipped into the mix. I hadn't had a plan when I'd handed it to Rupert other than to watch the faces of each person playing to see if I could gauge any sort of reaction. In my years as a portrait painter, I'd gotten quite used to studying faces and learning to read the myriad of emotions displayed on them. Back when we were children and he'd taught me to play cards, I used to beat Benjamin soundly every time we played poker because I could read his facial expressions so well. He'd apparently learned how to control that, because now, I couldn't get a read on him at all. He would have had to, to stay alive in his line of work.

It was Miss Loughty and Lord Belvoir's turn again, and she drew her slip of paper out of the hat Rupert held out to her. She stilled for just a moment, her eyes flickering to her cousin for a half second before she smiled and began to act. *Interesting. What did the word blackmail mean to Miss Loughty?* I glanced at Mr. Loughty beside me, but he hadn't seemed to notice Miss Loughty's hesitation, nor the desperation in her eyes when she'd glanced at Lord Belvoir. Did that mean that Miss Loughty was being blackmailed? Or perhaps she knew that Lord Belvoir was, and he'd killed to protect his secret?

I nearly started when I saw Benjamin watching me carefully. He likely suspected me of slipping the word in there and disapproved. I lifted my nose, and he shook his head at me, almost imperceptibly. In a few more seconds, Lord Belvoir had correctly guessed the word, though he was laughing and didn't seem at all perturbed by it. But he was an impeccable actor, after all.

Benjamin and Miss Price were on their final word of the game, and I had half a mind to go ahead and make my excuses to Sarah to see if I could search Benjamin's room before he retired for the night. He was currently acting out something that involved violent shooing away of what appeared to be imaginary mice. Finally, Miss Price called out "Rid!" and the rest of the party clapped for the first part of their word. I turned and was just about to slip out of the circle, when a hand grabbed my wrist and pulled me into the middle. Suddenly, I found myself being waltzed around the circle by Benjamin, who concluded our little dance with a low dip that took my breath away. For several seconds, I froze, staring into his eyes, wondering if it was affection or malice I saw glittering there. I might have stayed in his arms like that all evening, except I heard a rusty, creaking sound, like hinges on a neglected gate, and I realized with a start that it was laughter. Benjamin whipped me back up and to his side as if I weighed nothing, and I turned to see Miss Price cackling, laughing so hard that tears began to stream out of her eyes.

"Dance!" She managed to gasp in between gaffaws. Arthur and Rupert stared at their aunt, mouths agape, as if they'd never heard her laugh before. Perhaps they hadn't.

"Rid and dance! The word is riddance! What cheek you have, young man. I knew I liked you."

Benjamin just smiled and bowed, and I slipped away as soon as he let go of my hand, hoping the rest of the guests didn't notice my deepening blush.

Chapter 19

Despite all my agitation and conflicted thoughts about Benjamin, I was so exhausted when I reached my room that I could barely keep my eyes open. Quickly untying and slipping out of my dress, I laid it gently across the settee for Betsy to deal with in the morning and climbed into bed in my chemise. The last few sleepless nights had taken their toll, and the genial sounds of continuing parlor games downstairs lulled me into a deep and dreamless sleep within minutes. I awoke many hours later, feeling more refreshed than I had in days. It was still dark outside, and the maid had not yet come in to stoke the fire, but I was wide awake and determined to make some progress on our mystery today.

After a decent night's sleep, I was able to look more objectively at the possibility of Benjamin's guilt, and I had to confess that I had allowed my prior dealings with his duplicity to affect my judgement. Whatever I thought of his character, and whatever dark deeds he may have been forced to do for Queen and country in his current line of work, Benjamin Hadleigh was not a murderer. He was highly intelligent, cunning even, and murdering Mr. Emsworth before he found any of the incriminating evidence, to leave its location unknown where it could be found by anyone, well—that just wasn't logical. The more I thought about it, the fact that he had allowed me to help search the house, to be involved in his investigation in any way, suggested he was hellbent on finding that evidence. And that would have been a much easier task if Mr. Emsworth was still alive.

Still, just to calm my wildly conjecturing mind, I vowed to ask him point blank whether he had killed Mr. Emsworth the next time we had a moment alone. I used to be able to read him like a book, and while I didn't seem to possess that talent any more, I found it hard to believe he could conceal something as consequential as murder from me. Since I could hardly go to his room at this hour and question him, I decided to slip down to the library before anyone was awake and conduct a search of my own. I had no doubt Benjamin or Lord Worthington had already searched the library, as the many shelves and books would provide excellent hiding places for a letter or a photograph. But I knew the Cunninghams' house much better than they did—I'd been haunting the library for weeks now, after all, and perhaps I would notice something out of place that they had not.

I decided against dressing without Betsy's help, since none of the guests would be up for hours yet, and slipped on my warmest dressing gown constructed of a thick navy wool trimmed in crimson velvet. Thick wool and shearling slippers would keep my feet warm. I hadn't bothered to unpin my hair before falling into bed, and it sat like a wild rat's nest on the side of my head. Quickly pulling the pins out, I ran a comb through the unruly waves and braided it in one long plait down my back. Even if I ran into a servant doing their early morning tasks, they'd seen me wandering the house in my dressing gown often enough to not be shocked.

The house was quiet and dark, but I didn't bother carrying a candle as I padded softly through the halls. I knew the way well enough. Once I slipped into the library and softly closed the door, I turned the gas lamps on low, and a soft light filtered through the room. I noticed a few coals still glowing in the fireplace, but otherwise the room was cold and empty, as if the very books were still asleep on their shelves.

I shivered, able to see my breath in the chilly air, and quickly added some kindling to the fireplace until it began to warm the room. Glancing around, I wondered where I should begin my search. Shelves lined every square inch of the room, including around the door behind me and the fireplace in front of me, making the most of every bit of storage space. While Rupert and Sarah had added quite a few modern books to the collection, they hadn't removed any of the hundreds of historical and religious texts acquired by Rupert's forebearers, so there wasn't a bare spot in sight. On either side of the fireplace were the large window seats, curtains covering them to keep out the cold, and on each of the side walls, bookshelves were built out into the room like little peninsulas. Cozy armchairs and settees sprinkled about the room maximized reading nooks.

The Cunninghams had clearly put a lot of thought into making their library welcoming, but where would I start if I wanted to hide something? Backing away from the fireplace, I stood in the center of the room and looked around. I'd probably avoid the areas with the most popular books, the ones that someone might pick up to read and disturb whatever I wanted to hide. I would go for the dusty, ancient texts that looked like they hadn't been read in decades—and likely hadn't. I turned towards the back of the room, towards the door where the oldest books were kept. The alcoves were deep in the shadows cast by the book peninsulas and the now-crackling fireplace. I hadn't spent much time in this part of the library, as I had little desire to read a four-hundred-year-old sermon. The books here were brittle, the paper yellowed with age. If someone had moved one, there might be some evidence left behind. I grabbed a small step ladder from the corner, and began my slow and tedious search.

After about twenty minutes, I became aware of an odd sound coming from within the room. A soft rustling was coming from somewhere on the opposite wall. I froze, listening carefully. It sounded almost like the swishing of skirts, but a quick glance around the room told me I was still alone. Perhaps there was a secret panel somewhere, or a hidden servants door I was unaware of? I glanced at the shelves around me for anything that I could use as a weapon, just in case, and settled on a large, ebony bookend carved in the shape of a tall, thin elephant. Holding it firmly by the trunk, I began to advance slowly to the other side of the room, grateful for my wool slippers, noiseless on the carpeted floor. My eyes swept across the wall around the fireplace, landing on the drapes that covered the window seats. There, on the seat to the left of the fireplace, the curtain wavered ever so slightly, as if caught in the subtlest breeze. Perhaps someone had cracked a window and forgotten it? Or was there someone behind it, lying in wait for me? If that was the case, they surely would have surprised me long ago, when my back was turned and I was absorbed in my search. The elephant's trunk clutched tightly in my right hand, I braced myself and used my left hand to fling the curtain aside, suddenly and with great speed.

"*Auuuugh!*" I wasn't sure if it was I who was yelling or the figure in black who was suddenly hurtling itself out of the window seat and straight at me. Jumping back, I raised the bookend above my head to deliver a blow to my assailant, but stopped when he tripped on the rug, swearing in a loud and very familiar voice as he landed in a heap on the floor at my feet.

"Benji! What in God's name were you doing in there? Are you trying to wake the whole house?"

Benjamin sat up, rubbing red, bleary eyes, and looked around the room, blinking. He was still wearing last night's evening clothes, a shadow of stubble lining the normally clean-shaven portion of his face. He moved to get up and wobbled, crumpling back onto the carpet.

"Benjamin Hadleigh, are you drunk?"

"No! I mean, I was—a little. Mostly exhausted."

His words were slurring a bit, and I shook my head in disgust. Grabbing his arm, I hauled him back up to the window seat and sat down beside him, pulling my dressing gown tighter around me.

"Explain yourself. Why are you sleeping off your liquor in the library and not in your room?"

Benjamin rubbed a hand over his face, looking more world-weary than I'd ever seen him.

"After the parlor games last night, the gentlemen decided to play a few rounds of poker. At first, I intended to excuse myself and come search in here, as it's the only room we haven't been able to search in its entirety yet. But Cunningham brought out some sort of infernal Christmas punch, which was apparently much stronger stuff than it seemed. The atmosphere was jovial, and conversation flowing a bit freer than it has been since the murder, so I thought I'd stick around and see if I could learn anything, hear any snippet of information that could shed light on who our murderer is, or where those blasted letters could be hidden."

"And did you learn anything?"

"There's an odd current of tension between Lord Belvoir and his cousin, Mr. Loughty. Neither of them seemed acquainted with Emsworth, though, but that doesn't mean that he hadn't obtained some sort of incriminating information about either or both of them. He could have been blackmailing them, and perhaps the tension there is because one of them knows the other killed Emsworth."

"Hmm. That's interesting. Lord Belvoir was bragging about what a good job his cousin does managing their estates only this morning, but maybe all is not as amicable there as it seems to be. Lord Belvoir seems to count me as a friend. Perhaps I can ask him about his relationship with his cousin and see if I can dig a little deeper."

A loud snort issued from the lout next to me, and I gave him a hard look.

"And what is that ungentlemanly-like noise supposed to mean?"

"It means that you're very much mistaken if you believe Belvoir only wants to be your friend."

"Poppycock. He's a dreadful flirt, but he's not serious. Anyone can see he's not over his late wife."

Benjamin just grunted.

"And you still have not explained how you ended up sleeping off a hangover in the library."

"As I said, the punch was deceptively strong, and the gentlemen played cards until the wee hours of the morning. When the play ended, I told Worthington to go get some rest, but I decided to come search the library while everyone else was asleep."

Eyeing his haggard appearance, I suspected he didn't get far. "And how did that go?"

"I searched for a couple of hours, at least I think it was a couple of hours, before I found myself falling asleep on my feet."

He waved a hand to indicate the right side of the room.

"I think I managed to search most of that side of the room before everything started to get blurry. I don't think I've slept more than an hour or two since I've been here, and I suppose it caught up with me."

I hadn't seen Benjamin look this miserable since we were children.

"Benjamin, I have to ask. Did you kill Mr. Emsworth?"

Chapter 20

"Honestly, Freddie, I'm surprised it took you this long to ask." Benjamin sighed, tucking his legs up under him and leaning against the window, looking more like the lonely boy I fell in love with as a foolish girl than the confident and cocky young man I had married. "If my superiors had ordered me to do so to prevent the blackmail evidence from leaking out? I might have, but I don't think it would have come to that. I would have worked very hard to bring the man to justice before I resorted to violence."

He must have sensed my continued skepticism, because he went on.

"No. I did not kill Emsworth, and that is not why I was sent here. I hate… Freddie, I hate that you've been sucked into this mess. I would much, much rather Emsworth was here, alive."

I peered carefully at him, willing my rapidly beating heart to slow. I really didn't want to believe him. I wanted to keep him carefully in my little box labeled *Villain*, and the more blame I could heap on his shoulders, the better. But looking at him now, I knew Benjamin Hadleigh was telling the truth. He didn't kill Mr. Emsworth. I couldn't afford to keep second-guessing him because of what had happened between us in the past. We may never be friendly towards one another again, but I had to put that aside for now and trust him enough to work together, or Mr. Emsworth's killer may never be brought to justice.

Slowly, I nodded.

"I believe you. However you hurt me in the past, I don't think you're a murderer."

"Freddie, I've given you very little reason to trust me since I left you in Italy. Anyone is capable of murder, if something they hold dear enough is threatened. And that is why finding a murderer is so damn difficult. When—when someone I loved was threatened, I may have resorted to murder if I'd had the opportunity. But instead I was forced to give up everything, just to…just to keep that person safe."

I frowned, looking at the man in front of me that seemed so like the man I'd known and loved, and yet somehow so changed.

"Benji, what on earth are you talking about? Are you talking about when your mother was ill and you had to take her home?"

Benjamin just looked out the window at the growing light of dawn and groaned.

"No, not then. That's a story for another time. We'd best get out of here before anyone awakes and discovers us."

"Nonsense. You said yourself that the gentlemen were playing cards into the wee hours of the morning, and it sounds like the ladies retired quite late as well. They won't be up for hours yet. Let's search in here for a few more minutes."

I got up and walked quickly to the library door, locking it, and stuffed the key in the pocket of my dressing gown.

"If anyone had heard your hollering, they would have been here by now, so we've got more time. You searched the right side of the room, but I'm not sure we can trust your abilities while you were three sheets to the wind. I think we should focus on the back wall of the room, where the older, less popular books are. Letters or photographs would be more likely to go unnoticed than if they were tucked into the novels and newer works. It's winter, and this library has seen a steady flow of traffic from all the guests looking for their next cozy read."

Benjamin got up and stretched slowly. I was briefly distracted by a glimpse of hard, toned abdomen before he lowered his arms and tucked his shirt back into his trousers. Turning quickly towards the bookshelves, I hoped he hadn't noticed me staring and quickly picked up a few dusty tomes, checking behind them for any loose papers or signs of disturbed dust. The Cunninghams employed a talented staff to keep the house clean, but even the most meticulous housekeepers wouldn't take each book off the shelf and dust behind it very often.

Benjamin began doing the same on the opposite side of the door, and we worked in silence for several minutes. I was carefully checking inside and behind a set of burgundy-bound *Fordyce's Sermons*, when I noticed that one book was slightly different from the others. It was the same size and only a shade lighter than the rest of the set, and from even a few feet away I would have never noticed the difference. I squinted carefully at the faded gold printing on the spine, and my heart started to beat with excitement.

"Benji. Over here."

My voice came out as a hoarse whisper, and I pointed to the faint gold text.

"What is a book of Thomas Gray poetry doing mixed in with these *Fordyce's Sermons*?"

He shrugged.

"Likely a guest just accidentally returned it to the wrong spot. Look how similar it looks to the volumes of *Fordyce's*."

"Precisely. Almost as if someone was hoping it would go unnoticed. And apart from Miss Price, who of this group would even open a book of *Fordyce's Sermons* during this day and age?"

Benjamin stifled a yawn, took the book from my hands and shook it out by the binding. Nothing fell out of the book, and I knew a moment's disappointment before coming upon another idea.

"What if it's only meant to look like a normal book? What if there's a hidden compartment?"

I grabbed the book back from him and began to examine the cover closely. It was a thick, old binding, with plenty of room to hide a letter in if there were a way to open it.

"I hardly think someone not familiar with the Cunninghams' library could find a book with a false compartment amongst all these tomes, slip their evidence inside, and hide it back on the shelves."

"Of course they couldn't. And if they had, they'd put it back where they found it, which in this case would be over there in the poetry section." I waved my hand to the wall to the left of the window seat Benjamin had been napping in. "But if they brought their own book containing a secret compartment with them…"

Running my hands along the inside of the back cover, I noticed that the silk lining was slightly discolored in a line running close to the binding. I pressed up and down over the discolored area, and was finally rewarded with a soft click.

I couldn't help myself. Eyes wide, I looked up to Benjamin for his reaction. He was suddenly looking much more sober and alert. Not waiting for him to do the honors, I used the edge of my fingernail to pry up the hidden compartment out of the book's back cover, and revealed a thin hiding space, not more than a few centimeters thick. I carefully dumped the contents into the palm of my other hand, and stifled a gasp.

"Well, at least we know we've found the right thing, and not some hidden cache of a teenaged ancestor's love letters."

I held the two small photographs up for Benjamin to see. He grimaced, but made no move to take them away from me, and I appreciated that he wasn't expecting me to suffer a fit of the vapors. Both photographs contained the same two men in various states of dishabille, locked in passionate but rather shocking embraces. I had acquaintances in Paris who had had similar photographs taken, but as none of them had been couples of the same sex, the practice was considered risque but certainly not illegal as it was for these two gentlemen.

"I take it one of these men is a relative of the Queen?"

Benjamin nodded, grimly.

"The young man is certainly not burdened with an

overabundance of discretion. It's one thing to engage in such a relationship in private, but to have photographic evidence taken that could fall into the wrong hands…" He trailed off, shrugging. "It could ruin him and cast dispersion on the Queen's entire family, forcing her to choose whether to uphold the law or to save her relative from prison."

"It's certainly sufficient evidence for blackmail." I shook my head. "And here I was hoping you'd been mistaken about Mr. Emsworth. He spent a lot of time here in the library, and it would have been the most natural thing for him to walk in here with an extra book in his hands. No one would have questioned him or looked close enough to see if anything was out of place."

I handed him the photographs, but tucked the book back where I'd found it. Wouldn't Fordyce be shocked to know what had been hidden away in between his volumes.

"Best to leave the book here for now, just in case anyone else knows about it. Should we burn the photographs? If the objective is to protect the Queen's family, then that seems the most prudent source of action."

Benjamin nodded.

"That was always my plan of action. The letters too, if we locate them. While I'm sure the young man would like to have his love tokens returned, I can't risk them falling into anyone else's hands."

I followed him as he walked back to the fireplace and threw the photographs in amongst the flames. They curled and blackened quickly and were reduced to ashes in minutes.

"Now all we have to find are those letters."

"And a murderer. Which means there is still another secret out there, something someone was willing to kill Emsworth to keep quiet."

I sat still as Betsy buttoned a long row of tiny pearl buttons down my back. I hardly heard her as she chattered on about the goings-on belowstairs, so absorbed was I in my thoughts. Benjamin and I had searched the library for another half hour before we heard signs of the staff readying the house for the day and slipped back to our rooms to dress. We both thought it was unlikely that Mr. Emsworth had hidden the letters in the same room as the photographs, but with so many potential hiding places in the library, we needed to be sure. Benjamin planned to return to the library that afternoon and finish the one section we hadn't searched yet, but I was already wracking my brain as to where else in the house someone could have hidden the letters. The servants quarters were on the uppermost floor, but were locked during the day, so unless Mr. Emsworth had slipped into one of their rooms at night while the servants were sleeping in their beds, we could rule those spaces out.

It seemed so incongruous to me to think of Mr. Emsworth as a blackmailer, but as Benjamin had followed him here on that suspicion and I'd held the photographs in my hand, it was hard to deny it now. But, blackmailer or no, he didn't deserve to die, and I hoped we could find some answers to his death before the house party broke up and our chance was lost. I looked out the window and was met with the sight of gathering storm clouds. Good. The original snowfall had started to melt off, but perhaps more would fall today, making travel difficult for a few more days.

If Mr. Emsworth had indeed been blackmailing another member of the house party, or even a servant, and had gotten killed for it, would we find that blackmail evidence as well? A thought struck me so hard that I jerked my head up suddenly, throwing Betsy, who was attempting to pin my hair up, off balance.

"So sorry, Betsy. I just remembered something. Do continue."

She continued her story about Thomas, the footman she was walking out with, and I went back to my thoughts.

What if there was no other blackmail evidence, because the murderer was somehow connected to the Queen's relative and was there to ensure the damning evidence didn't get out? What if he or she was on the same mission Benjamin was, but didn't know it? It was worth looking into whether anyone there could possibly have a connection to either of the young men in the photographs.

"There ya go, Miss, now that's right lovely."

I took a quick glance at myself in the mirror, admiring the way Betsy had braided my hair into a becoming twist at the nape of my neck. My deep rose-colored blouse brought out the pink in my cheeks, and I looked more alive this morning than I had since finding Mr. Emsworth's body. I pinned on my favorite cameo, a lovely pearl and burgundy pin that had been a gift from Lady Hadleigh for my sixteenth birthday, and made my way down to the breakfast room.

By now, I'd been up for several hours, and my stomach rumbled in protest at the delayed repast. Arthur and Rupert, looking as cheerful as ever and not the least bit hungover, were the only persons in the breakfast room, so I filled my plate without regard for propriety and enjoyed their convivial conversation while I dug into it with enthusiasm.

"I heard some of the gentlemen were taken by surprise by your special punch recipe last night," I said with a smile after I'd eaten enough to dull the hunger pains a bit. "How is it you two are looking so bright-eyed this morning?"

Arthur grinned.

"I guess we're used to it. It's our great-grandmother's recipe; it's been keeping Cunninghams warm in the winter for generations. You know, that punch is probably even responsible for a couple members of that lineage."

I snorted, and Rupert laughed.

"It's the honey and spices that make it deceptively smooth. We also know to pace ourselves since it's much stronger than it seems. But have you seen any of the other gentlemen this morning? I thought we were only ones up, but I was hoping to rouse enough companions for an early morning shooting party."

Too late I realized my misstep. I took another bite of toast and gave myself a moment to think of an appropriate reply that was not, *Oh no, just meeting with my ex-husband in the library in my dressing gown to search for blackmail evidence.*

"A shooting party, this early, Rupurt? No, I haven't seen anyone else yet this morning, but Betsy was chatting about the deadly punch as she did my hair. You know how observant the servants are. I imagine they were extra quiet in the gentlemen's rooms when they were stoking the fires this morning."

I sent a silent apology to Betsy for blaming her for such blatant gossip, though with all she had talked about this morning while I got ready, she could have mentioned the gentlemen's over-consumption, and I had just been too lost in my thoughts to notice.

Arthur gave his brother a wry smile.

"I told you that you would struggle to find anyone up and about before noon today. And with that poor chap's accident, I can't say that I blame them. I appreciate that we're trying to continue on with the activities for the other guests' sake, but you have to admit that some stiff drinks and a good lie-in might be better served in this case."

Rupert shrugged.

"It'll be just like every holiday with our old man, then, eh?"

I couldn't help but smile at my friends, and we continued talking of the activities Sarah had planned for between now and Christmas, wondering which of them would be appropriate to continue under the circumstances. A steady snow was again falling outside the breakfast room window. It looked like the house party would continue on for the time being, a fact I would have loathed once Benjamin had arrived, but was now grateful for. I was relieved that it would give us some extra time to look into Mr. Emsworth's death, but also relieved that I wouldn't have to flee the company of my friends quite so quickly. And maybe, deep down somewhere was a feeling I could not yet put a name to.

Chapter 21

After another leisurely half-hour at the breakfast table, Sarah and Mary joined us, followed slowly by Miss Price and Miss Taylor, and last of all Miss Loughty. It seemed the gentlemen were, indeed, still sleeping off the effects of the famous punch. I hoped Benjamin would awake in a few hours with a clearer head. I wasn't really sure where to go from here in our investigation. I couldn't question Mr. Emsworth's valet by myself, but if anyone could shed light on the poor man's last hours, it was he. I wasn't sure where else in the house to search for the blackmail letters, as most of the house had already been covered. As loath as I was to admit it, I needed Benjamin's guidance on what we should do next.

I was roused from my thoughts by Sarah, who asked if I wanted to accompany them to cut down a Christmas tree.

"It's a Christmas Eve tradition started by Rupurt and Arthur's mother, that we cut down and decorate a tree on Christmas Eve. She was inspired by Prince Albert himself, you know. The children have been making popcorn strings for the last few days to decorate it."

I looked up, surprised. With everything going on, I'd lost track of my days.

"Christmas Eve, already? Time has been flying by! I'd love to go with you all to choose a tree."

Since there wasn't much more I could do to move our mystery forward at the moment, I decided to allow myself to enjoy the Christmas festivities. It was why I'd come all the way to England

128

after all. Mary, Miss Loughty, and Miss Taylor professed their eagerness to accompany us as well, with Miss Price saying she'd prefer to wait for us by the fire.

"I've no problem with such wholesome traditions," she said haughtily, "but at my age it would be madness to trudge around in the snow."

With Miss Price's blessing thus bestowed, we took half an hour for each of us to put on our boots and warmest coats, and the whole group made our way slowly through the snowy back garden to the woods that lay just beyond. The children had joined us, and they were chattering happily and throwing snowballs at one another as we walked through a light, swirling snow. It was quite picturesque, and almost made me forget the tragedy and struggles of the last two days.

The woods were magical when covered with a thick dusting of snow, like a childhood fairy tale. I breathed in the crisp air, allowing it to ease away some of the tension I'd been carrying since finding Mr. Emsworth's body. Arthur and Rupert were arguing good-naturedly over whether our tree should be tall and skinny, or short and fat, and soon had everyone in stitches over their antics. Arthur picked up little Fanny on his shoulders to approximate the height the tree should be, and the two ran about from tree to tree measuring, Fanny giggling all the way.

The sight unexpectedly made me a bit emotional. I'd long come to terms with never having a family of my own, and most of the time I was at peace with it. I supposed it was the heightened emotions of the last two days, with Benjamin suddenly appearing back into my life and a man being murdered. It was enough to make the most stalwart spinster a bit maudlin.

Miss Loughty worked her way over to me, holding the hem of her gorgeous bottle-green topcoat up over the snow. She must have sensed some sort of emotion on my face, for she smiled kindly.

"I remember you saying that you grew up with your grandfather. Did you ever cut down a Christmas tree together?"

"We always spent Christmas day at the Hadleighs—that is, at our closest neighbors' estate. Grandfather always hated to see a perfectly good tree cut down when we weren't there to enjoy it on Christmas, but we would hang greenery and mistletoe all around our house during the season, and put candles in all the windows. Lady Hadleigh would have a grand tree, and we children would spend the whole day on Christmas Eve decorating it. Grandfather once got so angry at us because we stole a set of maps from his office to fold into paper star ornaments."

"Hadleigh—do you mean Lord Hadleigh's family? You must know each other quite well, then."

"We did as children. I'm afraid we've lost touch over the years since Lady Hadeigh passed away, and Grandfather and I moved to Paris."

"What happened to your grandfather's estate? That is, your childhood home?"

I looked up at Miss Loughty, surprised by her question. I honestly hadn't thought about the estate at all since we'd left. When Grandfather died, it had passed to the next male heir, a cousin I barely knew, but I hadn't grieved its loss at all. My home was my grandfather, Lady Hadleigh, and Benjamin. When I'd lost all of them, the actual house seemed to matter little anymore. I supposed I did miss the Hadleigh estate, with the orchards we used to play in, the fields where we would go riding, and the library where we would while away long winter days.

"The estate passed to a distant cousin when Grandfather died last year, but honestly I haven't thought of it since."

It was Miss Loughty's turn to look surprised.

"You haven't thought once of your ancestral home? I don't know who I would be without the Belvoir estate. It has been our family's home for generations and always will be."

I thought it interesting that she didn't mention her actual home, adjacent to the Belvoir land. I supposed she'd grown to view the two properties as one and the same.

"You must love it very much," I said gently.

"Oh, I do. I consider myself so fortunate to come from such a noble family. Which is why I'm afraid I must ask you, Miss Osbourne, do you have designs on my cousin?"

I blinked at her in shock, momentarily unable to form any words. Glancing around, I noted that Miss Taylor was engaged in conversation with Mary, and Sarah and the children were dusting the snow off of a tree they had chosen, begging Arthur and Rupert to come see that it was the perfect one. I answered Miss Loughty's question slowly.

"I have no designs whatsoever on Lord Belvoir, other than those of friendship. I have a full life and career in Paris, Miss Loughty." I saw her shoulders drop just a fraction of an inch, and I knew then that my earlier suspicions had been correct. "I don't ever plan to marry, and if I were ever to change my mind, I would not set my sights on an Englishman. I find I like my life too much to give it up." Lowering my voice, I smiled wryly at her. "Since I have been candid with you about my feelings, I confess I've been wanting to ask you the same question. Are you in love with your cousin?"

Miss Loughty stiffened instantly, the openness in her face a moment earlier shuttering closed. I'd been too blunt, but her reaction confirmed her feelings.

"I don't know what you mean. I care for him very much, of course. We are family."

"You don't have to confirm or deny it either way. Suffice it to know that I have no desire to be the next Marchioness. Your cousin may flirt with me, but I believe it's because I'm a safe target. I'm not likely to lose my head like a starry-eyed young chit just out of the schoolroom. I learned my lesson the hard way, long ago. I promise that while I enjoy Lord Belvoir's company as a friend, I will not encourage his attentions in regards to anything else."

She nodded stiffly, a look of understanding passing between us. For a moment, I thought her eyes were going to fill with tears, but she squared her shoulders, and turned back towards the group.

"Let's rejoin the others, Miss Osbourne. It appears they've chosen a tree."

I laid a hand gently on her arm. "I have known the pain of a love not returned—from long ago, when I was a young, green girl. If experience has taught me anything, I would encourage you to talk to your cousin about your feelings. He might return them, or he might not, but I would not want to live forever wondering if I were you. You are quite a bit younger than him, are you not?"

She smiled a slightly wobbly smile at me.

"I am five and twenty."

"He may have no idea of the kind of regard you have for him. But either way, you still have a chance for a full life, with or without a husband. Don't put yours on hold waiting for your cousin to notice you."

In that moment, I realized just how grateful I was for the life I'd lived the last nine years. I hadn't sat around, a wilting wallflower waiting for Benjamin to come to his senses and take me back, but I'd pursued my dreams and fought hard for the full and independent life I had today. If we had stayed married and I had come back to England after my residency as originally planned, what kind of life would I have lived as Lady Hadleigh? It would have been lovely to have a family, to have children, but I wouldn't have had the experiences that I'd had in Paris—experiences that made me the woman I was today.

I smiled at Miss Loughty.

"If you ever need someone to talk to, truly—you can always seek me out."

"Thank you, Miss Osbourne." Her voice was so soft, I almost missed it, but she seemed genuinely grateful.

"Please, I believe we're well acquainted enough for you to call me Winifred. Winnie, even—it's what my friends call me."

"And you may call me Helen."

Rupert had pulled out a small hand saw from his bag and was starting to cut down a tree, to the excitement of all the children.

Their shrieks of delight rang through the forest, and Helen and I made our way over to them to watch. Soon, Rupurt and Arthur began hauling the tree back towards the house, the ladies traveling in their wake, stamping their feet to warm them and discussing where the tree would be displayed to the best advantage. With one more small smile at Helen, and a kiss on Sarah's cheek, I decided to stay outside a while longer and play with the children. They'd left the adults to take care of setting up the tree, and were busily beginning to build a snowman in the back garden.

I hadn't made a snowman since I was ten, when Benjamin had decided he was too old for snowmen and I'd promptly followed suit. We'd moved on to snow forts, from which we could conduct our vicious snowball attacks on Augustus whenever he came home for the school holidays. But until then, we'd made snowmen as often as we'd had the chance, dressing them up with old clothes from the Hadleighs' attic. Since we seldom had enough snow in Paris to build anything with, I wasn't about to pass up on the chance.

Thomas insisted on a rather artistic arrangement of the snowmen, fashioning them into carolers clustered around the back patio, which made Addie and Fannie shriek with delight. We built snowmen for nearly an hour, with the children making a run to the attic at my suggestion, coming back with armfuls of moth-eaten scarves and top hats half a century out of date. Our carolers were soon smartly dressed, and my toes were now so numb I couldn't feel them despite my thick, wool-lined boots.

"Children, I think it's time we went back to the house for some hot chocolate!"

"Nooooo!" Addie whined, despair on her face. "You promised we would make a snow dog for the carolers."

And so I had. I looked around at the area surrounding the house, but our carolers were so numerous that we'd scooped up all the snow around us. I spotted a large snow bank on the other side of some bushes near the corner of the house.

"I'll grab some fresh snow, though sculpting is not my medium and I cannot promise how dog-like this creation is going to look."

Crouching next to the snow bank, I rolled two medium snowballs for the dog's front and hind quarters, and a longer, oval shape for his abdomen. I was just scooping up snow to make something resembling a head, when my gloved fingers struck something hard towards the bottom of the snowbank.

I pulled back, startled, afraid I'd disturbed some poor creature hibernating in the snow, but curiosity got the better of me. I reached into the dwindling pile of snow once more, feeling around until my fingers brushed the object again, and pulled it out.

It was a small glass vial, no longer than half the length of my finger, and just as slim, with a cork stopper at the top. A small brass loop coming out of the cork would have allowed it to be held on a chain, or perhaps a ring of keys. Sadly, it was empty, and there were no distinguishing marks on it of any kind, but I had a feeling it had once held the foxglove, likely in the form of digitalis, used to kill Mr. Emsworth. Anyone in the household could have dropped it in the snowbank. It was far enough off the path that it wouldn't have been shoveled or salted. If it wasn't for Addie's snow dog, it would have likely stayed buried here until spring.

Quickly dropping the vial in my coat pocket and buttoning it with cold, stiff fingers, I grabbed a couple of the snowballs I had made and called to the children.

"Come grab these, children. Let's finish our snow dog, and then I simply must insist we go inside. I'm frozen to the bone."

At least we could stop searching for signs of the murder weapon. But who had hidden it in the snowbank?

Chapter 22

The entire house party was soon gathered in the parlor to decorate the Christmas tree. Sarah had brought several small cigar boxes full of decorations down from the nursery. The children had been industrious over the last few days. Piles of popcorn strings, paper stars, and shiny punched tin ornaments spilled over the edges of the boxes. Lord Belvoir, Mr. Loughty, Lord Worthington, and Benjamin joined us as Arthur and Rupert were setting up the tree, and I was relieved to see Benjamin was looking more rested and far less disheveled than he had in the library earlier this morning.

Sarah had hot chocolate and Christmas cake served while we began decorating the tree, and I was almost able to forget there was still a murderer somewhere in the house. Almost. I'd changed my wet shoes, stockings, and skirt upon returning to the house, but carefully transferred the small vial I'd found in the garden to my new skirt's pocket. I needed to find a time to show Benjamin and Lord Worthington while the other guests weren't looking. It took some time, as Miss Taylor kept finding excuses to ask for Benjamin's help decorating the tree, batting her eyelashes prettily all the while. With his back to Miss Taylor, Lord Worthington raised an eyebrow at me and grinned mischievously. Turning towards him as I showed him some tin stars I was threading onto a bit of red ribbon, I murmured in a low voice, "do you think we should step in and save him, my Lord?"

Lord Worthington's eyes twinkled, and he leaned over,

ostensibly admiring the ornaments, and said where only I could hear him, "Please, I believe we've been through enough together for Christian names, have we not, Miss Osbourne? You can call me Chester."

I smiled at him.

"And I'm Winifred."

"Not Freddie?"

Lord Worthington—Chester—had a mischievous streak, that much was clear. I couldn't help but chuckle at him.

"Benjamin is the only one that has ever called me Freddie, I'm afraid. It started when I was about seven and sadly, it stuck."

If Chester had guessed that the degree of intimacy Benjamin and I shared was unusual for that of mere childhood friends, he gave no indication.

"Well, Winifred—a lovely name, by the way—I'd say we let Hadleigh squirm a bit longer before we rescue him from the machinations of Miss Taylor."

He helped me hang a few of the tin stars higher up on the tree, and I couldn't restrain my curiosity.

"So, Chester, may I ask how you met Benjamin?"

"We are members of the same club in London. One day, I'd gotten a particularly frustrating letter from my fiancée, and was drowning my sorrows a bit too deeply."

Chester smiled self-deprecatingly, and I couldn't imagine the quiet, somewhat impish man in front of me in such a bad state.

"Benjamin saw that I'd had enough and that some of the other members of the club were beginning to mock me, so he stepped in, found my coat and hat, and walked me a few blocks to his home and let me sleep it off. He treated me with such kindness, and he hadn't even known my name before that day."

"He always did have a bit of a hero complex," I said with a wry smile. "He used to try to rescue me all the time when we were children. I was the one who would rush headlong into danger without thinking, so most of the time I actually needed it."

I thought of all the times in the last ten years that Benjamin wasn't there when I needed him, and my throat tightened. Still, I pushed that feeling of loss aside. Perhaps someday I'd get to the point where I could remember the happier moments from our childhood without hating the way our story ended. I felt more charitable towards Benjamin than I had in years, so I found myself suddenly hopeful of that feeling. Perhaps I would finally be able to put some of the more bitter memories behind me and focus on the happier ones.

"I confess, I am usually more circumspect, but I was grateful for Hadleigh that day," Chester admitted. "We've been fast friends ever since. When he found out I was going to be attending the same house party as his, um, let's say person of interest, I was happy to secure an invitation for him as well."

After a few more minutes of decorating, Benjamin was finally able to get away from Miss Taylor as she was summoned to converse with Miss Price by the fire. As soon as I was sure no one was paying attention to us, I pulled the small vial out of my pocket and showed Benjamin and Chester.

"I think this may have been what the digitalis was stored in," I said in a low voice, turning my back to the rest of the room. "I found it in a snowbank close to the corner of the house when I was building snowmen with the children this morning."

I held it out in my palm and Benjamin took it, holding it up to the light coming through the window behind us. We could see a film of fine, white powder dusting the inside of the glass tube.

"You're probably right. Good find, Freddie. We still have no way of knowing who it belongs to, but at least we know how they got it into the house."

"They likely got rid of it as soon as they'd emptied the contents into Mr. Emsworth's drink. They could have even thrown it out a window, trusting in the snow to bury it and keep it hidden until everyone had left the house."

"Whose rooms are at that corner of the house?"

Chester's question was a good one. If the vial had been thrown out a window, there were only a few within tossing distance of that snowbank.

"It's the gentlemen's wing," I offered. "Lord Belvoir and Mr. Loughty's rooms are down on that end, but it could have been thrown from Mr. Emsworth's room, too, if someone threw it hard enough. Perhaps the killer tossed it out when they pushed Mr. Emsworth out the window, too." I shuttered. "I hadn't given much thought to how Mr. Emsworth was pushed out the window, other than the fact that he was likely dead before he was pushed. But if that was the case, the killer would need to be strong enough to pick up the body and clear the sash."

Benjamin opened his mouth to comment, but Chester held up a discreet hand in warning as Mary approached us. Turning to greet her with a smile, he asked her to show him how the paper angel garlands were made.

"I would love to hang some in my own home next year," he was saying, deftly leading Mary towards the table where the garlands were stacked, waiting to be hung on the tree. When the two of them were out of earshot, Benjamin spoke softly as he pulled a popcorn string out of a box and we began looping it around the bows of the tree.

"Worthington is a smart one. I'm glad to have him around. But about the body. You're right, the killer would need to be strong enough to pick it up high enough to clear the sash. But Emsworth was a slight man. Even a strong woman could accomplish it."

I glanced discreetly about the room.

"I doubt Miss Taylor or Miss Price could accomplish it. But I think nearly anyone else here could."

"Don't underestimate Miss Taylor," he grimaced. "You didn't feel the way she gripped my arm going into dinner last night."

I snorted loudly and tried to pass it off as a cough. Benjamin patted me between the shoulder blades, a slight crease between his eyebrows.

"I've been meaning to warn you," he continued, "that you shouldn't eat or drink anything that the rest of the group isn't having. If you order tea to your room, make sure you take the tea tray from the maid yourself. Just to be safe."

I raised an eyebrow.

"I hardly think the murderer will try to target one of us. Unless they know why you're here and suspect you're on to them? I could caution you to take the same precautions, but I doubt anyone has even figured out that I'm helping you."

"Even being seen with me could be dangerous. We need to be careful."

"I doubt anyone else here would suspect us as being anything more than childhood acquaintances. We hardly need to worry."

Benjamin's face had turned all dark and stormy, but I cut him off before he could go off on a tirade and alert the rest of the guests to our conversation.

"Here, hold these."

I grabbed a crate of pretty glass baubles one of the servants had just brought down to the side table next to us and thrust it into his arms. As I carefully unearthed a bauble from the excelsior around it and climbed onto one of the small step stools that Sarah had provided to hang it on the tree, I turned back towards him, whispering.

"Did you talk to Mr. Emsworth's valet yet? According to the maid, the valet was likely the last person to see him alive."

"The valet, a young man named Smythe, was the first person I talked to yesterday. He claims Emsworth was fine when he'd left him for the night after he dressed him for bed and hung up his clothing—but Emsworth hadn't yet drank his cup of warm milk. The maid delivered the milk while Smythe was assisting Emsworth, and Emsworth told her to leave it by the door. It was another five minutes or so before Smythe left, and he brought the tray in for Emsworth and set it on the table. When he left Emsworth for the night, he said that he didn't seem sick in any way."

"So he says," I mused. "Smythe could have killed Emsworth himself and dumped him out the window, and no one would be the wiser."

Benjamin shook his head as he held the box up for me to grab another bauble, which I hung carefully from my place on the stepstool.

"I don't think so. The man seemed genuinely distraught. He liked Emsworth. He had only worked for him for about a year, but said he had been an extremely kind employer. This was Smythe's first position as a valet, and he was hoping to stay with the family for a long time. He said Mrs. Emsworth paid him very generously for an inexperienced valet and always on time. Besides, while he could have had an opportunity to slip poison into the milk, it's unlikely he could have made it back to the room later to push the body out of the window. The servants are sleeping two to a bedroom due to the full house, and his roommate, one of the footmen, claims he's a light sleeper and that Mr. Smythe was snoring across the room from him all night long."

"So unless he had an accomplice, it's unlikely he would have been able to poison Mr. Emsworth, wait for the poison to take effect, and then push Mr. Emsworth out the window without anyone noticing his absence." I thought for a moment. "I do find it interesting that Mrs. Emsworth paid Smythe's salary and not her son."

Benjamin shrugged.

"It's not uncommon for the woman of the house to take care of domestic matters, including paying the servants."

As I reached down to grab another bauble, I wobbled on the stool slightly. Benjamin started to grab me by the thigh to steady me, then, as if he realized the intimacy of such a gesture, just hovered his hand a few inches away in case I fell. Thankfully, I caught my balance, retrieved the bauble, and continued in my task.

"So if Emsworth was fine when Smythe left him, but he hadn't yet drank the milk, it seems pretty likely that the poison was put into his drink somehow."

"And likely that someone poisoned the milk while Smythe was preparing him for bed. Even five minutes outside the door would have been plenty of time to drop the digitalis in."

"What are you two whispering at?" I started at the sudden interruption, and this time I actually toppled from the step stool. Thankfully Benjamin had already put down the box of baubles, for he grabbed me by the waist and gently lowered me to the ground, quickly stepping away to put a proper amount of distance between us. I'd been so focused on our conversation, I hadn't even noticed that most of the guests had retreated to the sideboard on the opposite side of the room to build their plates for luncheon. Sarah's eyes glinted mischievously as she stood next to us. The wretch showed not a hint of concern for my welfare, and I wagged my finger at her.

"You silly goose! I could have broken my neck with you sneaking up like that while I was on a stepstool. You know how clumsy I am."

Sarah grinned at me, and I couldn't help but smile at her. I had never been able to be mad at her for long, even when we were silly schoolgirls.

"Well, it's a good thing Lord Hadleigh was standing so close to you then. Since the two of you were whispering so cozily behind the tree here, you missed my announcement that luncheon is served. I was just coming to warn you before Rupert and Arthur clean out all the sandwiches. Tromping around in the snow this morning has given us all quite an appetite."

As if on cue, my stomach rumbled.

"We'd better get Miss Osbourne some lunch before she expires," Benjamin said with a roguish smile at our hostess. "I'm sure it was her faintness from hunger that caused her to topple off that stool."

The wretch winked at Sarah, and she laughed. Looping her arm through mine, she led us over to the awaiting luncheon, looking as delighted as I'd ever seen her. I would certainly hear all about my cozy tête à tête with Benjamin later.

Chapter 23

The party assembled at luncheon was almost merry, with only a slightly subdued quality to indicate a young man had died at the house only two days before. I couldn't bring myself to begrudge the guests their festivity. It was Christmas Eve, after all, and Benjamin, Lord Worthington, and I were the only ones present that knew about the murder. Mrs. Emsworth had spent the morning in her room, but had made her way down to the parlor for luncheon, and everyone sat grouped around a few small tables. It was the older woman that I was most interested in watching. She looked ill at ease, not just grief-stricken, and I wondered again if she had any inkling that her son had been murdered. She was putting on a brave face, however, and attempting to converse quietly with the other guests, though she dabbed at her eyes occasionally with a handkerchief. I wondered if she would head home to London as soon as the roads were passable, or if she would take Sarah up on her offer to remain with the Cunninghams until Mrs. Emsworth's other son could make it back to the country. I decided that we should try to talk with her. As Benjamin and I were the last to fill our plates at the sideboard, I leaned over towards him and whispered softly as I offered him a sandwich filled with a creamy herb and cheese mixture.

"Mrs. Emsworth seems to be acting strangely. Almost jumpy. I think we should talk to her, and try to assess if she has any idea that her son was murdered."

"Everyone grieves differently, Freddie. She could be jumpy because her son just died."

"Last night before dinner she told me that she wasn't surprised that her son had an accident—apparently he was so absent-minded that he got himself into trouble frequently. He even fell out of a window once. She was grieved of course, but—I don't know. She looks different today. Let's go sit at her table."

"Are you sure you want to be seen with me after getting caught together behind the Christmas tree?"

He raised an eyebrow, and I snorted.

"You make it sound like we were doing something indecent. Come on, there are two chairs across from Mrs. Emsworth."

I grabbed a piece of fruit-studded pound cake, piled two pieces onto Benjamin's plate without asking, and made my way over to the table where Mrs. Emsworth, Sarah, and Mary were sitting.

"May I join you all?"

I smiled at the ladies as Benjamin pulled my chair out for me, then sat down beside me, and I noticed Sarah's eyes were still glittering with mischief. I'd deal with her later.

"Mrs. Emsworth, it's so good to see you downstairs. May I get you anything?"

The poor woman seemed to be pushing some vegetables around on her plate without really eating anything. Her sandwiches remained untouched.

"I can certainly recommend this fruit cake," Benjamin said, and I looked over in astonishment to see he'd already devoured half a piece. "It reminds me of the panettone they eat for Christmas in Italy."

"Have you spent much time in Italy, my Lord?" asked Mary politely.

"We went on holiday a few times when I was growing up. In fact, some of the happiest times of my life occurred in Italy."

I nearly choked on my sandwich, but managed to swallow and wash it down with some tea. When I could speak again, I offered, "Lady Hadleigh was in poor health, and I believe she felt the Italian weather to be beneficial."

"So they serve a Christmas cake like this in Italy?" Sarah looked towards Benjamin thoughtfully. "Our cook is as English as they come, but Rupurt's mother did love finding Christmas recipes from around the world. Perhaps that's where this particular cake claims its heritage."

Trying to steer the conversation to include Mrs. Emsworth again, I turned towards the older woman.

"I believe your younger son's wife is from Bavaria? Has she introduced you to any interesting traditions?"

"None that our own dear Prince Albert hadn't already introduced to England, though she is a dear. I do love the tradition of a Christmas tree, and I'm so glad you decided to cut one down today."

Benjamin, now warming to his theme, continued on about Italy, oblivious to my attempts to include Mrs. Emsworth in the conversation.

"In Italy, gifts aren't exchanged until after Twelfth Night, when La Bafana, a kindly old witch figure, is said to bring the gifts to children rather than Father Christmas. Legend has it that she tried to follow the wise men to Bethlehem but got lost, and decided to bring gifts to all the children she found in lieu of the Christ child."

"Well isn't that charming." Mary smiled at Benjamin, though I noticed her eyes flicked subtly between us a couple of times. "Perhaps you can tell that story to the children later this evening. I know they'd love a new Christmas tale."

"I would be delighted to." I was surprised that Benjamin actually looked pleased at the prospect. I was just thinking about another way to draw Mrs. Emsworth back into the conversation, possibly by talking about her grandchildren, when Sarah caught me off guard with a question.

"Winnie, darling, didn't you spend some time in Italy right after we left school? I seem to recall you traveling around there before you began that art residency in Florence."

I stilled. I felt as if I were treading on very thin ice. It wouldn't take a very clever person to put two and two together about our summer in Italy, and conclude that Benjamin and I had once been much closer than the childhood acquaintances we were attempting to pass ourselves off as. I needed to choose my words carefully.

"Yes, Grandfather and I spent the summer before my residency in Italy. I got to see much of the country. It's really very beautiful. Mrs. Emsworth, I know you've been to Paris, have you made it as far as Italy yet?"

Thus roused, Mrs. Emsworth was obliged to tell us about the trip she and her younger son took to Rome many years back, the poor, recently-departed Mr. Emsworth not inclined to travel abroad. She seemed to perk up a bit talking about her travels, and when we all departed to our various tasks and amusements after luncheon, she seemed more like herself.

"I don't think she has an inkling of how her son truly met his end," Benjamin whispered softly when he was sure we were alone again. We were returning our dirty plates to the sideboard for the servants to clean up, as the other guests had all finished their luncheon and moved on to other pursuits, some to play cards and some to rest or write letters in their rooms. "Not unless she's a very, very good actress."

"No, I think you're right," I agreed, "but there was definitely something different about her this morning. What do you plan to do this afternoon?"

"Worthington and I will discreetly question the rest of the servants. We've talked to most of them, but there's a few other valets and lady's maids that traveled here with the guests that aren't part of the Cunninghams' household nor work for the Emsworths. I don't see how any of them would have any motivation to kill the man, but they may have seen or heard something that could prove useful."

"Anything I can do?"

Benjamin thought for a moment, and I was pleased he was actually considering how I might be useful.

"If you have a few minutes, put all of your thoughts down on paper. Details of what the body looked like when you found it, where everyone was the night of the murder as far as we know. Your photographic memory may conjure up something we've overlooked before. If you notice anything, we'll speak again when we gather before dinner."

I agreed that it wouldn't hurt to try, and we parted ways, Benjamin heading down towards the servants' areas. I walked up the main staircase back towards the women's wing and stifled a yawn, thinking that maybe I should take a short rest before I began putting all of my thoughts on paper. I felt as though there were some details I was missing, something important, but I'd been up since long before dawn, and my tired brain was refusing to think straight. Perhaps Benjamin was right, and if I wrote down everyone's names and possible motives for murder, something would jump out at me. Lost in thought once again, I failed to pay attention to my surroundings.

I didn't notice the danger until a clawlike arm reached out and grabbed me at the top of the staircase, pulling me roughly into the hallway and slamming me up against the wall.

Chapter 24

Taken by surprise, I had the wind knocked out of me and stood gasping for breath for a moment, my back still to the wall.

In front of me, and still clutching my arm like a bird of prey, was Miss Taylor. It took a moment for my brain to catch up with the fact that this slight, delicate looking creature was the one who had snatched me from the top of the stairs. One wrong move and I could have tumbled down the grand staircase. I would have been lucky to come out of the incident with only a few broken bones.

I looked at her hold on my arm, and then back up into her pretty face, now stormy with rage. She was slightly taller than me, which I'd never realized since she had such a delicate air about her. The fingernails digging into my arm told me it was all a show.

"Stay away from Lord Hadleigh," she hissed quietly in my face, but a quick glance around me told me we wouldn't be interrupted. Everyone else was in the parlor playing cards or resting in their rooms.

"Miss Taylor, this is hardly appropriate. I have no idea what you're talking about." I raised an eyebrow, trying to keep my voice quiet and calm but firm. I was the adult in this situation, and I didn't want her to see how much she'd just unnerved me.

"Don't act like you're some kind of innocent. I saw you two, whispering behind the Christmas tree. I saw you the other day, sneaking out of the conservatory together. I know the game you're trying to play. Lord Hadleigh will be my prize, and I won't have some old spinster take that away from me, just because you wear fancy gowns from Paris and pretend to be all high and mighty and sophisticated. I will do whatever has to be done to secure my future, and I'm not about to let you get in my way."

The girl's eyes flashed, but she took a step back from me, allowing me to shuffle slightly away from the wall. She still held my arm in a vice grip, so I waited, trying to breathe normally.

"Whatever you think you saw, Lord Hadleigh and I are just old childhood acquaintances. He was asking my opinion on a matter this morning, that is all."

"You two thought you were so sneaky because you didn't leave the conservatory at the same time, but I saw you come out a few minutes later. I know you were in there at the same time."

"I was in the conservatory to draw, to calm my nerves." I injected a note of steel into my voice, hoping I sounded authoritative. "Lord Hadleigh came for a stroll in the warm conservatory, and we bumped into each other there, then went our separate ways. Nothing more."

Miss Taylor gave an unlady-like snort. "Don't get all high and mighty and pretend to be any better than me just because I have matrimonial ambitions. As women we have two possessions to our name: our beauty and our wit. I'm sure you've had to use both to get anywhere in your profession. You're no different than me."

In one sense, she wasn't wrong. I knew plenty of women artists that had to compromise their morals in order to make a living in our field. I was thankful that Grandfather's wealth and connections in the art world had allowed me to succeed without being one of them. While I didn't agree with her methods, I understood her need for them. As women, we were relatively powerless. Marrying well at any cost was one of the only ways to make it ahead in life.

I looked at the girl—for that's all she was really, a girl—with her fingernails digging into my arm through the fabric of my blouse. I would have to choose my words carefully.

"Miss Taylor, I completely understand the need for your ambition. I sympathize with why you would have the need for it, even. But you have to understand that I am in no way your competition in regards to Lord Hadleigh's affections."

Miss Taylor scoffed, an ugly sneer marring her delicate features.

"I've seen the way he looks at you. Like he's a drowning man and you're the only one that can save him."

I blinked, startled. I wasn't sure Benji had ever looked at me that way, even when we were on our honeymoon. I replied to the girl as gently as I could, not wanting to provoke her further.

"Anything you think you see, is just the nostalgia of old friends who have long since lost touch remembering their childhood. I haven't seen Lord Hadleigh in years, Miss Taylor. He has no desire for any sort of relationship with me."

"You two were looking awfully cozy in the parlor this morning. Hardly like indifferent former friends. You have to swear to keep your distance from him."

"I will do nothing of the sort—" I held up my free hand when she started to protest. "Not because I have any intentions towards Lord Hadleigh, but because this is a small house party, and I can't feasibly keep my distance from any of the other guests without raising questions."

Glancing me up and down with a wary eye, she finally loosened her grip on my arm.

"I may not succeed in my efforts with Lord Hadleigh, but if you decide to be my competition, I will make your life a living hell. I will stop at nothing to secure a title for myself."

Shocked at the malice in her eyes, I believed her. Taking a small step back, I rubbed at the claw marks in my arm through my sleeve. *What if Mr. Emsworth had found some compromising information about Miss Taylor and decided to blackmail her?* I could easily imagine this wrathful young woman in front of me slipping poison into a cup of milk on a tea tray, even entering Mr. Emsworth's room after everyone was asleep in bed and tossing his lifeless body out the window. Judging from the grip she had just had on my arm, she certainly could have been strong enough.

"Miss Taylor, does Miss Price know of your… ambitions? I know she desires to see you well-married, but I can't imagine she would approve of these sorts of methods."

Miss Taylor let out a rough bark of laughter.

"That prejudiced old fool! She has a talent for seeing only what she expects from people. She hates you because you're an artist, but she thinks that because I'm a young heiress from a good family with a sterling reputation, that I could not possibly act like anything other than a perfectly demure young ninny. I bow my head and bat my eyelashes at the right times, affect a blush now and then, and I have the old bird eating out of my hand. And don't you dare threaten to tell her! I won't be blackmailed."

Startled, I had to plant my feet on the floor to force myself from taking another step backwards. I looked at her thoughtfully.

"I don't plan to tell Miss Price anything, Miss Taylor. I don't think she would believe me anyway. As you said, she hardly would take the word of someone she believes to be morally loose just because of my profession, much less over the word of her beloved ward."

For a moment, Miss Taylor was silent, and I felt that we understood each other, just a little. We were both orphans, both forced to make our own way in the world. I was just fortunate I'd had Grandfather and Lady Hadleigh to raise me rather than Miss Price. Then, she straightened and took a step back, finally putting a proper amount of distance between us.

"Just remember, I will be watching you." The girl's voice came out in a soft, snake-like hiss.

"Watch me all you want, Miss Taylor. I have nothing to hide and no desire to marry Lord Hadleigh. I like my life very much the way it is, and I have no wish to move back to England to be at the mercy of any man, not even a wealthy and titled one. Your machinations have nothing to fear from me."

Except for the fact I would be warning Benjamin to tread very, very carefully around this girl. And that went for Lord Worthington and Lord Belvoir as well, just to be safe. Which reminded me of something that I was now dying to know.

"Miss Taylor, may I ask you something? Purely out of curiosity, of course."

She nodded, still eying me warily.

"Why set your sights on Lord Hadleigh, and not Lord Worthington or Lord Belvoir? Lord Belvoir has an even more prestigious title than the other gentlemen."

Miss Taylor sighed, pouting and looking as though she were discussing something as demure as unfortunate hat trimmings.

"I tried entrapping Lord Belvoir first. But what they say about his past as a terrible rake must be true, because he saw through all my tricks and wasn't shocked in the least. And while I have not the least scruples in securing a man whose affections are otherwise engaged—after all, men are such fickle creatures, are they not?—Lord Worthington is engaged to be married, and an actual engagement carries some legal precedence that would more likely see me ruined than the next Viscountess. And besides, Hadleigh is by far the most attractive gentleman here, and Miss Price says he's filthy rich. He's the most obvious choice."

I stared at the girl again, noticing the cold calculation in her eyes, and a chill ran down my back. I'd certainly met other women who were ambitious when it came to marriage, cunning even, but Miss Taylor put them all to shame.

"Well, Miss Taylor, you have nothing to fear from me."

How odd, that I'd said those same words to Miss Loughty only that morning. What was this house party turning into? I found myself longing to run to Sarah and tell her everything, but she'd have too many questions of her own—questions I wasn't prepared to answer just yet. But perhaps, when this was all over, I'd tell her the whole story—everything about the murder investigation, and everything about mine and Benjamin's aborted marriage. It was the first time in years I'd contemplated telling another soul, and I found the idea didn't hold as much dread for me as it used to.

"One word of caution, Miss Taylor. As you've pointed out, I'm an artist, and I've seen all sorts of behavior that some would consider shocking. But I've seen enough to know that the line between success and ruination here is very thin. Please do be careful."

Still glaring murderously at me, Miss Taylor nodded, then turned abruptly on her heel and marched back towards her bedroom. I stood at the top of the stairs, lost in thought for a few moments as I watched her go. The girl had just proved herself strong and determined enough to be moved to the top of my list of murder suspects.

Chapter 25

All thoughts of rest now far out of my mind, I still decided to spend some time writing down all of the information I had gathered so far. Surprised to find my hands shaking as I opened the door to my room, I reasoned it wasn't an altogether unreasonable response after finding oneself grabbed and slammed against a wall. Taking a few deep breaths to calm my nerves, I locked the bedroom door and assembled my writing supplies at the escritoire by the window.

As I sat in the cushioned wingback chair and leaned forward against the desk to write, I noticed the hard glass vial in my pocket. Removing it, I held it up to the dim light coming through the window. The day was still overcast, but the snow had ceased. Turning the vial around and around, I looked again for any identifying marks. Surprisingly, Benjamin had handed it to me to slip back into my pocket while we were talking behind the Christmas tree. There hadn't been much time to examine it in the parlor without being seen by one of the other guests, and on some level, I appreciated him trusting me with such a valuable piece of evidence.

I noticed for the first time that the vial had a flat bottom with a slight etching a millimeter or two above, as if it were made to go in a holder of some kind. Perhaps it was part of a set like the kind commonly used for household apothecary. If that were the case, wouldn't it have a label to distinguish the potentially deadly poison for other, more benign substances? I turned it over again, looking for any evidence that there'd once been a label affixed to the vial, and I noticed a small set of notches in the cork. There were three, too uniform and evenly spaced to be made by hazard. This must have been how the owner of the vial kept its contents straight. I supposed it was too much to hope that *foxglove* or *digitalis* was printed on the side in incriminating letters.

I set the vial on the desk in front of me and took up pen and paper. In a few minutes, I had a list of every person that had been in the house the night of Mr. Emsworth's murder, including most of the servants. The only people that weren't accounted for on my list were servants and staff members that traveled here with the other guests, and hopefully we would have some information to add after Benjamin spoke with them this afternoon. Next, I added any possible motives everyone on the list could have had to kill Mr. Emsworth.

Mrs. Emsworth was distraught, and could hardly be suspected of killing her own son. Rupurt and Sarah were more acquainted with Mrs. Emsworth than her son, and as far as I knew, didn't have any sort of secrets that could expose them to possible blackmail. Arthur and Mary had never met the Emsworths before they arrived here for the house party. For that matter, neither had any of the other guests. I sighed, staring at my notes forlornly. This exercise was getting me nowhere.

Miss Taylor certainly had information she wished to keep quiet—if Mr. Emsworth had somehow witnessed her attempt to entrap Lord Belvoir, whatever that had been, he could have tried to blackmail her about her unladylike and promiscuous behavior. Miss Price did seem unaware of her ward's true character, but if she had somehow found out about the blackmail, I wouldn't put it past her to take matters into her own hands.

I thought back to our game of charades the night before, and of Miss Loughty's strange reaction to the word *blackmail* as she played with her cousin. That was probably nothing, a mere hesitation as she thought about how to best act out the word—but what if it wasn't? Had the Loughtys ever crossed paths with the Emsworths before? It was a question worth asking.

In a little section under the title *Evidence*, I listed the two photographs we had found and destroyed. Somewhere in the house there were incriminating letters as well, if Benjamin's information was to be believed. They could be kept on someone's person, sewn into a skirt lining or—if there weren't too many of them—tucked into a waistcoat pocket. But finding the photographs hidden in the library told me they were probably also hidden somewhere else in the house, though we'd searched nearly every room.

After an hour, my nerves had calmed enough that my hands were no longer shaking, and I had all the information I knew so far in front of me. It didn't shed any light on our mystery, but perhaps we would learn more by the end of the day. I knew that Benjamin and Lord Worthington were probably still talking to the guests' servants. I longed to tell them about Miss Taylor's threats and warn them to be on their guard, but it would have to wait. What could I do to make myself useful in the meantime?

I didn't much feel like playing cards, but I decided to go back down to the parlor and sit with the others. At least I could talk to someone. I certainly wasn't going to learn any more information just sitting in my room. I stifled a yawn. Perhaps Sarah could procure me a cup of tea or coffee, since I wouldn't be getting that nap in any time soon.

Thankfully, I arrived in the parlor just as a generous tea tray was brought in, laden with more of the fruit-filled pound cake and several other sweets. I was excited to see a pile of the colorful little macarons that I favored in Paris, taking several and pouring myself a cup of strong black tea to revive my flagging energy levels.

Pulling a chair up near one of the card tables, I found Sarah, Rupert, Mrs. Emsworth, and Miss Price playing All Fours. Mr. Loughty, Helen, and Lord Belvoir were playing whist at the next table with Miss Taylor, and I smiled and waved at the cousins. I deliberately ignored Miss Taylor, hoping the others wouldn't notice.

"Do you want to play, dearest?" Sarah asked. "You can have my place."

"Oh no, not right now, I'm just here for the company and the tea." I stifled another yawn, then popped a macaron in my mouth. "I decided against a nap, and now I must find a way to keep myself awake this afternoon."

"Well, you've certainly come to the right place." Rupert leaned over and snagged a macaron off my plate, then held his hand of cards up to defend himself as his wife smacked his arm for his thievery. I chuckled at their antics. "Don't worry, Sarah, darling, I just wanted one. I'll bring treats over for everyone after this hand is over."

"Oh, macarons!" Mrs. Emsworth's face brightened over her cards. "They're so lovely, too, I must try some."

"I hate to be the bearer of bad news, but macarons are made with ground almonds, Mrs. Emsworth," I said gently.

"So?" Mrs. Emsworth blinked at me, a confused look on her face, and it was my turn to blink right back.

"Oh, I must have heard you wrong the other day. You said you had *une petite allergie d'aumande*. A little almond allergy."

"I did? When?" The poor woman looked confused.

"When I almost ran you down outside of Mrs. Hudgins' office. You said you were leaving a note for her about your almond allergy."

"Oh, Mrs. Emsworth, I'm so sorry!" Sarah exclaimed, looking worried. "Mrs. Hudgins never told me, or otherwise I would have made sure the menu didn't include any almonds."

Mrs. Emsworth smiled, a sudden look of understanding on her face.

"Oh no, Mrs. Cunningham, please don't think anything of it. In fact, almonds are just fine for me. It's chestnuts I have trouble tolerating." She turned to me. "I should have said, *une petit allergie de châtaignes*, Miss Osbourne, but my French is a little rusty."

I smiled reassuringly at her.

"I've lived in France for years, and there are still words that I get mixed up sometimes. Why, one time, I thought I was asking this kind old woman at the market for jam, but I ended up accidentally asking her for something quite different."

We then spent another half hour sharing our worst translation mishaps, and Rupert had us all in stitches over his recounting of a trip to the Scottish highlands that went terribly wrong due to a mispronounced village name, landing him in a dilapidated cottage with a smelly sheep farmer overnight, rather than at his school friend's hunting lodge. Eventually, Helen, her brother, and Lord Belvoir joined us, their card game at an end, and we passed the tea snacks around, conversing amiably and enjoying the now fully-decorated Christmas tree. I was not disappointed that Miss Taylor excused herself when the rest of her table came over to join us, though she was likely off to roam the halls in search of Benjamin again, since he hadn't made an appearance since luncheon.

"Do you think we'll be able to make the ride into the village for Christmas services at the church tomorrow morning?" asked Lord Belvoir when there was a lull in the conversation. "The snow looks deep, but it's not coming down anymore."

"Why Felix, I've never known you to be such a religious man," teased Rupert.

"Well, you know me, I'm the very model of propriety," Lord Belvoir retorted, with a wink at me, and we all chuckled. "It's a tradition that Katherine started, taking the whole family to Christmas morning services, for she loved to see the church all decorated in greenery."

"The church in our village is so lovely this time of year," Helen added with a shy smile and a quick pat on her cousin's arm. "It's been a tradition that I've grown to love as well."

"We were planning on going before all this snow started," said Sarah, "and the church isn't far. If it's too deep for the carriage, we can always walk if the weather isn't too bad."

I hadn't been to an English Christmas service in years, and it did sound like a lovely idea, but the thought of sitting in a church service with a murderer made my stomach clench. But everyone else looked enthused at the idea of morning services, so either no one else at the table had murder on his conscience, or they were just excellent at pretending.

After a few more minutes, everyone began to excuse themselves to go get ready for dinner, and I found myself alone with my friend and hostess for the first time in days. I held my stomach as I helped Sarah carry the tea cups and dirty plates to the sideboard.

"Sarah darling, I don't know if I'm going to be able to eat dinner in two hours. Your cook certainly knows her way around a macaron. I ate far too many."

Sarah frowned, looking at the dirty plate she was picking up off the table.

"Wasn't this Mrs. Emsworth's plate?"

"I believe so. Why?"

"She ate some of these chestnut biscuits. I didn't realize what she was nibbling on at the time. She said she was allergic! We should check on her. She could be terribly sick."

"She's been sitting here with us for nearly an hour since she ate them, and she was just fine," I pointed out. "And you know how attentive Mrs. Hudgins is. She would have never served something with chestnuts if Mrs. Emsworth had warned her about it. Maybe it's another nut that troubles her, and she misremembered."

"That must be it. Come to think of it, I saw her eating roasted chestnuts at dinner last night. It seems like a dangerous thing to be so cavalier about. I had a friend with a nut allergy once, and it nearly killed her."

"Perhaps Mrs. Emsworth's isn't that severe." I shrugged. We had much bigger things to worry about than Mrs. Emsworth's shifting dietary requirements. She was a grown woman and could keep track of those things for herself.

"Before I go up to dinner, I have something extraordinary to tell you."

I gave her a brief summary of my encounter with Miss Taylor, omitting that she'd used physical violence against me and that I now suspected her capable of murder.

"Isn't it shocking? I feel as though we need to warn the gentlemen of her plans so they can be on guard."

Sarah's already large and expressive eyes had turned to the size of saucers as I told her the story, and she stood with a hand over her mouth as we both leaned with one hip up against the sideboard.

"Winnie! She seems so demure and sweet. I can hardly believe her capable of such a thing."

"I know. She caught me quite unaware," I admitted. "She puts on a good act to be sure."

"But darling, I do believe she has the right of it about Lord Hadleigh. You may not have set your cap at him, but I also saw the way he was looking at you this morning. He is certainly much warmer towards you than a mere childhood acquaintance."

I felt my cheeks burning, but I held her gaze.

"Maybe at one time, long ago—" I held my hand up at the sudden look of joy on her pretty face, and continued—"perhaps he had some feelings for me many years ago, Sarah, but anything that was there is long gone and buried. He hasn't even done so much as write me a letter in nine years."

"Oh, Winnie, do you have a history with him? What have you not told me?"

I bit my lip. Part of me wanted to tell her the whole thing, but if I started now, I suspected I'd soon be a sobbing mess in her arms and neither of us would make it to dinner tonight. That wasn't exactly how I wanted to spend my Christmas Eve, and I had yet to find Benjamin or Lord Worthington and ask if they learned anything from their afternoon interviews.

"There is a story there—" I stopped again as Sarah jumped up and down and threw her arms around me as if I'd just swum the English Channel. "Darling, do get a hold of yourself. It's not a happy story, and though I do think I'm finally ready to tell someone all about it, I need more uninterrupted time with you than we have now—and perhaps a bottle of sherry."

Sarah stepped back, nodding solemnly, but her eyes still sparkled.

"We can arrange that."

"Let's get through Christmas first, and then it's you and me, the sherry, a roaring fire, and perhaps another plate of those delicious macarons."

"You have yourself a deal."

Sarah linked her arm through mine as we left the parlor and headed up the stairs to dress for dinner.

"Let me come in and help you pick out which of your delectable gowns to wear to dinner."

"Sarah," I warned, "whatever there may have been between Benjamin and I in the past, that ship has sailed. As I told Miss Taylor earlier, I like my life. I'm not looking to rekindle anything in that department."

"And I fully support you in whatever your ambitions. But just because you have no desire to marry any of the gentlemen here, doesn't mean you can't make them all fall in love with you."

"Sarah!"

"Oh, humor me, Winnie. It's Christmas Eve. Let's have fun getting dressed up like we used to when we were girls."

And so I let her, and we ended up having so much fun picking out dresses and hairstyles for each other that we would have been late for dinner had Sarah's lady's maid not intervened. She ended up bringing Sarah's things down to my room, and we laughed and giggled like we were schoolgirls again. At one point, Addie came down looking for her mother and joined us, and the three of us had to do several twirls around the room in our pretty dresses. For a moment, I just stood looking at them while they were twirling, my eyes growing misty. It wasn't that my heart ached for the family I once thought I would have, but that had never come to be. It was that a little piece of my heart felt at home, here, with one of my dearest friends and her family, and yet I had deprived myself of her company for so long just because I'd been afraid to come back to England. I'd built a life for myself in Paris, yes, but I was beginning to see that my life could be even fuller if I let go of some of the weight of the carefully-concealed hurt I'd been carrying around for so long. I'd faced my biggest fear—coming face to face with the one person who had so deeply wounded me—and I'd survived. Perhaps it was finally time to move on.

And so it was, with my head held high, and small sprigs of holly that Addie insisted we wear tucked into my coiffure, that I walked arm and arm with Sarah back down the steps to dinner.

Chapter 26

Christmas Eve had all the guests decked out in their most festive clothing and assembled early in the parlor for pre-dinner drinks. I'd hoped to have a chance to talk to Benjamin quietly before we went into the dining room, but he was in conversation with Miss Price and Miss Taylor when Sarah and I walked into the room. Sarah squeezed my arm and went over to talk to Mary and Mrs. Emsworth, who were sitting on the sofa by the fire, and I made my way over to Lord Worthington, who was standing near the drinks trolley.

"Good evening, Chester. How was your afternoon?"

Looking around to make sure the other guests were far enough away not to overhear us, he answered me in a low voice.

"A bit tedious. Most of the servants we questioned were annoyed that we took them away from their important duties on Christmas Eve. Most had never met Mr. Emsworth, and all of them had others that could vouch for their whereabouts during the hours between when he was last seen by the housemaid and the valet, and when you found him in the garden."

"So we're pretty much where we left off this morning, then."

"We did learn one interesting thing. Several servants overheard an argument between Smythe, Mr. Emsworth's valet, and Sommers, Mrs. Emsworth's lady's maid, shortly after the body was found."

"What did they say they were arguing about?"

"Apparently Smythe is quite the gossip, and was spreading

rumors about one of his old employers belowstairs. Sommers believed that Smythe's gossiping painted the Emsworths in a bad light and took exception to it. We'll have to ask Benjamin more about it. He had to remain and talk to Sommers about it when Arthur summoned me for something. We'd both been absent for most of the afternoon, so one of us needed to make an appearance before our routine death inquiry began to look a little suspicious."

Chester grimaced, and I nodded in understanding.

"If Smythe is as much of a gossip as Sommers believes him to be, perhaps that is where Mr. Emsworth got his information to blackmail people with."

"That's what we were thinking as well. We had hoped to talk to him further, but since he doesn't have a master to dress at the moment, Mrs. Emsworth gave him the evening off, and apparently he's walked down to the village pub."

"Understandable under the circumstances. I'm sure he's eager to get back to London as soon as he can so he can look for other employment."

Rupert walked over to us with two glasses in his hand and a smile on his face, and we were forced to abandon our conversation as he handed us each a glass. At the bottom of each was about an inch of reddish brown liquid garnished with an orange peel. I eyed it warily.

"Please tell me this isn't the infamous punch I was hearing so much about at breakfast this morning."

Chester winced.

"Sip slowly," he offered in a mock whisper, and Rupert laughed.

"It is, but this version has been, let's say, lightened up a bit for mixed company. I would still advise you to partake carefully since we haven't eaten yet, but as long as you don't fill your glass you should be plenty safe."

I took a cautious sniff. It smelled of oranges and spices, with a hint of vanilla. Taking a small sip, my eyes widened as the sweet, thick liquid hit my tongue.

"Goodness, Rupert, it's delicious!"

"Therein lies its danger, Winifred, my dear. Just stick to what's in your glass, and you'll be quite all right."

Chester and I stood sipping the delicious drink, a small smile threatening at the corner of his mouth. Rupert continued around the room, handing out small glasses of punch to the other guests.

"After the debacle during which I met Hadleigh, I rarely drink much anymore, so I had a small glass last night and immediately called it quits. But I confess, I've never seen Hadleigh quite so drunk."

"He was still quite soused when I found him in the library early this morning," I said with a chuckle, forgetting for a moment to censor my encounters with Benjamin. "I hadn't seen him that bad off since he was sixteen and decided to break into his father's liquor cabinet. I was only twelve, but I gave him a scolding like a fishwife. It was one of the few times our roles were reversed—usually I was the one dragging him into scrapes. But I held his hair back while he cast up his accounts and sponged off his forehead. It was enough to warn me off ever drinking to excess."

Chester grinned at my tale, and I reveled in this strange new freedom I had to remember my childhood with Benjamin without having to remove every trace of him from the story of my past. Before I could regale Chester with any more tales of delinquency, however, the dinner bell sounded, and he offered me his arm to go into the dining room. I spotted Miss Price clinging to Benjamin's arm, Miss Taylor trailing along behind them looking smug. She didn't even so much as glance my way, for which I was grateful.

Unfortunately, I was seated at the opposite end of the table from Benjamin tonight. From the glare Sarah shot towards Miss Taylor and the apologetic look she gave me, I suspected the girl had switched our place cards around. I found myself again seated between Lord Belvoir and Mr. Loughty, as I had been on that very first night of the house party before Benjamin had even arrived. I felt as though I had lived half a lifetime in those few short days. While I enjoyed conversing with Mr. Loughty and with Felix, who continued to flirt mercilessly with me throughout dinner, I found myself wishing I'd had the opportunity to discuss Mr. Smythe and his fight with Sommers the lady's maid with Benjamin. There was something there that didn't sit right with me. Who would be worried about household gossip when a man had just fallen to his death?

After much encouragement from Felix, Mr. Loughty spent most of the dessert course telling me about the extensive collection of exotic botanicals housed in his three conservatories. It was clear he was passionate about the subject, and his face was alight with enthusiasm as he described how he had continued the collection his father had started. I was only half listening however, because something was niggling at the back of my mind. It was something that had happened today that I knew in my gut was significant somehow, but I couldn't quite place what. I felt as I had when Lady Hadleigh had tried to teach me how to embroider—like I had all the pieces in front of me, I just couldn't figure out how to put them all together into the final picture. Though I loved a good conservatory as much as the next artist, I soon grew weary of Mr. Loughty's descriptions and was grateful when the meal was over and the women adjourned to the sitting room for tea.

Though it was late, the children joined us along with their nanny. We were to read Christmas stories aloud before bed, accompanied by more of Rupert's punch for the adults and hot chocolate for the children. When the gentlemen joined us, Rupert and Arthur took turns reading aloud to the whole group, with Thomas, Addie, and Fanny snuggled up in a quilt by the fire. The fire and candlelight around the room glittered off of the tin stars and baubles hanging on the tree. For a few moments, it was a delight to forget everything and revel in how very English this evening felt.

After the stories were read and the children sent up to bed, Sarah told everyone that while the roads were still not passable, the footpath to the village was, and anyone who wished to could join them for the Christmas morning church service.

As I climbed the stairs towards my room, sleepy and warmed through from the punch, I heard raised voices coming from one of the women's bedrooms. Concerned, I stopped at the end of the hall and listened. Determining that the voices were coming from Mrs. Emsworth's room, I crept closer, pressed my ear to the door and listened.

"But where did that letter go, Sommers? I had left it here on the writing desk, debating if I should send it, but I'd forgotten all about it after poor Harold's accident."

That voice belonged to Mrs. Emsworth.

"I told you, ma'am, I'm not sure. You said it had a name on it, but not an address? Perhaps one of the maids saw it and accidentally put it in the letters to be posted?"

"No, no, no!" Mrs. Emsworth's voice sounded panicked. "This desk has been locked since the morning Harold died, and I haven't opened it since."

"Your son was in here the other night, the evening before his accident. He was sitting right at that desk penning a letter while you were getting ready in the dressing room. Do you remember? Perhaps he knew the address of the intended recipient and posted it for you."

I heard a muffled thud, then, and Sommers voice again. "Ma'am! Mrs. Emsworth, are you all right?"

I was about to knock on the door and see if I could offer any assistance, when I heard her weak voice inside.

"Yes, Sommers, I'm fine. Just a bit of a shock…I need a moment…moment to think."

"Yes, ma'am, let me help you to the bed, then."

I heard muffled noises as Sommers readied her mistress for bed, but when it was clear they were finished talking, I took my leave.

I wondered what in the world that could have all been about. Mrs. Emsworth was missing a letter, but one without an address. She'd grown so upset when Sommers suggested that perhaps

Mr. Emsworth had finished it and delivered it for her, that she'd apparently had her legs buckle right out from under her.

What was this letter, and was it somehow linked to Mr. Emsworth's death?

I needed to tell Benjamin. Glancing around to make sure the hallway was empty, I slipped across the landing to the bachelor's wing and knocked softly. There was no answer, and the door handle was locked, so I made my way quietly back to my room and rang Betsy to help me ready myself for bed.

I had just drifted off when I was jolted awake, sitting upright. Something was wrong, and I looked around the room with bleary eyes. The fire still crackled merrily in the fireplace, so I'd only been asleep a few moments. What then had awaked me? I heard a few soft clicks, the sound of metal on metal. Immediately, I turned towards the door, looking around for a weapon of some sort. Was someone trying to pick the lock? Was it the murderer, coming to silence me for my part in the investigation?

Wide awake now, I grabbed the brass candlestick from my nightstand. It would have to do, as the fireplace and accompanying fireplace poker—the mainstay of self-defense according to novels, at least—were too far away. I climbed out of bed and inched towards the door, finally daring to bend down and peer through the keyhole. There was no one in front of the door. The hall appeared empty. Where then had the metallic sound come from? I turned back towards the bed, wondering if I had dreamt the whole thing, when to my horror, my window shutters were suddenly wrenched open from the outside and the window flung open.

Chapter 27

An icy wind blew into the room, and I stifled a scream as a man climbed through my bedroom window.

"Bloody hell, Benjamin! Are you trying to make a habit of nearly giving me an apoplexy?"

Shaking fresh snow from his hair, Benjamin closed the window behind him and shut the drapes for good measure. He was still fully dressed in his evening wear, but he'd swapped his shoes for outdoor boots, telling me his little excursion into my bedroom was planned.

"How did you get up here? We're on the third floor!"

"When I was examining the outside of the house the other day, I noticed you had a very convenient rose trellis not too far from your window. It's as easy to climb as a ladder."

"Somehow that doesn't make me feel any better."

I shivered, and looked down at my flimsy lace nightgown. Benjamin followed my gaze and went very still, the movement of his Adam's apple as he swallowed hard the only sign he hadn't frozen in place like a statue.

Rolling my eyes, I grabbed my dressing gown from its place on the coat tree near the door.

"Don't worry," I said airily, trying to look nonchalant as I slipped my arms into the warm wool and cinched the belt up tightly. "It's nothing you haven't seen before."

And that was exactly the problem.

I waited, staring, for Benjamin to tell me why he was here, but he just stood there, still frozen, a look of utter torture etched on his face.

I sighed.

"Come sit by the fire and tell me what madness you're up to now. You must be half frozen, running around outside like that without an overcoat."

I led the way to the settee by the fireplace and sat down. Benjamin followed me, still mute, and stood staring into the fire. I grabbed a warm quilt from the settee and threw it at him.

"Sit. Talk. Tell me why you're climbing up to my tower like Rapunzel's prince."

Gingerly, he sat on the lambswool rug in front of the fireplace, wrapping the quilt around his shoulders. He did not make a move to join me on the settee, and I didn't offer.

"Why didn't you use the door like a normal person? Are you afraid I wouldn't let you in?"

Benjamin rubbed his hand over his face and quietly came back to life, blood seeping back into a face that had gone the color of parchment. Either he'd been out in the cold longer than it seemed, or he was that affected by the sight of my sleepwear. It was something to mull over later.

"Miss Taylor is apparently lying in wait at the top of the stairs in a state of undress, waiting for me to pass by on my way to bed so she can faint into my arms or some other nonsense. Worthington noticed her lurking behind the potted lemon tree in the hall on his way up to bed and sent a note down via his valet to warn me."

I sighed again. "Unfortunately, I don't doubt that it's true in the least after what she did to me this morning. But how did Chester know she was lying in wait for you?"

He grinned ruefully.

"I was the only gentleman left downstairs. Everyone else has retired for the night. Worthington and I had been discussing the details of the case in the library, and I planned to retire shortly after him. Lord knows what the chit would have gotten me into if Worthington wasn't an exceptionally observant fellow. I owe him."

"You could have been well on your way to being leg-shackled to Miss Taylor for the rest of your life."

Benjamin looked carefully at me, his expression unreadable.

"No, I couldn't have. But it would have been a damned unpleasant situation."

Something in his gaze made me uncomfortable, but I couldn't fathom what was going on just under the surface of those stormy blue eyes.

"So why here? Why not climb up to your own room? Or better yet, why not send a note to Miss Price to come take charge of her harridan of a ward? Perhaps a lecture from that old dragon is exactly what she needs."

Now it was Benjamin who sighed. "I needed to talk to you about something. I tried to find a chance all evening, but we kept getting interrupted."

Leaning forward, I felt my heartbeat quicken.

"Did you find the letters?"

"Not yet, but I did learn something very interesting from Sommers, Mrs. Emsworth's lady's maid. Apparently Smythe, Mr. Emsworth's valet, used to work for the Loughty family."

I sat up, surprised.

"The Mr. Loughty that's here? Was he a valet?"

"No, apparently Smythe was a footman at the Loughty estate. But it's an interesting coincidence, is it not?"

"Interesting, but not all that unusual," I mused. "A valet is a much more prestigious position than a footman, and it's not unheard of for an ambitious young man or woman in service to move up into the position of valet or lady's maid."

"But don't you think he would have mentioned it when I talked to him?"

"It may not have seemed relevant."

"Worthington told you about the other staff overhearing

Smythe and Sommers arguing about Smythe's gossiping the morning after Emsworth's murder. What if Smythe heard a choice piece of gossip while working as a footman for the Loughtys, that he then told to Mr. Emsworth? Emsworth could have used that information to blackmail the Loughtys. This house party seems to be the first time the Emsworths and the Loughtys met in person—maybe one of the Loughtys had just been waiting for the opportunity to do him in."

"It's an interesting theory. You definitely need to talk to the valet again, and I want to come with you."

Benjamin nodded slowly.

"It wouldn't hurt to have you present."

I was just beginning to feel a warm sense of pride in my investigative skills when Benjamin added, "Smythe strikes me as a ladies' man, he might be willing to share more details with you in the room."

"*Bof.*"

Benjamin raised an eyebrow.

"That's French for I think you're ridiculous."

He grinned at me then, a warm, rich smile that reminded me of our childhood and sent a pang to my heart.

"Well, Smythe likes to think himself a bit of a Lothario, if the stories of the other staff are to be believed, so it can't hurt to bat your eyelashes at him a few times and see if he can remember anything of importance for us."

"There's also something I wanted to tell you, something that might be related." I straightened in my seat. "I overheard Mrs. Emsworth talking to Sommers on my way to my bedroom. Mrs. Emsworth was so distraught that she was nearly shouting. She was looking for a lost letter, one that hadn't yet been addressed. When Sommers suggested that perhaps Mr. Emsworth had addressed and posted it when he was in her room the evening before his death, she took it very hard and seemed to have a breakdown of some sort."

Benjamin looked thoughtful.

"Perhaps Mrs. Emsworth knew about her son's inclination to blackmail," he suggested, "and the letter had some sort of incriminating evidence in it. Perhaps she was afraid that he'd read it."

"If that were the case, he could hardly make use of that information from beyond the grave. And the post hasn't been able to go out for days, so even if he did read the information, he wouldn't have been able to share it with anyone."

"Unless they were already here in the house."

Benjamin rubbed a hand over his face, looking weary.

"I don't know, Freddie. I'm ready to be done with this whole business. In fact, that's one of the things I've been wanting to talk to you about."

He fell silent, looking into the fire, and for a long moment I wondered if he was going to speak.

"I need to tell you about why I left."

My blood ran cold.

"It's pretty obvious now, isn't it?" I tried to keep my voice light, but it wavered slightly despite my best efforts. "Augustus needed you to work for the Home Office, and he knew being married to me would spoil those plans, so he dragged you home and forced you to annul our marriage. You could have at least written, though, after you got back to England, and explained what you felt you had to do. Not that I would have agreed with you, but at least I would have known why you had our marriage annulled."

Benjamin's face hardened, and in that moment he looked every bit the blackguard I'd believed him to be these last nine years.

"Freddie, they threatened to murder you."

"I'm sorry, what?!" Looking around the room, I realized I had nearly shouted. I waited, but no sounds came from out in the hall. Just the crackle of logs burning in the fireplace in front of us. I lowered my voice back to an appropriate whisper. "The Home Office threatened to murder me? You'd have me believe Her Majesty's government would…would have me killed, just to keep you from being distracted doing, well, whatever it is spies do?"

Benjamin closed his eyes, looking old and suddenly tired.

"Not officially, no. But Augustus' superior was a nasty piece of work. The man had no morals whatsoever. I underestimated the value our family's position and contacts offered to the government. They'd just lost two of their best men of high rank, one on a mission and one through apparently natural causes, though they couldn't be completely sure. They couldn't afford for me to bow out, too, and wouldn't risk me having a civilian for a wife. Augustus' superior…Jameson was his name—is his name—though thankfully he's moved on from the Home Office, and we don't work for the same department anymore. One night shortly after I arrived home from Italy with Mother and Augustus, he cornered me on the street in front of our London townhome and threatened me. He told me about another operative who decided to get married without the Home Office's consent. That man wasn't even an aristocrat, just country gentry, but his wife died in a mysterious carriage accident a few months after the wedding. Freddie, I knew the man Jameson was talking about. He was a friend of Augustus', and I even went with him to the wife's funeral."

I shivered in a way that had nothing to do with the cold as Benjamin continued.

"That night I saw the complete lack of human emotion in Jameson's eyes, and I knew I—*we*—were just pawns in his chess game. He would do whatever he had to do to achieve his objective. If he was responsible for that poor woman's death just because she'd dared to marry an operative… Freddie, I couldn't risk it. The next day, they brought me annulment papers, and I signed them. I promised that I wouldn't try to contact you again. Losing you gutted me. Knowing what you must think of me for abandoning you nearly ruined me. But at least I knew you were safe."

Benjamin was staring at the fire, his jaw set in a hard line.

"At the time I thought that perhaps, in a few years, after my contract was up, I could help them see that I wasn't nearly as useful to them as Augustus, leave the service, come live with you in Paris, and marry you again, properly this time. That was my plan, Freddie."

I willed my heart to keep beating. I had so many questions, but one jumped to the forefront.

"But nine years is more than a few, Benji. You never intended to run into me here. We would have kept on living our separate lives if we hadn't both shown up at this house party. What happened?"

Benjamin groaned and got to his feet, crossing to stand by the quickly dying fire.

"This damned work happened. It changes you. Makes you distrust everything and everyone. After my contract was up, I considered stepping away from the job. I still wanted to. But by then, Augustus had died, and it turned out I was even more valuable to them as the Earl than my brother had been. I wasn't nearly as ruthless as he was, but I could be charming, persuasive even. I felt I was being useful to my country, and I still feared the danger my work could put you in if I came back into your life. I needed some wise council, but my mother was long gone, and I didn't even have Augustus to talk to anymore. There was no one I could share our secret—and my dilemma—with. So before I signed on for another five years, I came to see your grandfather in Paris."

"You what?!" I spluttered, nearly falling off the settee, and wrapped my dressing gown tighter around my body as I steadied myself. "But you—I never saw you!"

"I found where you and your grandfather were living, and I met with him while you were at the *académie*. I told him everything. The nature of my work, the threats on your life. I told him that I wanted to leave the Home Office, but I wasn't sure if you wanted anything to do with me anymore. This was four years ago."

My breath caught in my throat.

"I didn't want anything to do with you at that point. I hated you. You hurt me more than anyone else ever could. Turning you into a villain was the only way that I knew how to cope."

"Yes, your grandfather told me as much, and told me to tread carefully, but he was hopeful you might eventually come around. I came to the *académie* to see you, and I stood across the street watching you in the courtyard." He turned away from the fireplace, and held up a hand. "It's creepy, I know. But let me finish. You were laughing, talking with a group of young artists, and then a man showed up. You were so excited to see him that you ran to him and embraced him. I thought—I thought he was your paramour. Perhaps he was?"

My mouth quirked in a rueful smile.

"No. That must have been Antoine. One of my dearest friends, but he would be more likely to fall in love with you than with me."

Benjamin chuckled softly.

"I was mistaken, then, but perhaps it was for the best. Losing my mother, working for the Home Office, distrusting everything and everyone—I was in a dark place, Freddie. Augustus died, and for a while I wondered if someone had murdered him too, though the doctor said he just drank himself to death. I was going insane, seeing dark and sinister shadows in every corner. I saw you in Paris and you were just so…happy. Full of life and light. You seemed just fine without me, and I knew then and there that I could not ask you to shackle yourself to the Hadleigh name once again. For a long time, I thought we were cursed. I was determined that I would not bring you down with me."

Chapter 28

Benjamin fell silent, his confession complete. We sat there, both of us staring into the fire for some time. Eventually, I trusted my voice enough to speak.

"Maybe if you had trusted me and told me the truth sooner, I could have decided for myself what kind of future I wanted, if the risk of your job was worth it. Then at least I wouldn't have spent the last nine years thinking it was somehow my fault, that I was somehow terribly unlovable, that you wanted a more docile or biddable or conventional wife—"

I broke off, surprised at the tears that were now flowing freely down my face.

"Oh, God no, Freddie—no."

In an instant, Benjamin was on the settee next to me, pulling me into his arms and stroking the top of my head, like he used to do when I was a child and fell and scraped my knee. This small act of comfort nearly made me come undone, and I cried harder. I cried for my eighteen-year-old self, newly abandoned and wondering how she would cope. I cried for the decision Benjamin had been forced to make. I even cried for Mr. Emsworth. But most of all, I cried for all of the last nine years that could have been. I hadn't had anyone to comfort me like this since Grandfather died, and somehow it made the tears flow even more freely. I don't know how long we stayed like that, Benjamin holding me and stroking my hair, me crying tears all over his jacket, but eventually the tears slowed and I was left bleary and puffy-eyed, and utterly spent.

"I am so, so sorry, Freddie. I am so sorry for everything."

And those were the words I never thought I would hear, and for a moment I was afraid I would start sobbing all over again, but instead, I let out a small giggle that was halfway to a sob.

"I certainly never thought I would hear you apologize."

"I should have done so long, long ago. I was only trying to protect you, Freddie, doing my best in a strange new world that I never really wanted to be a part of. I was so young and foolhardy, I see that now."

"So… What do we do now?"

"I don't know. I really don't. We find Mr. Emsworth's murderer. Make sure he or she doesn't have the opportunity to hurt anyone ever again. I have a few months left on my current contract for the Home Office, and I don't plan to continue this line of work after that. I have no idea what's next, but I know I don't want to stay away from you forever, and soon, I won't have to for your safety."

"Benji, I like my life. I like the work that I'm doing in Paris. I don't know if I could just up and leave it, even if it were suddenly safe for me to come home."

Home. That was a term I hadn't thought of in regards to England in a long, long time. In a way, it would always be home, but I wasn't sure I even belonged here anymore. *Home* was irreparably tied to this reprobate with his arms still around me. I elbowed him in the side.

"You're a cad, Benjamin Hadleigh. You know that, right?"

"Undoubtedly. A knave of the worst possible kind."

I could hear the smile forming at the corner of his lips.

"I don't know where exactly we go from here, but I don't think I want to avoid you for the rest of my life, either," I admitted in a small voice, then let out a small burst of laughter that was mostly air.

"If you told me that I'd say that just three days ago, I would have laughed all the way to the train station to get as far away from you as possible. I was thinking of fleeing, you know, as soon as you walked into the sitting room that night."

"I had a similar reaction. I was about to make my excuses, run back to London, and send a colleague to investigate Emsworth in my place."

"Why didn't you?"

"Besides the snow? Honestly, even if the roads would have been passable, I don't think I could have left. Just being in the same room with you after all this time was torture, but I was also so grateful to see you looking happy and whole and fulfilled. It was like I was getting a little glimpse of the woman you'd become, and I just couldn't turn away. I still planned to find the blackmail evidence and head back to London as quickly as I could, but I thought it would probably be the last time I ever laid eyes on you, and I couldn't bring myself to end it so quickly."

"We never did get to say goodbye before." My voice was barely above a whisper now, my throat tight. "When you left, we thought it would only be a couple of months before I returned home to England."

"I was always grateful for your grandfather's academic contacts in Paris that made it possible for you both to build a life there. I don't know what I would have done if you had come home to the house right next door to me, and I was still not supposed to have any sort of contact with you."

"Likely you would have had to become the blackguard I believed you to be, renounced all connection to a lowly miss with a modest dowry, and moved on with your life."

"You knew those things didn't matter a fig to me. You would have seen right through me. I could have never played the dashing spy if you had been nearby to see me. You've always known me better than anyone else."

We sat quietly for a moment, then gazed into the embers glowing in the fireplace grate. When I finally looked up into his face to respond, Benjamin put a finger to my lips.

"Enough words." He searched my face, and he must have found what he sought there, for he continued in a quiet voice. "There's more I need to tell you, but my poor, bruised heart can't take any more tonight." He quirked a smile in the semi-darkness, and I stifled a laugh. "I'd rather not climb back out of your window. Let us hope Miss Taylor has grown tired of her ambush by now and retreated to bed."

I looked at the clock above the mantelpiece, amazed that it was already half past two in the morning.

"I'll check the hallway before you go out, just in case. If I run into anyone, I'll just tell them I couldn't sleep and was venturing to the kitchen for a snack."

I stood and began to make my way to the door, but Benjamin grabbed my hand and pulled me back towards him. He stood as I looked at him with questioning eyes, and pulled me back into his arms. My heart thudded wildly in my chest, and I both feared and eagerly awaited whatever he was about to do. After several agonizing seconds, he bent his head slowly and carefully towards mine, giving me plenty of space to pull away if I wanted to. I did not. At long last, his lips met mine, and he kissed me as slowly and gently as if I were made of glass.

For a moment I thought I would shatter, but I did not. I pulled in closer, and held my back straight as I kissed him back as fervently as I would have all those years ago. After several minutes, he pulled away, resting his forehead against mine and closing his eyes.

"I missed you, Freddie." His voice was the merest whisper, and if I hadn't been so close I wouldn't have heard him. "I've missed you so, so much."

My throat was clogged with emotion, and I couldn't speak. I simply nodded against his forehead, hoping he understood my meaning.

"I need to go now. Let's check the hallway?

Part of me longed to beg him to stay, to not leave, not now after everything I'd just discovered. But my thoughts were too jumbled, and my nerve endings were on fire. I needed some space to think.

"Come on, I'll go first." I grabbed his hand, and we made our way quietly over to the doorway. When we reached it, he leaned back and gave me one more soft, chaste kiss that almost broke my resolve. Then he opened the door and pushed me through, and I found myself blinking in the dark hallway. I stood there for a moment to let my eyes adjust, then double-checked the hallway, the landing, and the gentlemen's hallway, my bare feet padding softly on the thick carpeting. There was no sign of Miss Taylor or anyone else, so I slipped back inside my room.

"I trust you've kept your room locked, so she's not lying in wait for you there?" I whispered into his ear before he opened the door again.

"What kind of amateur do you think I am?"

And with that he kissed me one more time, turned, and disappeared into the darkness.

Chapter 29

Betsy came in to stoke the fire and help me into my warmest wool dress and matching jacket long before the first light of dawn. I'd told Sarah to have me woken up with the churchgoers that morning, and even though I couldn't have slept more than two or three hours since Benjamin had left, somehow I vibrated with energy as Betsy buttoned the long row of buttons up my back and twisted my hair into a simple chignon. There would be time for fancy Christmas attire later today, but walking the half mile into the village for the sunrise church service wasn't the place to sacrifice warmth or comfort.

I was the first down to the breakfast room, and I helped myself to more of the fruit-studded poundcake laid out on the sideboard, adding extra sugar to my cup of tea. I was ravenous. Within a few minutes, Sarah joined me, yawning into her fawn leather gloves.

"I can't even manage a bite this early." She waved a hand at the footman who came in with a platter loaded with biscuits and scones. "Put it over there with the cake, please, Frank."

I eyed the spread of sweets even as I was polishing off my slice of cake.

"For someone who can't stand the sight of food before ten o'clock, you've certainly supplied plenty of it."

"We can't have people growing faint on their walk to the church, can we? Of course, we'll have a proper Christmas breakfast served when we arrive home. Ham and eggs and sausage rolls, and everything else."

I laughed.

"Maybe I should rethink a second slice of cake. I won't be hungry enough for all of that in a couple of hours."

"Have one of the scones instead," Sarah offered. "Oh, drat! I forgot to tell Cook not to send the chestnut biscuits back up today. We must remind Mrs. Elmsworth not to eat any, just in case she does have an allergy. I can't have any more accidents befalling another one of my guests."

I looked over to the chestnut biscuits that Sarah was pointing to, and my hand froze with my teacup halfway to my mouth. I stared, pieces of what had been nagging at the back of my mind suddenly falling into place. *Almonds. Then Chestnuts. Mrs. Hudgins office. The missing letters.* I set my teacup back down with a clatter, my appetite suddenly ruined as my stomach roiled. I knew where the missing blackmail letters were, or at least where they *had* been. And I knew who the true blackmailer likely was.

"Winnie, darling, are you quite alright?"

I managed a weak smile.

"Yes, dear, I just have to take care of something really quick before we leave for church. I won't be long."

I took the stairs down to the servants quarters two at a time, stopping in front of Mrs. Hudgins' office. I knocked softly, but heard no answer. Gratefully, the door was unlocked as Mrs. Hudgins had said it usually was. There was no sign of the housekeeper or any other staff, so I slipped inside and looked around. I glanced at the desk and the sturdy wooden shelves lining the office walls. If someone was going to hide a letter somewhere where it wouldn't be stumbled over during the busy preparations for Christmas, where would it be? I decided that Mrs. Hudgen's desk was too obvious a hiding place, and that she would have likely stumbled across anything put on or in her desk during the last few days. A quick peek in and behind all of the baskets hanging on the wall told me there was nothing to find there.

I turned to the large wooden shelves, not wanting to waste a minute. Working quickly, I ran my hands between large stacks of folded linens, sorted through baskets of extra candles, and moved jars of preserves around on the shelves to peer behind them. When I spotted a collection of large ceramic containers filled with dried herbs and teas, I opened each lid and stirred them around with a wooden spoon I found nearby. The aroma of thyme and dill wafted up at me. To the housekeeping staff's credit, there was no dust on any of the containers, so it was hard to tell if anything had been lately disturbed. I was just about to give up and move my search to the desk after all, when I found I couldn't quite stir the container of dried rosemary—something was blocking my spoon.

Sticking my hand down through the herbs in the jar, I was rewarded with a small stack of paper tied with a blue ribbon. They were obviously letters. With shaking hands, I untied them and glanced at the first one, then breathed a sigh of relief. They were exactly what I'd hoped to find—and hoped not to, since it meant that we'd been wrong this entire time.

And that someone I truly liked was guilty of blackmail.

I shut the door quickly behind me, not bothering to even glance in the direction of the kitchen, a fact I would soon bitterly regret. Not even registering how quiet the house was without the usual hustle and bustle of the servants, I ran up the hall and back up the stairs towards the guest rooms. Coming to an abrupt stop in front of Mrs. Emsworth's room, I paused to catch my breath, wishing I'd instructed Betsy to lace my corset looser than usual this morning. I really should be looking for Benjamin, but I had to be sure of something first. I felt I owed Mrs. Emsworth that much at least. Taking a deep breath, I raised my hand and knocked softly.

"Who is it?" Mrs. Emsworth's voice called out softly.

Thankfully, she was awake. I hadn't been sure if she was among those planning on going to the Christmas morning services or not. If I had to delay speaking with her, I thought that I might lose my nerve.

"It's Miss Osbourne. Do you have a moment?"

Mrs. Emsworth answered the door herself, fully dressed for the day, and ushered me in.

"What can I do for you, Miss Osbourne?" She offered me a seat by the fire, smiling warmly. "I understand that Sarah has some refreshments downstairs, but I had planned to wait until breakfast later."

"Mrs. Emsworth, I'm afraid I'm going to have to be very direct, and I ask you to forgive me. There isn't time for anything else."

She frowned, confused.

"Why of course, dear, whatever is the matter?"

"You aren't allergic to any nuts, are you Mrs. Emsworth?" I tried to ask as gently as I could. "You gave me that excuse that day outside of Mrs. Hudgins office, because you didn't want me to know what you were really doing in there—what you were hiding."

I pulled the letters out of my pocket and held them out for her to see. All at once, the color drained from Mrs. Emsworth's face, and she sat down heavily beside me.

"Ma'am!"

Sommers, who had been tidying the dressing table, rushed towards her, but Mrs. Emsworth waved her off.

"I will be fine, Sommers. Please leave us."

Sommers looked doubtful, but nodded her assent.

"I'll just take the dirty tea things back down to the kitchen, then."

She grabbed a tray holding an empty tea pot and dirtied cup and saucer, and closed the door quietly behind her.

Mrs. Emsworth sighed, her face looking weary as she sank back into her chair.

"You know, then. You're a clever one. I confess, after my discovery last night, I am grateful to discuss it with someone."

"It's possible you might be in danger, ma'am." I wanted to warn her as gently as I could, but it was likely she'd already realized the state of things.

"I confess, I no longer care." An errant tear slipped down her cheek, and I felt my heart clench. No matter what she had done, no mother deserved to see her son murdered, much less in her place.

"I overheard you talking about a misplaced letter last night. I take it it was another blackmail attempt?"

She nodded miserably.

"I'd all but decided not to send it. The information was too much, too volatile. I left it, unaddressed, on my desk, but Harold— dear boy."

I paused as she broke into sobs, and I reached out to hold her hand as she continued the best she could.

"Harold must have seen it and thought it was the most natural thing in the world to deliver it. He had no idea, you see."

"May I ask why? Why you've been resorting to blackmail?"

"Why does anyone? It was the money, of course. Harold had no head for business, and I took care of everything. Running the estate, managing our finances. The estate had been losing money terribly since my dear husband died. I tried my best, but poor Harold—he just didn't care. He just wanted to read his books and be left alone in peace. And I had grown accustomed to a certain lifestyle—trips abroad, the finest gowns. A full social life in town."

She grimaced, and I actually felt sorry for her. While I didn't agree with her methods, I'd seen many well-born women who'd had to resort to desperate measures to maintain a certain standard of living.

"The first time, the information fell to me quite by accident," Mrs. Emsworth confessed. "A middle-aged woman, no matter how well-connected, just tends to blend into the background of society events. People say things around you and don't think anything of it. No one would expect the society matron that was on the fringes of that ball they went to to be the source of the blackmail letter they've just received." She smiled bitterly. "The first woman I blackmailed was truly horrible. I'd planned to divulge how terribly she was treating her daughter, just to protect the girl, whether or not she paid me. But to my astonishment, she did pay me. Quite a lot of money too, and I was able to encourage one of the girl's suitors to go ahead and offer for her to get her out from under her controlling mother, so that the whole situation ended well for everyone. But suddenly, I had found a way to support myself and our estate, and Harold was none the wiser. I just told him our tenant farmers had a better yield than expected that quarter, and he never thought to question it. Poor, sweet, trusting Harold." She sighed, tears filling her eyes again. "He was never quite right, you know. Didn't understand people or social situations like most boys. Always shied away from any sort of touch or affection. But he was my son, and I still loved him fiercely."

"Understandably." I sat very still, still clutching the letters in my lap, not wanting to interrupt Mrs. Emsworth at such a crucial moment. "He seemed like a very kind man to me."

"He was, in his own way. But I've been supplementing our income this way for years. Mostly my information was just about little things: whose supposedly devoted husband had a mistress on the side, who claimed aristocratic heritage but really came from trade. Minor things, for which I requested minor amounts. I only had a couple of people who couldn't or wouldn't pay, and for those, I turned the information over to a relative of Sommers who works at one of the scandal sheets. I had a very tidy system going."

"And you hid these letters from the Queen's relative in Mrs. Hudgins office, that day I ran into you, and you made the excuse about having an almond allergy you wanted to inform her of?"

If Mrs. Emsworth was surprised that I knew about the blackmail of a member of the royal family, she didn't show it, or even ask me how I knew. I suspected she was just ready to unburden herself.

Chapter 30

Mrs. Emsworth nodded and said, "I suppose it was you who found the photographs I hid in the library—you and Lord Hadleigh, if I'm not mistaken? I was quite distracted at dinner the other night. I'd gone to retrieve them the other day, after Harold died. I wanted to keep them with me in case I needed to leave quickly. But they were gone. I confess, I'm rather glad it was you all who found them. I was afraid it could have been someone with far fewer morals."

Mrs. Emsworth was observant.

"Yes, we found them. We destroyed them."

"It's for the best. I will do the same with these letters. I don't want anything to do with blackmail ever again. Not after last night. I learned about that young man—" she gestured to the letters in my lap, "because I heard him and his lover arguing beneath the terrace at a Duke's ball once. The lover threw the packet of letters and photographs at the young man, saying he wanted nothing more to do with him, but the poor fellow was so distraught that he forgot them outside, and I retrieved them. I waited a few weeks—just long enough that he must have thought he was safe, that a servant must have picked them up and disposed of them. Just long enough that no one remembered who'd been around at that ball.

"I'm not proud of that decision, if I'm honest," she continued. "The poor young man was so distraught, and I'd never blackmailed someone who hadn't truly deserved it before that. But I'd just

187

gotten another dismal report from my banker, and with the young man being related to the Queen, well, I thought it was fate giving me a way out of my precarious financial situation. The amount of money that I could have gotten for that information—if invested wisely, I would have never had to resort to blackmail again. But, the money never came, even though I sent two more demands. I was about to give it up. I brought the letters here with me to keep them from falling into anyone else's hands, but I'd just about decided to destroy them if I hadn't heard any response to my letters by the time I returned back home. But seeing as how you're here, and you know—I'm guessing Her Majesty wasn't quite ready to give it up, then?"

I shook my head sadly.

"No, ma'am. I'm afraid not."

"It's no matter—not any more. I deserve every possible consequence for my actions."

The woman's eyes filled with tears again, but I had to press on. Mrs. Emsworth's life could be at stake.

"I need you to tell me about the lost letter. The one that may have cost Mr. Emsworth his life."

She nodded, though it took a few more minutes for her to dry her tears and continue.

"My son's valet used to work in the Loughty household. He is a terrible gossip, and it wasn't the first time I'd used information he told me to blackmail someone. But when we arrived here and he saw who the other guests were, Smythe told me about something Mr. Loughty had done. It was so incredibly shocking, I thought there had to be some mistake, some great exaggeration to the story. But as is often the case, with every rumor, there's often a shred of truth at its core. I wrote the blackmail letter while the information was fresh in my mind, but I didn't intend to send it until I got home. Indeed, I wasn't sure I was going to send it at all. I left the letter on my desk, intending to pack it away with my things later, and I honestly forgot all about it when Harold died. When I remembered it last night, I went looking for it, but I couldn't find it anywhere. That's when Sommers told me my son had been sitting at this table before his death, and that perhaps he had seen it and delivered it."

She sniffed, tears welling in her eyes again.

"That's just the sort of thing poor Harold would do. He would surmise that letters are meant to be delivered, and not even think about why someone would leave an unaddressed envelope on their desk."

"You think it's possible that Mr. Emsworth delivered this blackmail letter for you, not knowing its contents, and that someone thought he was the blackmailer?"

I found it sadly ironic that the poor man would be suspected of blackmail twice. And one of those times may have gotten him killed.

Mrs. Emsworth nodded sadly.

"That's why I wasn't going to send it, at least not yet. I was worried that if the information were true—well, it was so much worse than anything else I've ever blackmailed someone about."

"Mrs. Emsworth," I asked carefully, "what did Smythe think Mr. Loughty had done?"

She lowered her voice almost to a whisper, though we were the only ones in the room.

"He killed Lady Belvoir's unborn child. And possibly Lady Belvoir herself."

I sat there for a moment, shocked. I was aware that my jaw was hanging open, but I was unable to close it for several seconds.

"But Lord Belvoir said that she had been sick for a long time before she died."

"Yes, well, according to Smythe, she was with child, and Mr. Loughty put something in her tea for a few days in a row that caused her to lose the baby. But she died only a few weeks later."

My heart pounded as I thought of how affectionate Felix was towards his cousin, how much he seemed to appreciate him. There was no way he could know that his cousin had killed his unborn child—and possibly caused the death of his beloved wife.

"But…but why? Why would he do such a thing?"

Mrs. Emsworth wiped away another tear that was trailing down her cheek.

"I have no idea. And you can see why I doubted the truth of such a claim. But even though Smythe is a gossip, he is an honest man. He would never make something like that up. But he said that was why he left the Loughtys' home and came to work for us. He didn't feel safe there any more."

I sat quietly for a moment, digesting everything that Mrs. Emsworth had told me. It was going to be time to leave for church soon, but I couldn't leave Mrs. Emsworth.

"Does Mr. Loughty have any reason to suspect you might have been the one to send that blackmail note? If so, you might be in danger."

Mrs. Emsworth wrung her hands fretfully.

"He might. I was going to go down to Mrs. Hudgins office last night, to remove the blackmail letters that I'd hidden there and burn them, but I ran into Mr. and Miss Loughty on the way. They looked like they'd been arguing, and they were polite enough, but I'm afraid I let out a small squeak when I ran into them unexpectedly in the hall. It may have been nothing, but I felt as if that young man looked at me as though he knew. Even if he didn't know I was the true source of the blackmail, he may have become suspicious that Harold or Smythe told me about what he'd done because of the way I reacted. I gave up on the letters and returned to my room instead, intending to destroy them today as soon as I had the opportunity."

"I think we need to fetch Lord Hadleigh now, Mrs. Emsworth. If you can tell him everything you told me, he can keep you safe from Mr. Loughty, if indeed there is even a need to. It's still possible the story you heard from Smythe was exaggerated or a rumor, and it's also still possible your son's death was an accident."

Given my observations about Mr. Emsworth's body, I didn't believe that second part was true. But we didn't know for sure yet that it was Mr. Loughty who had killed him, even if he had indeed poisoned his cousin's wife.

"A wise course of action, my dear. I will wait here. I'll lock the door after you leave, and I'll be perfectly safe."

I nodded, still hesitant to leave the older woman alone, but I also didn't want to wait here with Mrs. Emsworth until Sommers returned. We needed to act quickly, before anyone left the house for the Christmas service. If we could walk to the church, someone could easily walk on to the train station and be out of town before we even realized they were missing.

"Just one thing first."

I took the letters in my hand and tossed them into the crackling fire, turning away only when I saw them beginning to blacken and curl.

"Good riddance," Mrs. Emsworth whispered softly.

"I'll be back in just a couple of minutes," I promised as I walked to the door. The rest of the house had to have risen by now, so hopefully I would catch Benjamin dressed and ready. I pulled open the door, and froze in my tracks. For a moment, I forgot to breathe.

Mr. Loughty stood in front of me in the hallway, pointing a pistol straight at my chest.

Chapter 31

I stood frozen in the doorway, unable to comprehend what was happening. I heard Mrs. Emsworth gasp loudly behind me, and I slowly backed into the room, my hands raised at my sides in what I hoped was a non-threatening gesture. Mr. Loughty was fully dressed, his dark hair perfectly styled despite the still-early hour. He looked completely calm and in control as he waved me further back into the room with the gun. It was that icy self-control that caused me to finally regain my voice.

"Mr. Loughty, please tell me what is the meaning of this? Put that gun away at once!"

I tried to inject every inch of Miss Price's outraged superciliousness into my voice, but Mr. Loughty didn't seem a bit concerned.

"I'm terribly sorry, Miss Osbourne, but I'm afraid it can't be helped."

He smiled apologetically, looking as though we were discussing something as harmless as the weather and making the gun seem terribly out of place in his hand. My eyes darted to the still-open door behind him into the hall. Surely if I screamed, someone would hear me, and send help? I didn't have a chance to test my theory, however, as Mr. Loughty kicked the door shut with his foot and pointed the pistol straight at my face.

"I'm afraid I can't have you screaming, Miss Osbourne. Things have already gotten much too complicated as it is. And don't think your gallant Lord Hadleigh will come to your rescue, either. I've already been forced to get him out of the way."

At the horrified look on my face, he waved the gun dismissively.

"Oh don't worry, he's still alive—for now. You two have created far too many messes for me to clean up, so I'm going to have to orchestrate everything very carefully. I have plans for the two of you later."

"Now, see here, young man—" Mrs. Emsworth began, but Mr. Loughty interrupted her, pointing the gun in her direction.

"It would be a shame to have to shoot you now. Not that you have long to live, mind you, but a gunshot wound is a lot harder to explain away than a distraught mother overdosing on laudanum."

Now it was my turn to gasp.

"Mr. Loughty, you're mad! I won't let you near her."

With my hands still raised at my sides, I backed up slowly a few steps so I was standing slightly in front of Mrs. Emsworth and reached out slowly and grasped the older woman's hand.

"While it's kind of you to champion a despicable blackmailer, there's no need, Miss Osbourne," Mr. Loughty continued calmly. "The deed is already done. I took the liberty of dropping a little something into Mrs. Emsworth's morning tea pot, you see. Our lovely hostess has indeed thought of everything, including the little personalized name plaques on each guest's morning pot, so they can have everything exactly how they enjoy it. It was a small matter to pass through the kitchen early this morning while the maids were out stoking the fires."

I felt Mrs. Emsworth's hand trembling in mine, and my stomach clenched in dread at the thought of the empty tea things Sommers had already taken away. Mr. Loughty had already poisoned Mrs. Emsworth, and there was nothing we could do about it now. To her credit, Mrs. Emsworth simply tugged me behind her, positioning her body to protect me the best she could.

"What happens to me matters not, Mr. Loughty. You have no need to harm Miss Osbourne. She has done nothing to you."

"On that point, we agree madam, but I'm afraid I can hardly let her walk away if I have any hope of making it out of here with no one the wiser. I made a mistake, you see."

I cleared my throat, finding my voice again through the haze of panic that had started to grip me.

"And was that mistake killing Lady Belvoir, or killing Mr. Emsworth?"

Mr. Loughty shook his head as if I was a delinquent child.

"Neither, I'm afraid." I wasn't sure if he meant that he hadn't killed either of them, which was a little much to hope for since he was still pointing a gun at me, or if neither of them was a mistake. I opted to keep my mouth shut in the hope that he would keep talking and buy us some more time, and he did.

"The only oversight on my part was that I thought it was your pathetic son who was blackmailing me." He looked at Mrs. Emsworth, and I thought I saw his mask of calm slip slightly. "I never imagined a *woman* could be so clever! Simpering fools, the lot of you. I saw a letter being slipped under my door late one night, so I opened the door and saw Emsworth retreating back down the hall towards his room. Imagine my surprise when I saw what the note contained! I have no idea how you two got this information, but I should have gotten rid of both of you just to be safe—although it would have been so much harder to make two deaths look like an accident."

He doesn't know about the footman-turned-valet then. At least Mr. Smythe was safe for now. I decided it was best to keep Mr. Loughty talking.

"So you poisoned Mr. Emsworth, thinking the blackmail note was from him?"

"It was far too easy. The little maid left a tray right outside his door every evening. A little foxglove in the convenient form of digitalis was easy to dissolve in the teapot."

"You just happened to be carrying a deadly poison?"

"I just happened to be carrying an important heart medication.

I don't take it, but if ever questioned I could claim I did. I carry it with me everywhere."

I shuddered at the thought of a man who felt he had the need to always carry poison with him.

"And then what? You slipped into Mr. Emsworth's room and pushed him out the window?"

"People look less closely at a tragic fall than a man found dead in his bed with no history of previous illness. It was a simple thing to slip into his room in the middle of the night after I knew the poison had had enough time to work, and push him out the window."

Mrs. Emsworth stifled a sob, and I squeezed her hand.

"As pleasant as this little chat was, we've got to get moving, Miss Osbourne," Mr. Loughty demanded. "Lord Hadleigh is waiting for us. The churchgoers should be off by now—don't worry, Miss Osbourne, I told Mrs. Cunningham that you'd decided to stay and keep Mrs. Emsworth company because she wasn't feeling up to an outing this morning, so they won't be waiting for you. Mrs. Emsworth, I wish I could say it has been a pleasure, but you and your son have caused me no end of headaches with that ridiculous blackmail letter." He sighed long-sufferingly, and waved the gun to indicate I should follow him. It appeared I had little choice, and I was afraid he was going to shoot one of us accidentally just by waving the weapon around so much. Turning to Mrs. Emsworth, I gave the older woman a hug, surprised when tears began running down my face. She may have made a mistake by resorting to blackmail, but she didn't deserve to have her son murdered or to be poisoned by this madman.

"Don't worry about me, dear," she whispered in my ear before I could pull away. "I'm not going to go without a fight."

I nodded, looking into her eyes, though my vision was blurred by the tears streaming down my face. If her tea had indeed been poisoned, she likely didn't have long if we couldn't get a doctor here quickly.

"Come along, now, Miss Osbourne. You can scream and cry all you want after we leave, Mrs. Emsworth, but I imagine you're already beginning to feel rather sleepy and heavy. You can't tell everyone about my crimes without confessing to your own role in all this, including your hand—however unintentional—in your son's death. I think, rather, that you'll accept your fate, and sink into a dignified and dreamless sleep from which you'll never wake up. The others will assume that you couldn't handle the grief of your son's death and overdosed on the laudanum that your doctor so helpfully provided for you the other day. The symptoms will be the same, so it's not an unlikely conclusion."

To Mrs. Emsworth's credit, she held her head high, though her eyes were filled with tears. Reluctantly, I moved towards Mr. Loughty, who was motioning for me to walk in front of him.

"We'll take the servant's stairway, just in case, but everyone who isn't already gone to church should still be fast asleep at this hour. I'll remind you not to scream, because I'd hate to have to shoot you right now, but I will if I have to."

I nodded my understanding, took one last look at Mrs. Emsworth as she slumped, exhausted and deathly pale, back into her chair, and I opened the door. Unfortunately, Mr. Loughty was right, and the halls were deserted. Everyone left in the house was still sleeping, and I didn't want to put Mr. Loughty to the test and scream. Hopefully, he'd take me to wherever Benjamin was, and we could figure out a way to overpower him together.

I decided to keep him talking as we walked down the servant's stairs.

"Where is Lord Hadleigh? Where are you taking me?"

"He's out of the way where no one could hear him for a while. I'm afraid he stumbled onto me as I was lacing Mrs. Emsworth's tea, and I had to act."

I swallowed hard. Had Mr. Loughty shot him? Likely not, or we would have heard a gunshot in the house.

"Is he—is he okay?"

"Just fine—for now."

I held my tongue as we walked through the now-deserted kitchen. There were signs of a struggle: trays and baskets overturned, a chair at the large kitchen work table on its side, and a pewter teapot—with what appeared to be smears of blood on it—on the floor by the back door. *Where are Mrs. Hudgins and all of the staff? Why isn't Cook preparing the Christmas breakfast even now?* Surely someone had to be around to see what Mr. Loughty was doing. Again I contemplated screaming, but until I was sure someone was within shouting distance, I couldn't risk it.

"Where are all the servants?" I asked Mr. Loughty quietly as we went through the back door and down the frozen gravel in the back garden, our footsteps crunching softly through the early morning frost. The first light of dawn was on the horizon now, and I could see my breath coming out in great billows in front of me. Blinking at the cold air suddenly enveloping me, I wrapped my arms around myself. My dress was warm, and I was still wearing the thick, velvet-lined jacket over top of it. I was grateful for these warm layers at least, but Mr. Loughty had hardly given me the chance to retrieve my overcoat before we went outside, and the morning was a cold one. I was not going to be able to endure the frigid air for long.

"Our thoughtful hosts gave them the early morning hours off to attend church services. I confess, I wasn't planning on having to do all of this this morning, but the lack of servants wandering about makes everything so much easier."

He still spoke calmly and cordially, and I marveled at a man who could seem so normal, despite having killed at least one person. I was itching to ask him about Lady Belvoir, about whether or not he really poisoned her, but I didn't want to provoke him just yet. If the scene in the kitchen was any indication, then he had indeed encountered Benjamin and had likely injured him in the process, since I couldn't see blood on Mr. Loughty anywhere. I knew there was a possibility that Mr. Loughty was lying, that he was leading me away somewhere to my doom, and Benjamin was just fine, tucked in a pew at the church and none the wiser. But then, whose blood was on the teapot? And if he was going to shoot me either way, I'd play along for now. If there was a chance that he had Benjamin somewhere, I figured we had a much better chance of escaping this madman together than we did alone. I just prayed he was still alive.

After what felt like an eternity but was only a few minutes, Mr. Loughty indicated that we should stop in front of the gardener's shed. He took the long, wooden bar off the door with one hand, still holding the gun on me with the other. The gray light of dawn was just beginning to filter through the trees around us, but inside the shed was pitch black.

"Okay, Miss Osbourne, in you go."

I hesitated. Mr. Emsworth's body was still in that shed somewhere. I wasn't squeamish, but all that work documenting corpses for Poisons had taken its toll. I shivered involuntarily for reasons that had nothing to do with the cold.

"Go on then. I really can't have you making my plans difficult."

Willing my feet to move forward, I took a small step towards the darkness. Then I heard a deep groan, one that belonged to someone very much alive. Stepping quickly into the shed, I didn't even look back as the heavy wooden door slammed shut behind me.

Chapter 32

"Benji?" I called out into the darkness, standing still for a moment to let my eyes adjust. I heard another groan to my left, and I slowly began to shuffle in that direction, my hands stretched out in front of me to avoid running into anything. "Benji, where are you?"

I heard a muffled curse from the direction of the floor, so I crouched down on my hands and knees and began to crawl towards it, bunching my skirt up in one hand the best I could. The shed wasn't a large one, so I reached Benjamin within a few feet. Blinking rapidly, I tried to assess his injuries the best I could in the dark.

His feet were bound and his hands tied behind him, so I quickly untied those ropes, feeling my way as my eyes began to slowly adjust to the dark shed. The side of Benjamin's face was sticky with blood, and I could just make out a nasty gash on his right temple. There was dried blood all over his head and neck, but his pulse was strong, and the bleeding appeared to have slowed for now. Pulling my handkerchief out of my pocket, I pressed it to the wound, and he stirred and groaned again.

"Confound it, Freddie!" Benjamin rasped, his voice hoarse, and relief flooded over me. "Why did you let him throw you in here with me?"

"Oh, I don't know," I said dryly, stopping to catch my breath a moment now that I knew he was somewhat coherent. "It could have had something to do with the pistol he was pointing at me.

And anyway, how did he overpower you? You're supposed to be the spy here."

He groaned.

"It was a stupid mistake. I couldn't sleep, so I was walking the perimeter of the house again, just to check things out. I wanted to see the spot where you found the vial. When I came in, I stumbled onto Loughty in the kitchen, standing over the teapots. He caught me so off guard—I'd just walked in the kitchen door, said good morning and asked him if he was as in need of a cup of tea as I was, and before I knew it, he'd bashed me in the side of the head with one of those heavy teapots. I fought back for a minute after that, but my damned head was bleeding so much that I must have passed out."

Tears welled up in my eyes again at the thought of what Mr. Loughty had put in one of those teapots.

"Benji, he poisoned Mrs. Emsworth." Benjamin uttered another curse. "She was the real blackmailer, not Mr. Emsworth and—well, it's a long story. I'll tell you everything in a moment, but Mr. Loughty began to suspect she was involved, so he dosed her morning tea with laudanum—or maybe it was something that acts like laudanum, I'm not entirely sure on that account. And I don't know how she's going to get help to find a doctor. I think everyone's already left for the church, and the servants were all given time off to go to the service, too."

I dabbed gently at the wound on Benjamin's head, just to give myself something to focus on other than the fact that Mrs. Emsworth was likely dying in her room right now if she hadn't found someone to help her.

"Honestly, as I was lying here coming in and out of consciousness, I couldn't figure it out. Other than the fact that Loughty must have been the one that poisoned Emsworth and was trying to poison someone else—that part was pretty apparent."

Benjamin took the handkerchief from me and felt his head gingerly, wincing.

"Here, let me help you sit up. Put your arms around my neck."

Pulling gently, I tugged him into an upright position, helping him lean against a wooden shelf filled with flower pots. Realizing that I could now see better in the dark, I stood up quickly and examined our prison, being careful not to look too closely at the man-sized shape draped in a sheet lying atop the worktable against the opposite wall. Mercifully, thanks to the cold, I couldn't detect any odor of decomposition, and for that I was grateful.

"There isn't much we could use as a weapon," Benjamin said through gritted teeth from his spot on the floor. "I tried to search when I first regained consciousness maybe an hour ago, but I got so dizzy I passed out again."

"You've got a head injury. You may have missed something."

I took a quick inventory, but maddingly, Benjamin was right. The small building was quite old and made out of solid stone—the walls were impenetrable. A shelf and a few small work tables around the room contained hand tools, a collection of clay pots, and burlap sacks filled with soil and seeds, but that was about it. If we could catch Mr. Loughty by surprise, maybe we could bash him in the head with one of the clay pots, but they weren't large or heavy enough to do much damage. I shivered again, this time from the cold that had begun to seep into my bones, and gave up on my search.

"C'mere Freddie. We've got to stay warm."

Sitting down next to him on the cold dirt floor, I scooted as close as I could, and Benjamin tucked an arm around me. He was still wearing his evening clothes from the night before, but thankfully he had on his woolen overcoat. Wincing again at the movement, he shrugged his arms out of the coat and pulled it around both of our shoulders.

"Now what?" I whispered, though our only company was a dead man. Tears clogged the back of my throat, and I was finding it hard to speak. My pulse was racing, and I was sure Benjamin could feel it through his shirt and waistcoat. The room was beginning to spin, and I found my breath coming in short, shallow gasps.

"Hey—hey Freddie."

Benjamin turned towards me under the shelter of his greatcoat, and cupped my tear-soaked face with his bloodied hands.

"Do you remember that time when we accidentally got locked in the vegetable cellar?" he asked gently.

I hiccuped a sob.

"Of course I remember. I was terrified of that place. It was dark, and there were spiders, and it smelled like turnips."

"Well, what did we do?"

Ever so gently, Benjamin wiped the tears off my cheeks with his thumb.

"You told me stories to get my mind off of things," I answered feebly, "and fed me pieces of apple you carved with your pocket knife."

"So now it's your turn to tell me a story. You're going to tell me all about one of your favorite things—why I was wrong. Tell me about Mrs. Emsworth and the blackmail, and why I was wrong about her son."

His request slowed my tears, and slowly and shakingly, I began to tell him everything I knew. First, seeing Mrs. Emsworth outside Mrs. Hudgins' office that day, and the excuse she'd given me about an almond allergy, which then changed to a chestnut allergy later when I'd seen her eating almonds. Everything I'd overheard between her and Sommers last night, and what she told me about writing the blackmail letter to Mr. Loughty but then losing track of it. How she'd first started writing blackmail letters to help pay her expenses, where she got her information, how her son knew nothing about the blackmail, and how distraught she was when she learned that he may have delivered the letter—and gotten killed for it.

Eventually, my breathing slowed too, and I felt less panicked.

"I'm sorry," I whispered. "I think it's being in here with . . . with Mr. Emsworth. My work on illustrating *A Physician's Illustrated Guide to Poisons* really helped launch my career, but I had to look at more dead bodies than most policemen do in a lifetime, many of which were in a terrible state. I—" I broke off, unable to finish, but Benjamin understood.

"You've been a rock, Freddie. An absolute gem. You don't have anything to apologize for. I'm the one who should be apologizing for dragging you into this mess, for allowing you anywhere near my investigation."

I shook my head vigorously.

"I would have continued looking into it even without your permission, you know."

Benjamin sighed. "I know. It's what I love and loathe about you."

My heart thudded in my chest, this time for something entirely different than panic. It wasn't a declaration of love, exactly, but my emotions were so raw after the revelations of last night and the turmoil of this morning that my foolish, battered heart leapt at any sign of hope. Now was hardly the time or place to determine if we had any possible future together—first, we needed to ensure we had a future to begin with. Looking around us, I noticed that light was slowly filtering in through the shed's dirty windows.

"It must be about dawn. The church service should have started by now. I'd say we have maybe an hour before everyone gets home. Surely then someone will come looking for us?"

"Perhaps once they even notice that we're missing, which could take time. Loughty could be long gone by then."

"I don't think he's planning to just leave us here. He said that he had plans for us." Shuddering again, I leaned my head on Benji's shoulder.

"For what it's worth, Benji, I'm glad you're not the villain I thought you to be. I want—well, I don't know what I want, not yet. But I don't want to be enemies anymore."

"I was never your enemy, Freddie. I just had to let you think I was, and it was the hardest thing I've ever done."

Leaning over, he kissed me gently on the forehead.

"C'mon, help me up. Let's check the windows."

We examined the narrow, paned glass openings in the shed.

"I can break the glass," he determined, "but they're too small for me to fit through. Perhaps you can make it?"

I looked up at the window, then down at my hips.

"Maybe when I was twelve, but certainly not anymore. Why don't we break one out anyway—maybe we can yell for help when the servants get back, or use a shard of glass as a weapon."

Benjamin took an empty burlap sack from the shelf, wrapped it around his hand, then punched through one pane—two, three, then four, carefully pulling a few of the larger shards out and setting them on the shelf with the flower pots. While he hammered the wooden window divider out with a clay pot, I ripped a piece of burlap off of another empty stack and gingerly wrapped one of the largest glass shards in it and stowed it in my pocket. Joining Benjamin at the window, I looked out into the snowy woods surrounding us. All was quiet.

"It's possible that someone who didn't attend church is awake by now, and might be able to hear us if we shout," Benjamin offered. But I was doubtful.

"It's also possible Mr. Loughty will hear us and come and shoot us," I added with a grimace.

Benjamin looked suddenly livid.

"He's likely to do that regardless of whether we scream, so I think it's worth a shot."

I felt like I was going to throw up, but I nodded. I hated this helpless feeling of waiting, and we didn't have any better options at the moment.

"On three, ready? One…two…three."

We screamed ourselves hoarse for several minutes, until Benjamin held up a hand for me to stop.

"Now, we wait," he croaked grimly. "But you're not going to like this next part."

"What?"

He looked towards the body I'd been so carefully avoiding.

"We're going to have to move Emsworth."

"What?! Hell, no."

"You need a place to stay hidden, just for a moment, and that's the only spot."

"No, Benji, I refuse."

"When Loughty comes back, he might be angry enough to shoot at anything that moves, and that's the only place where he can't see you."

"A sheet is hardly going to protect me from a bullet. Besides, I have a better idea."

A few horrific minutes later, everything was in place. I crouched in the darkest part of the shed, near the figure slumped over in the corner by the shelves, where Benjamin had been when I first entered the shed. I shivered from the cold, but thankfully I didn't have to wait long. Within a few minutes, I heard the scraping of wood against the shed door, and light flooded the small space. I put a hand over my eyes at the sudden brightness, and called out to Mr. Loughty.

"Please, Mr. Loughty, you have to help Lord Hadleigh, I can't wake him."

I motioned to the figure next to me.

"You have to help him," I repeated, injecting a note of desperation into my voice that wasn't entirely feigned. "I know you said you have plans for us, but I hardly think those plans include him bleeding out from a head wound in the gardeners shed."

As I'd hoped, Mr. Loughty took a step forward towards me, into the shed.

In a blink, Benjamin jumped off of the worktable, the sheet that had been draped over him now flying over Mr. Loughty's head. For a moment, I couldn't see anything except the white of the sheet flailing around, and the cries and grunts of the two men struggling on the floor. A gunshot went off, and I screamed and ducked. Even though Mr. Loughty was armed, there were two of us. Surely we could overpower him. Pushing up off the ground, I felt for the shard of glass still wrapped in burlap in my skirt pocket. In such close quarters, I'd be just as likely to injure myself or Benjamin as I would our captor. The two struggling men straightened then, the sheet left in a pile on the floor, and I was just making a move to jump on Mr. Loughty's back when I heard the unmistakable sound of a shotgun being cocked behind me in the still-open doorway.

My heart lept, and I was turning to thank our rescuer when I saw Benjamin still and raise his arms above his head. As my mouth dropped open, he gave a little shake of his head. Turning slowly, I saw Miss Loughty, a shotgun held comfortably in her arms.

"Enough."

She spoke firmly, with only the slightest tremble to her voice. She was a few steps away from me, blocking the door to the shed. I saw then why Benjamin had given up so easily. The shotgun was pointed directly at my heart.

Chapter 33

"**H**elen, what is going on?" I gave her a cautious little smile, being careful to keep my hands at my sides non-threateningly.

"I'm afraid I have to ask you to come with me, Miss Osbourne. My brother has gotten us all in quite a fix, and I'm not sure what else to do. I cannot allow you all to continue on in such a manner."

She sounded like a proper schoolmistress, and I breathed a sigh of relief.

"Thank you, Helen, I'm sure if we just go back to the house, we can talk this over with the Cunninghams and figure out a way—"

"I'm afraid I can't allow you and Lord Hadleigh back to the house—not now. The others will be returning soon, and I cannot allow my cousin to learn of my brother's indiscretions. It would ruin…ruin everything, you see."

"Indiscresions? You mean murder?" I felt my blood boiling, and I took deep breaths in an attempt to control my temper. I'd thought Miss Loughty was my friend, and more sensible than this.

"Helen, you would be willing to cover up two murders, possibly three, because of a *tendre* you hold for Lord Belvoir?"

I risked a glance back at Benjamin, who was still standing as still as possible, his arms above his head, though he was starting to slowly sway on his feet. The tussle with Mr. Loughty had certainly not been good for his head injury.

Miss Loughty laughed, a choked, strangled sort of sound.

"A *tendre*? My cousin and I share a bond that a spinster like yourself couldn't possibly understand. My brother's actions are regrettable to be sure, but I don't see why I should have to suffer for them."

"They also had the added bonus of getting Lady Belvoir conveniently out of your way," I said, my teeth gritted. I knew I was goading a woman who held a gun on me, but I couldn't help it. I was furious now. "Not to mention the fact that he killed an entirely innocent man in an attempt to cover up his own crimes."

"You will stop berating my sister, this instant." Mr. Loughty's voice was smooth and cold as ice. "Out of the shed, both of you."

"And if I refuse?" Benjamin still held his hands aloft, but I heard the note of steel in his voice, and I knew he was angry too.

"Then I am afraid we will go ahead and shoot Miss Osbourne and figure out how to clean up the mess later."

And without any further warning, Mr. Loughty drove his fist into Benjamin's face with a sickening crunch, and he collapsed to the floor as blood began gushing out of his nose.

I let out a scream of rage, but I could not move towards him with Miss Loughty's shotgun still trained at my heart.

"Very well, Helen," I emphasized her Christian name, hoping my voice was laced with all the anger now coursing through my body. "Lead the way. Though you made a mistake in knocking out Lord Hadleigh, Mr. Loughty. Now you'll have to carry him, and believe me, he's no lightweight."

After maybe ten minutes of walking away from the house, through the woods, we reached a small clearing. A fallen log and a circle of large stones, all covered in snow, told me we weren't the first to set up camp here. Mr. Loughty proved himself deceptively strong once again, half-carrying a mostly-unconscious Benjamin behind him. Tossing him unceremoniously against the trunk of a tree, he then tied Benjamin's wrist with some rope he produced out of one pocket. Then he once more trained his pistol on me as he tossed another rope to his sister.

"Sit, Miss Osbourne." He pointed to a tree near Benjamin's,

just far enough away that we couldn't reach each other to offer any sort of assistance. I obeyed, and Helen pulled my arms behind the tree and then tied them with her piece of rope.

"Now, Helen, darling, it's time for you to go back to the house," her brother ordered. "I will take care of everything here, and you don't need to see this."

His sister inhaled a shaky breath and picked up her shotgun.

"Just take care of everything this time, Theodore. This cannot continue."

"Helen, please—" I began. I knew I had a better chance of getting her to let us go than her brother. She may be terrified of losing her cousin, but I didn't think she was as utterly mad as her brother, just at his mercy.

Tears filled her eyes as she shook her head.

"I am so sorry, Miss Osbourne. I did truly want to be friends. But my brother leaves me no other choice."

"There's always a choice!" I called out to her as she turned and began to walk back to the house. "You can still help us!"

She ignored me, but I saw her shoulders slump in defeat. She was not going to save us from her brother. She was too afraid of him.

Mr. Loughty smiled at us as she walked away, and I felt my blood run cold. This man was as crazy as they came. When he was sure his sister was out of earshot, he brushed the snow off the fallen log, sat down, and crossed his long legs, as if we had all come out into the snowy woods on Christmas morning for a nice chat.

"I had planned to bury your bodies in the woods and write a note saying you'd run off together, but I'm afraid your little performance back there in the shed put a bit of a rush on things. I'm very good at handwriting, you see. I've been forging my cousin's hand for years to get anything done around the estate—without me the place would have gone under years ago, but that's neither here nor there. It would have been a simple matter to retrieve a piece of your correspondence and forge a letter informing our dear hostess that you've decided to run away together—back to Paris, or wherever it is you're from. Anyone with eyes has seen you two sneaking around together all week like schoolchildren." He rolled his eyes and sniffed in disdain, reminding me suddenly of Miss Price. "But no, now I'm thinking that getting to be around to see their faces at the sad tale of your murder and suicide—well that sounds so much more satisfying."

Benjamin groaned loudly, and I saw that he was beginning to regain consciousness. Thankfully the blood coming out of his nose had slowed to a mere trickle, and with what looked like great effort, he wiped his face on the shoulder of his coat.

"Ah, Hadleigh, glad you could wake up enough to join us. I believe that if we work together, we can set it up so that you get so angry at your pretty little side piece here that you're going to shoot her dead, then take your own life out of guilt. Yes, yes, that sounds believable. After all, you are a gentleman. A lonely spinster and a charming Earl—it won't be a stretch to conclude it was a lovers' quarrel."

"You're a sick bastard," I ground out between clenched teeth as I began loosening the knots around my wrists behind the tree, trying not to make any sudden movements that would give my purpose away.

"Or should you be the killer, Miss Osbourne? Heaven knows you have a bit of a bite to you. Perhaps it would be easier to believe you went hysterical. The sight of Mr. Emsworth's body, then being at his mother's bedside when you learned that she had overdosed on laudanum—it was too much. When your precious Earl jilted you, you snapped, killing him and then yourself. Well, then, I think I like that version even better."

"Let her go!" Benjamin's voice was muffled from his broken nose, but he sounded desperate now, and I found myself blinking away sudden tears. "It's me you want. I'm the one with the power to throw you in jail for your crimes—to make you disappear altogether. Winifred is no threat to you."

"No threat to me? No, no, you misunderstand, my Lord. She is the greater threat to my future. I've seen the way my cousin looks at her—much the way you do. She's far too young, far too pretty, and far too fertile. At least Katherine was already an invalid. It was all too easy to hurry her along."

I gasped, momentarily distracted from my own plight by his callous disregard for the life of Lady Belvoir. He didn't seem remorseful in the least.

Mr. Loughty waved a hand dismissively.

"I didn't intend for her to die—just the child. But her death was a fortuitous bonus."

"But … but why would you do such a thing?"

"Why? Because I'm the heir! Me! The heir to the Marquisate. I couldn't let that be put at risk. I grew up knowing it would one day be mine, that I was being groomed for it. My cousin was a hellion from the time he was fifteen and I was still in short pants. For a long time, it didn't matter how many women he bedded. He claimed he would never marry, and with no legitimate heirs, the title would eventually be mine. He always drank too much, lived too fast. Even he always said he was destined to go to an early grave and leave me the Marquisate. It is what I was born for, what I was trained for since I was barely out of leading strings."

I scanned the woods around us, desperate to delay him a little bit more as I tugged at the rope around my wrists. Miss Loughty had obviously not had as much tutoring on rope tying as I had with Benji, and the knot was a simple and flimsy one. I needed only a few more moments to free myself and to think of what I should do once I was free. Our friends were surely on their way back from the church service by now, and perhaps someone would be lucky enough to stumble onto us. Or even better, perhaps Mrs. Emsworth had found a doctor and was still alive to tell them what had happened—or perhaps Miss Loughty would have a change of heart and lead our friends this way after all. I decided it was in our best interest to keep Mr. Loughty talking as long as I could, and clung to hope.

"So when your cousin fell in love and married Lady Belvoir, it must have been quite the shock to you." I saw Benjamin also struggling silently against his ropes, and tried to keep Mr. Loughty's attention. "You suddenly had an unexpected obstacle between you and the inheritance."

Mr. Loughty sighed, leaning forward as if he was enjoying telling the tale of his great misfortune.

"My only consolation was that he married a sickly little wretch with no chance of bearing him a natural heir. The doctors all said there was no way she could ever conceive a child, but he didn't mind. He had me for an heir, after all, and he didn't need one. For two years, everything was safe, and life proceeded nearly as normal."

Suddenly the mild smile was wiped off his face, and he sat up straighter, eyes blazing, his mask of calm slipping once again.

"But then one day, she came rattling over to tell my sister the happy news: despite everyone's predictions, she was with child. She hadn't even yet confided in my cousin. She knew he would be worried sick the whole time, and wanted to spare him the agony until the secret could no longer be kept. But she wanted to tell someone, so she came to us—and she expected us to rejoice with her! The wretch.

"She likely wouldn't have survived the pregnancy, but if the child somehow did, it could have ruined everything. I had to do something. It was an easy thing to slip some special herbs into her tea a few days in a row. That should have just ended the pregnancy, but apparently she was too weak, and it carried her off as well. I dare say she wouldn't have lived much longer anyway. But my cousin—my cousin hasn't been the same since her death, and he never even knew about the baby."

Oh, God. Lord Belvoir's wife and unborn child had been murdered by his heir and closest friend, and he didn't even know.

"Thankfully he was so in love with her that he's been too devastated to ever marry again, and all has been well lately. But the way he looks at you—no, no, I can't take the risk that he will decide to move on and remarry."

The rope finally fell free from my wrists, though I was careful to keep my arms wrapped out of view behind the tree.

"I can promise you," I said, "I have no desire to marry Lord Belvoir. But even if your cousin never marries again, are you planning to wait another forty years to inherit? Your cousin is still young and in excellent health. Or were you planning on poisoning him too?"

He waved a hand, as if the question of possibly murdering his cousin as well wasn't important enough to merit an answer.

"I'm just doing what my father should have done years ago. He was the one that traveled extensively and introduced me to all of the exotic and dangerous plants. If only he'd had the guts to use one of them to get rid of my uncle before he'd married! Then I wouldn't be in this mess! But no, he was a small-minded man, content with his adjoining estate and his gardens. He didn't care one jot about the Marquisate! But he never had to grow up in the shadow of my wastrel cousin, left to do all of the work but receive none of the glory. My father never cared for the man he could have been but for an accident of birth."

As if feeling as though he had shared enough, Mr. Loughty stood, dusting off his coat, and checked his pistol. I didn't dare draw attention to him by looking directly, but I could see out of the corner of my eye that Benjamin was still and focused, staring straight ahead. He was likely almost out of his ropes as well. If I could just keep Mr. Loughty occupied for a few more minutes, maybe we would have a chance.

"You know they'll never let you get away with four deaths at one Christmas house party," I pointed out unhelpfully. "Scotland Yard will tear this place apart looking for evidence."

"It's unfortunate, yes, but don't think I haven't thought this through. There's absolutely no evidence to point to me. My cousins and I will stay for as long as the inquests take. It will be a hardship, but you saw the incompetence of that magistrate first hand. There's nothing that will point to the heir to a Marquisate being responsible for a careless man's accident, a mother's grief, and a sordid affair gone wrong."

And with that, Mr. Loughty swung towards Benjamin with his pistol and cocked the hammer. A few short days ago, being married to Benji again would have been the worst thing I could have possibly imagined. Now, watching him die in front of me was.

"Noooo!"

I screamed as loud as I could and launched myself up off the ground, flinging myself at Mr. Loughty with all my strength. The jagged piece of glass was clutched in my already bloodied hand. I knew I was about to get shot, knew this was probably the last thing I would ever do, but I found that I cared very little.

Mr. Loughty turned suddenly, the report of the gun echoing through the woods. I felt a hot, searing pain graze the top of my left shoulder, but I kept moving, bringing my right arm up and then down again with all the force I could muster. A flash of confusion, then surprise crossed Mr. Loughty's face as I stabbed my makeshift weapon into his right arm as hard as I could. He screamed, dropping the pistol, then dove for it at the same time as I did. For one horrible minute, we rolled together on the ground, both struggling to reach the weapon. But even with the glass in his arm, he was much larger and stronger than I was, and soon had it in his grasp. I struggled to take it from him, clutching the barrel of the gun with both hands, but, inevitably, he wrenched it away.

The last thing I heard was the sound of Benjamin yelling my name as the world exploded in a haze of gunfire and smoke.

Chapter 34

When I awoke, my head was in Benjamin's lap, his arms supporting my shoulders. I blinked in confusion, my vision partially obscured by something hot and sticky running down my face. Bile rose in my throat, and my head throbbed. Turning quickly, I emptied the meager contents of my stomach into the snow beneath us. When I finished, I felt slightly better, and settled myself gingerly back into Benjamin's lap. My voice came out in a hoarse croak.

"Benji, what happened? Where is Mr. Loughty?"

Benjamin produced a handkerchief from somewhere in his pockets and attempted to staunch the flow of blood from my forehead. I didn't think I had been shot a second time, so Mr. Loughty must have clubbed me with his pistol. Glancing at the graze on my shoulder, I was relieved to see that it wasn't bleeding much. Thankfully, I'd taken him by surprise when I charged him, and the bullet had nearly missed me. When Benjamin had finished mopping up my head a bit, he pulled me up gently into a sitting position, one arm around my back to support me in case I passed out again.

From this slightly higher vantage point, I noticed all the activity in the woods around us. Rupert was there, looking grimmer than I'd ever seen him, a rifle at his side. Arthur was with him, tying a rope tightly around Mr. Loughty's feet while a burly man I recognized as one of the Cunninghams' estate staff sat on the madman's back, tying up his arms. Lord Worthington bent over the prone form of our assailant, pressing a handkerchief to a wound in the back of one shoulder, while Lord Belvoir stood next to them. The Marquess's face was ashen, and my heart ached for the shock I imagined he must be going through.

"Well it's about bloody time," I murmured through clenched teeth as another wave of nausea hit. "But when did they get here? How long was I—"

"Only a minute or two. You scared the hell out of me, Freddie. I'd nearly finished untying my rope, but I couldn't get the last knot free. I could see Worthington and the Cunninghams making their way cautiously through the woods, tree by tree, but I didn't want to draw any attention to them, so I kept my head down and worked on my rope. I appreciated your effort to keep Loughty distracted as long as possible, but then you charged him, you little maniac! What on earth were you thinking!?"

"He was going to shoot you! I couldn't just sit there and watch you die."

"So you thought getting shot yourself was a better option? That's a crazy thing to do for your sworn enemy, Fred."

I couldn't help it. I burst out laughing, stopping abruptly when my head began pounding and the world started spinning again. Breathing heavily, I leaned back against Benjamin's chest and closed my eyes.

"You know you're not my enemy, Benji," I murmured when I could speak again. "I don't think you truly ever were."

"I know."

"Benji?"

"Yes, my love?"

"Can we go inside now? This ground is freezing."

"Absolutely. I would carry you, but I might need some assistance myself."

"Some spy you are. Letting a concussion and a broken nose slow you down."

"I know. I'm truly the worst."

Rupert pulled me gently to my feet as Lord Worthington helped Benjamin up and steadied him. Arthur and the gardener were turning Mr. Loughty over to the local magistrate, who had arrived amidst the chaos. Before we headed back to the house, I limped gingerly over to Lord Belvoir and grasped his hand. I felt Benjamin hovering at my back, whether protectively or because he was worried I would black out again, I wasn't sure. I didn't know how much of his cousin's crimes Lord Belvoir was truly aware of, apart from mine and Benjamin's attempted murders, but that was enough to tear his whole world apart. My heart went out to him.

"I'm so sorry, Felix," I told him truthfully. Even though we had suffered for Mr. Loughty's crimes and his sister's complicity, it was nothing compared to what the Marquess was going to suffer in losing his closest friend, confidant, and heir all in one blow.

"It is I who should be apologising to you, Winifred." Tears clogged his voice, and he looked away to wipe his eyes. "When I think of what Teddy has put you through this morning, I cannot bear it—"

"When you get back to the house, I will tell you all we learned," Benjamin offered, stepping forward slightly. "I cannot say it will be easy, but you deserve to know the truth."

Lord Belvoir nodded, and turned back to the magistrate, who was hauling Mr. Loughty to his feet like a sack of potatoes. His wounded shoulder was bandaged up, as was the arm that I'd sliced open with the piece of glass. He was conscious and staring down at the forest floor, all the fight having seemingly gone out of him. I resisted the urge to go over and give him a good kick in the groin.

"Who shot Mr. Loughty?" I whispered as Rupert hooked an arm underneath my shoulders and Lord Worthington did the same for Benjamin, and we began our slow and agonizing walk back to the house, strung between our friends' shoulders like a half-drunk and bloodied load of laundry. Wiping ineffectually at the dried blood on my hands for a moment, I gave up and focused on putting one foot in front of the other without falling over. I was sure my head looked even worse than the rest of me, but at least the bleeding had mostly stopped. Sarah was going to have a heart attack when she saw me.

"We all carried rifles, but it was Worthington that fired the shot," Rupert informed me grimly. "He's an expert marksman, and the way you were fighting Loughty for the gun, Winifred, I didn't trust anyone else not to hit you."

I looked gratefully up at Lord Worthington.

"Thank you, Chester. Two more seconds, and I think my time might have been up. I owe you one of my best paintings, if you ever find yourself in Paris."

His cheeks pinked, and he nodded in acknowledgement.

"I would like that very much, Winifred."

"Why on earth did you charge him like that?" Arthur asked, slowing his stride to keep up with our sad little party. His eyes were once again twinkling, and I knew his question came without judgement.

"Well, since our rescuers were taking their sweet time in reaching us, and I couldn't just sit there and watch Mr. Loughty shoot Lord Hadleigh, once I'd freed my hands from the ropes, I had to try something. The piece of broken glass was the only weapon I had, and I couldn't exactly throw it at him. I had to take him by surprise, and given how little Mr. Loughty thinks of women, I knew he wouldn't be expecting an attack from my direction."

Rupert whistled.

"You're a hell of a woman, Winifred Osbourne," he added with a grin. "If you don't mind my saying, Hadleigh, you're lucky she was around."

Benjamin smiled at me then, a true smile that, despite his bloody face and swollen nose, warmed me to my core.

"I was just thinking the same thing."

All was chaos once we reached the house. Servants were running this way and that, the Christmas day festivities clearly thrown into turmoil. From the sounds of loud conversation in the parlor, all the women were gathered there, anxiously waiting for news on what was happening. Sarah, who'd been pacing the entrance hall, immediately burst into tears at the sight of me and ushered me towards the stairs.

"The doctor is waiting for you upstairs. I sent him up as soon as Rupert sent word that you were safe but injured. Oh, Winnie, I'm so sorry, if only I'd known that you hadn't truly decided to stay home to comfort Mrs. Emsworth as Mr. Loughty had told us!" Tears flowed down my friend's pretty face, but I was distracted from any attempt to comfort her or ask for more of the story by the sight of Mrs. Emsworth coming down the stairs alive and apparently well.

"Mrs. Emsworth!" I gasped as the older woman rushed down the stairs towards me, grasping my hands in hers despite the mess. "You're alive!"

"Quite so my dear. And I must say, I'm exceedingly glad to be able to say the same of you and Lord Hadleigh." She looked to Benjamin and Lord Worthington, who were just behind us on the stairs. "Once I figured out that I was not about to drop dead, I ran to the church to alert everyone. I'm afraid I caused quite a commotion during the service, bursting through the doors and telling everyone you'd been kidnapped by Mr. Loughty. But thankfully, they all believed me, and we rushed back here!"

"But how did you survive the poisoning?" I asked her, still incredulous that she stood in front of me, quite whole and healthy.

"It was only due to the attentiveness of Sommers, but I was, in fact, never poisoned." She motioned to the lady's maid, who I now noticed standing a few steps behind Mrs. Emsworth as if reluctant to leave her side. "She'd been wary ever since my son died, having heard Smythe's gossip about the Loughty family before, and had taken it upon herself to wash the pot of tea out every morning and make it again for me herself with tea that she brought with her and kept locked in her trunk, just to be safe. Why, Sommers even prepared my breakfasts with her own two hands and made sure that I wasn't eating anything else the other guests weren't eating at other meals. I have her to thank for my life." Mrs. Emsworth's eyes filled with tears, and she turned towards Benjamin. "Whatever that may be from now on. I am fully prepared to pay for my crimes, Lord Hadleigh, however you see fit."

Benjamin grasped her offered hand in his, kindness in his eyes, and I found myself letting out a breath that I wasn't aware I'd been holding.

"Since the evidence against the Queen's relative has been destroyed, and the suspected blackmailer is deceased, that is the only instance of blackmail with which I am concerned profession-ally. Personally, I think you have already paid quite enough for your indiscretions, ma'am—provided you reform your ways and resist the temptation to resort to blackmail again in the future, however deserving one might appear."

Mrs. Emsworth stifled a sob.

"Knowing how it cost my son his life, I would never be tempted again. My younger son has been trying to convince me to come live with him and his wife's family in Bavaria for some time, and if I am not to be sent to gaol, I think I am going to accept his kind offer. I will be close to my beloved France, and I have no desire to ever move about in society again. Perhaps, Miss Osbourne, I could even come visit you in Paris, sometime, provided that you plan to remain there?"

She looked between me and Benjamin, and I knew what she was suggesting, but I hardly knew how to answer her.

"I plan to return to my home and my studies there after Christmastide, and you are welcome to visit me any time," I answered her.

I didn't know what role, if any, Benjamin would have in my life going forward, but I did fully intend to return to my own life.

Judging that we'd been sufficiently filled in on Mrs. Emsworth's survival, Sarah linked her arm through mine and began to pull me up the rest of the stairs.

"We will see you again soon in the parlor, Mrs. Emsworth, but we must have Winnie seen by the doctor immediately, before any kind of infection sets in."

Despite my protestations that I had merely a scratch on the shoulder and a concussion, she propelled me upwards with such force that I was obliged to obey. I took pity on her, as she'd grown up with all sisters and hadn't had the benefit of the rather rough and tumble education I'd been given by Benjamin as a child and was by nature far less adventurous. More than anything, I was looking forward to a hot bath, as I was soaked through and thoroughly chilled. We parted ways with Benjamin and Lord Worthington at the top of the stairs, Benjamin promising to check on me as soon as he'd cleaned himself up a bit.

"Not too soon, Lord Hadleigh," Sarah instructed. "I don't plan to let Winnie up and about until she is thoroughly warmed through and the doctor has assured me she is in no danger."

True to her word, she sat in a chair by my bed as I soaked in a warm bath by the fire until the water was cold, then was gently and carefully wrapped by Betsy in my warmest dressing gown. The doctor entered then and examined the graze wound on my shoulder, the cuts on my hands, and the gash on my forehead, cleaning them thoroughly and then treating them with iodine and wrapping them carefully. He pronounced all nothing to worry about except for the gash on my forehead, which would need several stitches.

As the kindly old man readied his needle and thread with hands that I thought were remarkably steady given his age, a knock sounded at the door, and Benjamin poked his head in. The doctor had seen to his wounds while I was bathing, and he was now dressed in a clean shirt, trousers, and waistcoat. While his broken nose was still obviously swollen, the gash on his head had been cleaned and thankfully proved not to be too deep, as the bleeding had already stopped without the need for a bandage.

"Did I miss another injury, young man?" the doctor asked with a wry grin. "I am nearly finished. I only have to see to these stitches."

"I thought Miss Osbourne might need stitches on that head wound, and she hates needles." He looked over to where I'd gone rather still on the edge of the bed, and likely white as a sheet. He wasn't wrong. I'd never been able to bear the thought of a needle piercing my skin. I was equal parts touched that he'd remembered, and irked at him for pointing out my weakness.

"I'm sure I can manage just fine without your assistance," I managed with an attempt at haughtiness, but I'm afraid my shaking hands gave me away, for Benjamin just laughed.

"If you can charge a gun-wielding maniac with only a shard of glass, you can certainly manage a few stitches without me," Benjamin consented. "But you don't need to."

Nodding against the lump in my throat, I held out my hand for Benjamin's as he sat next to me on the bed. If Sarah was surprised at this sudden show of intimacy, she didn't say anything, merely taking my other hand in hers and murmuring soothing things as the doctor began stitching up my forehead. I felt distinctly woozy, and clenched my eyes tightly shut until it was over.

"Now, may I suggest a draught to help you sleep?" The doctor smiled at me as he poured a few drops from a vial into a glass of water before handing it to me. "You're young and healthy, and as long as you keep your wounds clean, I don't foresee any infection setting in. But you've had quite a morning, from what I've heard, and I advise you to rest."

I thought about protesting, but I was tired now down to the bones, and my throat was parched. I longed to see what had become of Miss Loughty and Lord Belvoir now that Mr. Loughty was sitting in the magistrate's cell, but it could wait a couple of hours. I drained the glass, then climbed into bed, sighing happily as my head hit the soft pillow.

"Sleep, love, and I'll have a plate of food sent up later," Sarah offered, tucking me in under the covers. "We've canceled the

Christmas breakfast under the circumstances, and the others are having a cold collation in the parlor." I could see the curiosity in her eyes as she looked from me to Benjamin, and I knew she would have a million questions later, but I was grateful for the momentary reprieve.

She ushered the doctor out and slipped out behind him, leaving it cracked open behind her, though as Benjamin still sat on the edge of the bed next to me, we were hardly observing the proprieties.

"Freddie, you saved my life." He spoke quietly, whether afraid someone would overhear, or hoping I would start drifting off to sleep, I wasn't sure.

"I would have been tempted to shoot you myself a few years ago," I admitted groggily. "But now that I know the truth, I couldn't just sit there and watch you die."

There was a long silence as Benjamin tucked the covers around me and smoothed my damp hair against my forehead. Then he spoke in almost a whisper.

"You might be tempted to shoot me again, once you know the whole truth."

But what that truth was, I didn't hear, for I was already drifting into a deep and dreamless sleep.

Chapter 35

A few hours later, I awoke feeling sorer than I'd ever been, but refreshed. I rang Betsy, who helped me dress into a light green velvet dress, and then let her attempt to style my hair to cover the stitches on my forehead. She was only partially successful, but as my bandaged shoulder wound was covered by my dress and the cuts on my hands hidden by dark green evening gloves, I looked nearly respectable. Betsy informed me that dinner had been moved up by an hour to account for the lack of a proper breakfast and lunch, but I still had some time to kill before I needed to present myself. I planned to find a comfortable chair by the fire in the parlor and admire the Christmas tree until the other guests gathered for pre-dinner drinks. I heard raised voices coming from that very direction, however, as I descended the stairs, and was surprised to find nearly everyone else already gathered.

Miss Price, from her chair by the fire, was lecturing Benjamin about something as he stood by the Christmas tree.

"I've never seen anything so shabby in all my days," she was saying imperiously. Benjamin was standing there calmly, resplendent in his evening clothes despite his bruised and swollen face, holding two glasses of sherry. His face, quickly on its way to sporting two black eyes, lit up when he saw me, and he handed me one of the drinks in his hand as I entered the room.

"How are you feeling, Freddie?"

I was momentarily taken aback that he would use my nickname here among all these people, but not entirely displeased.

"Remarkably better than Miss Taylor over there," I answered as I pointed to the debutante slumped over on the sofa next to Miss Price. "What happened to her?"

The older woman was fanning her charge with her fan, but otherwise made no effort to rouse her and seemed little concerned. Mary, who was sitting on Miss Taylor's other side, was gently chafing the young woman's hands in an effort to wake her.

Benjamin grinned.

"She fainted dead away at the sight of me when I walked into the room," he said. "There wasn't even an eligible man nearby to catch her, which is how I know her swoon was genuine."

"Oh, the poor thing. I supposed the sight of your bruised face was just too much for her. You're lucky you were not kidnapped with her, or you may not have fared quite so well."

"There is no woman I'd rather be tied to than you, Freddie, literally or figuratively."

Benjamin winked at me, and I felt my face growing hot.

As Miss Taylor stirred and Mary pulled her back up to a sitting position, Miss Price returned her attention to my former husband.

"You put that young woman in a compromising situation, my Lord! It is not to be borne."

As she continued on her tirade, it took me a few moments to realize that I was the young woman to which she was referring. I'd hardly expected Miss Price to defend my honor, as morally loose as she already saw me, but here she was, pointing her finger at an Earl's chest as if he were a schoolboy. I stifled a giggle that was more of a hiccup, and winced as my stitches strained, and the pain in my forehead blossomed anew.

Rupert and Arthur appeared on my other side, Arthur offering me a plate of cold cuts and nuts. My stomach rumbled in thanks, and I realized suddenly that I hadn't eaten since that slice of fruitcake early this morning. True to her word, Sarah had sent up a plate of snacks while I was sleeping, but up until now I'd been too exhausted to care.

"You'll have a nasty scar from that, Winifred the Brave," Rupert said, pointing to the wound on my forehead.

"But if she wears her hair in a fringe, it should nearly cover it," added Arthur with a grin. "Betsy is a marvel, that one, you can barely notice those stitches."

Miss Price's lecture was reaching a fever pitch now, and my aching head could bear it no longer. Just a few days ago, I never would have thought that my darkest secret would barely even matter anymore. After a man's murder, an attempted murder, and having such a close call myself, I didn't even care that the whole room was about to know what was formerly my greatest fear. I heaved a sigh. It was time for me to speak up.

"Miss Price, while I appreciate the defense of my virtue from a rather unlikely avenue, I think an exception to propriety can be made in this case. You can hardly blame Lord Hadleigh or me for being kidnapped by a madman and locked in a shed together."

Miss Price sniffed indignantly.

"She's right, Aunt Maureen," Sarah added kindly as she breezed over with a plate of biscuits and added a couple to the plate in my hand. "Mr. Loughty is entirely to blame for the whole situation. We're just grateful Winifred and Lord Hadleigh are safe and that Mr. Loughty was apprehended."

"We will all rest a little better tonight knowing that no murderer is on the loose," Miss Price agreed. I looked around to see if Miss Loughty or her cousin were present but they were still absent, as was Lord Worthington.

"But no matter whose fault it is," Miss Price continued, "the fact remains that the two were alone together for some hours without a proper chaperone. Lord Hadleigh must marry Miss Osbourne to save her reputation."

Miss Taylor, who had regained her wits and was sipping

on a glass of sherry provided by Mary, choked and sputtered on her drink.

"Lord Hadleigh!" she exclaimed, a dismayed expression on her face. "Marry that spinster? What a waste."

"You forget yourself, child." Miss Price glared at her charge, and I wondered then if she knew more about the girl's improper behavior than she let on. "It is the right thing to do. Propriety demands it."

Everyone began talking at once then, most of them to defend my lack of need to marry anyone, of which I was grateful, but I found I didn't have the energy to enter into the argument myself just yet. I sank gratefully into an armchair Rupert pulled over for me and nibbled on my biscuits, wishing I had something stronger than the glass of sherry to wash them down with.

Finally, Benjamin held out his hands in a demand for silence.

"While I appreciate all of you advocating for Miss Osbourne, I'm afraid that it won't be possible for me to marry her at this time." Benjamin spoke in an authoritative voice, but there was the ghost of a smile at the corner of his mouth. The wretch was enjoying this, and I would never admit to anyone how much my heart fell at his pronouncement. He was right. We'd tried it once, and it hadn't worked. I was a fool to think Benjamin would want to marry me again, and I didn't even know if that was what I wanted. Why, then, did it sting so much?

"There, you see?" I turned to Miss Price, brushing crumbs off my fingers and trying to look nonchalant. "Lord Hadleigh has no wish to marry me, and no need to. I am a grown woman, and since I don't even move about in English society anymore, my reputation is hardly in jeopardy."

Benjamin cleared his throat, and the whole room turned again to face him. He sent me an apologetic look. What was that reprobate up to now? It was clear that we were going to have to go ahead and tell everyone the whole story. They would see just how ruined I actually was, but that I had been living perfectly adequately all these years without any need for a savior—and we could move on with more important things, like checking on wherever Lord Belvoir and Miss Loughty had gone.

"It's rather a long story but, many years ago, in fact, Lord Hadleigh and I—" I began, but I was interrupted by Benjamin.

"I cannot marry Winifred Osbourne, Miss Price, because I am already married to her."

The collective gasp that came over the room was almost entertaining, but I had to clarify, and quickly, as I felt the narrative slipping out of my control.

"*Was*—married to me," I nearly shouted, setting my plate down on the floor with a clatter, suddenly heedless of my rumbling stomach. "We were married, when we were much younger, but it was annulled after only—"

Benjamin took my hand and pulled me to my feet, a sad little smile on his face.

"*Are* married. *Still.* I am so, so sorry, my love."

"But—that's not possible. The annulment papers, I saw them—

Turning back to the room, Benjamin kept a hold of my hand.

"Friends, may I present to you all my wife, Lady Winifred Hadleigh?"

The room erupted in chaos around us. Lord Worthington, who had just walked into the room with a plate of champagne, dropped the tray with a deafening crash. As the servants rushed to clean up the mess, and Sarah looked torn between rushing to me or Lord Worthington, Benjamin took both my hands in his.

"I'm so sorry, Freddie. I've been trying to figure out a way to tell you for the last few days."

I heard his words like they were coming at me from far away. Vaguely aware that the room had gone suddenly silent, I felt my knees growing wobbly as I peered into his face, trying to make sense of it all.

"You utter scapegrace."

I felt myself mouth the words, rather than heard them, for I'm not sure any sound had actually come out of my mouth. And then I did the only thing left to a worldly, independent woman of twenty-eight in the face of such a shock.

I fainted.

I came to a few minutes later, my head once again resting in Benjamin's lap, with Sarah at my side, anxiously smoothing my curls as Mary waved a vial of smelling salts around in front of me.

"Winnie, darling! What a fright you gave me. Shall we carry you back up to your room for some rest?" Sarah asked anxiously.

"No, my love," I groaned, "but I'm afraid if I don't get a solid meal in me after all of that blood I lost, you may have me expiring in earnest. Just help me back into my chair."

Sarah and Mary pulled me back onto my feet, but instead of helping me back into my chair, they led me to the chair by the window, on the other side of the Christmas tree and away from all the shocked and curious faces of the rest of our house party.

"I'll send word to have dinner hurried along, but why don't you and Lord Hadleigh sit here for a bit of privacy and talk things over first."

Benjamin moved a second chair to the little alcove, and sat down next to me.

"I know I owe you the whole story."

"At the very least! I could have accidentally become a bigamist."

"As could I, though I had no intention of ever marrying again."

He dropped his head in his hands.

"After the Home Office forced me to sign that annulment, I believed that was it, that there was nothing else I could do, even though I had a moral objection to the annulment as our marriage had already been, erm, consummated."

I felt myself blushing to the roots of my hair, but motioned for him to continue on just the same. On the other side of the room, I saw Lord Worthington telling a lively story to distract the other guests, and I was immensely grateful to him.

"I had to continue on with my word and break all contact with you, as I've said, to keep you safe, and I continued believing that our marriage had been dissolved for several years. Then, one day not long before Augustus died, he had been drinking heavily and was thoroughly foxed. He was laughing his head off at me, claiming you and I were still married! I demanded that he explain himself, but he was so far gone that all I could get out of him was that our marriage had been conducted in Italy, so the British government had had no authority to dissolve it. He didn't remember a thing about the conversation the next morning, but I sent a solicitor—not my usual solicitor but a man I'd known since Eaton and trusted to be discreet—to Italy to learn what he could."

"A few weeks later, he sent word that you and I had been married in a civil ceremony through the Italian government, rather than through an Anglican priest like I'd thought. Honestly, Mother made all of the arrangements, and I was so eager to marry you as quickly as possible, I don't even remember the details. The Anglican priest had been arranged, and the legal contracts drawn up, but the man became ill at the last minute and mother had arranged for a friend of hers, a minor Italian governmental official, to conduct the ceremony and sign the paperwork instead. While we could have gotten the marriage legally recognised by the English government when we'd gotten home, we never had the chance. Neither the Home Office nor the Queen had any authority over a marriage conducted via civil contract in another country. Therefore, according to Italy and the rest of the world, we are still married."

"But you've known this for how long? Four years?! Benjamin Hadleigh, you guttersnipe!" I closed my eyes, fighting the urge to start throwing things at him. I shouldn't have sat down so close to the Christmas tree with its shiny, very breakable glass baubles. "Why didn't you tell me? What if I had tried to get married again?"

"You remember I told you when my contract was up, before I signed on for more time, I went to see your grandfather? I had just learned that we were still married, and I wanted to let you know right away. Your grandfather told me that you hated me so much, that if you found out that we were still married you would be outraged and never want to speak to me again. Then I saw you with your friend, and thought you were happy and didn't need to be burdened with me ever again. I fully planned, then, to apply for a divorce and dissolve the marriage properly, and I told your grandfather as much. I told him to let me know if you were soon in a place where you wanted to remarry, and that I would take care of everything and you would never have to know about it. But then I just…couldn't. I kept putting it off, telling myself that it was a lot of hassle to send a solicitor to Italy, that it wasn't really important until you were ready to remarry, but deep down I knew it was the only little piece of you I still had. I know it was wrong of me, Freddie, but I beg of you to forgive me."

I sat there, dumbstruck. After a few minutes of staring at the silver tinsel stars twinkling in the room's soft gaslights, I sighed wearily. This day had certainly been full of surprises, and I wasn't sure yet if this was a good surprise or a devastating one.

"So," I sighed, "our deepest, darkest secret is out. Now what do we do?"

He shrugged, looking more distinguished than I'd ever seen him despite his injuries. Suddenly, I noticed a few strands of gray at his temples that I'd never seen before. Idly, I wondered what he'd look like in twenty years, or in forty. I suspected the years would be kind to him.

"To be honest, I'm not sure. I don't expect to—want to—change or control you. You can go about your life, live it however you want to, but, I have one request—please don't divorce me just yet. You can live your life in Paris as Lady Hadleigh, or Miss Osbourne, or however you see fit, but I am humbly asking to see you again, to spend time with you—to court you properly, if that's what you would like. We never even got that chance the first time around, when everything happened so fast."

"So you're going to come to Paris then?"

"I'd like to, if that's acceptable to you. Now that this matter with the Queen's relative is settled, my work will change. I've been planning for months to take a step back, to retire back into the life of a wealthy and titled gentleman now that my second contract is about up." He smiled wryly at me. "Maybe I can come visit you, and see what your life in Paris is like, and we could just—see what happens?"

I smiled and shook my head in wonder.

"Somehow I can't imagine you strolling the Champs d'Elysee or sitting in a Montmartre cafe with my artist friends."

"I fit in just fine in Italy, didn't I?"

"Actually, we hardly left our pensione in Italy, so I wouldn't be able to tell you." My face heated again as his eyes flashed, and I held up a hand. "Not that you can expect to resume…marital intimacies just yet, you rake. I have too many conflicting feelings to sort through, first."

Something in his expression made me catch my breath, and I held very still as he picked up my hand, turned it around, and kissed the slender patch of skin on the inside of my elbow, where my glove ended and my sleeve began. I felt a delicious shiver run up and down my spine, and I was suddenly grateful to Rupert for picking such an overlarge Christmas tree, as its branches largely hid us from the other side of the room. As much as I tried to remain expressionless, I knew he knew how much his physical presence affected me. I wondered how long I would be able to commit to my hasty vow of celibacy during this second courtship, if there was to be one.

Benjamin lowered his voice to the merest whisper, his eyes twinkling beneath the bruises.

"Just say the word."

I knew I wasn't going to get a wink of sleep that night, and it had nothing to do with being kidnapped and attacked by a murderer, and everything to do with the suspense of what could happen when we returned home to Paris.

Chapter 36

Christmas dinner was subdued but peaceful. It seemed that every-one had breathed a sort of collective sigh of relief. Even though no one besides Benjamin, Lord Worthington, and I had known that Mr. Emsworth had been murdered before today, knowing that his killer was safely behind bars and would be brought to justice seemed to lighten a bit of the glum pallor that had lingered on our party. The Christmas breakfast, abandoned amongst the morning's excitement, had been repurposed into extra dishes at dinner, and we feasted on ham, roasted duck, game pies, vegetable dishes, and every manner of pudding I could have imagined. Lord Belvoir and Miss Loughty, who had joined us at the last minute before dinner, were understandably grim. When I sat at my place, with Benjamin next to me, I stiffened, surprised and not altogether pleased to find Miss Loughty on my other side, with Lord Belvoir sitting across from her.

"I asked Sarah to sit me near you tonight, Winifred," Miss Loughty said quietly. "So that I could apologize. I have lived in awe of my brother for so long that I have never been able to refuse him anything. I truly did have a bad headache this morning, which is why I decided to stay home from church while my cousin went with the group, but I realized later that it was a premonition of sorts—somehow I just felt that my brother was going to do something terrible. I caught him sneaking about belowstairs last night, and we argued, and something about the look in his eyes just didn't sit right with me."

She dabbed at her eyes as the first course was served, and I confess that I was too tired and hungry to listen to her excuses, but I let her go on and unburden herself while I tucked into a pumpkin soup.

"I knew about his crime with Katherine, yes, and I should have said something much sooner, but I justified it—telling myself it was an accident, and that she may have died soon anyway even if my brother hadn't poisoned her."

As she wept into her dinner napkin, I knew she was sincere, though I wasn't sure that even she realized how much of her actions were driven by her unhealthy obsession with Lord Belvoir. Her cousin, while he looked stricken at her confession, nodded encouragingly for her to continue.

"When I discovered what he'd done today—how he'd kidnapped you and Lord Hadleigh to cover up his crimes—my first inclination was panic. I panicked that my cousin would find out and would banish me. If Theodore was in jail, and my cousin refused to acknowledge me—well, I would certainly not last long with only my own two hands to provide for myself. I panicked and I made the wrong decision. I should have run to the others and alerted them immediately, and for that, I will be forever haunted at the pain and fear you must have suffered. I am so sorry."

"I acknowledge the tough position you found yourself in, Miss Loughty," I admitted somewhat stiffly, still furious that the woman had held me at gunpoint and abandoned us to her brother even knowing him to be a murderer. "I would not have made the same choices in your situation, but I suppose I can try to accept your apology. If your cousin," I looked hard at Lord Belvoir, who was obviously supporting her and not disowning her, "can forgive your actions today and in the past, then I will attempt to as well."

I highly doubted that Lord Belvoir's forgiveness towards her could ever extend to the love she so desired—especially since he now knew that she willingly covered up her brother's murder of his beloved wife and child. But at least he would see that she was provided for, since her brother was bound for prison, and eventually, likely the gallows. Perhaps he could set her up in a small cottage somewhere away from the family estates, so he wouldn't constantly be reminded of his terrible loss. A bit of exile would be a fitting punishment for her transgressions.

I wanted to say as much, but a quick squeeze of my knee under the table from Benjamin told me to keep my mouth shut. Their family problems would be their own to work out, and Miss Loughty would have to live with her choice to remain silent about her brother's crimes, whatever that would cost her in the future.

Lord Belvoir, obviously satisfied that his cousin had apologized, then changed the subject, and I was glad to turn my attention away from Miss Loughty.

"So, Miss Osbourne, I mean, Lady Hadleigh, I hear congratulations are in order." He raised an eyebrow, and there was the ghost of a smile on his lips, though his usual sparkling good humor was understandably dimmed. "When, pray tell, did you find time to get married during the morning's excitement?"

"I confess, I wasn't aware that we were still married until less than an hour ago," I explained, still in awe at how nonplussed everyone seemed to be at the secret I'd thought would prove my ruin for so many years. But maybe that was because Benjamin and I were, at least legally, still married. Divorced women were still looked on quite unfavorably in our society, but a secret marriage—well, that seemed to be another matter entirely. I thanked the footman gratefully as he slid a huge slice of roast beef and a small meat pie onto my plate. I wasn't sure I'd ever been this hungry in my life, but I continued to tell Lord Belvoir our story in as ladylike a manner as I could manage between bites.

"I was just eighteen when we were married in Italy, but Benjamin's older brother, the Earl at the time, disapproved. For the last nine years, I was under the impression that our marriage had been annulled. Lord Hadleigh only recently learned that that was not the case." I was feeling generous this evening, and decided to stretch the truth a bit when it came to how long Benjamin had known. "We met here again this week quite by chance."

"What a remarkable love story. It's a pity, then, that the rest of us eligible English gentlemen never even had a chance."

"No, I suppose you did not."

"Well, if that ever changes, Winifred, do send me a letter."

I looked at Miss Loughty, who was regarding her cousin's flirtation with a bemused expression, and shook my head.

"No, Felix. I don't think I shall."

Benjamin let me focus on my meal through the rest of dinner as he talked quietly with Mary, who was seated on his other side. After I'd eaten as much as I could hold, I felt greatly restored. As the men took their port and cigars, the women retired to the sitting room, where Sarah took my arm and led me immediately to the settee by the fire. The other women filtered in and gathered around us while Mary poured tea and handed out biscuits to those who wanted them.

"Dearest, you don't have to tell me now in front of everyone, but you know I'm going to have to have the whole story," Sarah said in a low voice. "I still can't believe that you married Lord Hadleigh! Though now that I know he was your Benji, I should hardly be so surprised."

I sighed and looked at the curious faces around me. A few days ago, I wouldn't have shared my secret for the world. Now, despite my frustrations with Benjamin keeping it a secret for so long, our botched annulment had given me more social grace than I could have expected. Suddenly, I found that I wanted to tell the story that I had been holding inside for so long.

So I told them, at least, I told them as much as I could without revealing Benjamin's role in the Home Office. I told them that Benjamin had been my best friend and my first childhood love, and that we'd married while traveling in Italy with my grandfather and his mother, but that Benjamin's older brother had disapproved and forced us to annul the marriage. That he'd dragged Benjamin back to England while I stayed behind on the Continent. That much was true, and if anyone else thought that Benjamin had given in too easily, no one mentioned it. I told them that he'd found out a few years ago that the annulment hadn't been legal, so we were still technically married, but that he knew that I'd hated him and was reluctant to tell me. I told them that I had indeed hated him, that I thought him the worst kind of scoundrel—including up until the point where he walked through the Cunninghams' sitting room door just a few days ago.

"Oh, Winnie, that must have been so dreadful for you!" Sarah cried. "To have him here, knowing that you couldn't tell anyone the truth—no wonder you were so dreadfully pale that evening. I should have known something was amiss."

"I even contemplated running back to France, but I thought that would make me appear a coward. And I didn't want to miss out on my English Christmas with you just because Lord Hadleigh had shown up. And then I found poor Mr. Emsworth, and I knew something wasn't right."

I explained to the others, briefly, about my work on *Poisons* and how I'd suspected Mr. Emsworth had been murdered and demanded that I be allowed to assist Benjamin and Lord Worthington in their hunt for the killer.

"Oh, Miss Osbourne," said Mrs. Emsworth, overwhelmed. "You mean to tell me that no one would have known that my son was murdered if you hadn't been the one to discover him? I am forever in your debt!"

"No, ma'am. It's possible someone else would have realized eventually. But you and your son had both been so kind to me. I felt compelled to do something."

I continued my story, telling them very briefly about Mr. Emsworth's mistaken identity and how Mr. Loughty believed that he'd attempted to blackmail him for his part in Lady Belvoir's death. I deliberately left out the identity of the true blackmailer and Miss Loughty's part in her brother's deception. If they wanted to tell the others in their own time, those were their stories to tell, not mine.

Surprisingly, everyone except Miss Taylor—who'd huffed off to the opposite corner of the room when I started telling my story, declaring her intention to read in peace—voiced their admiration for my part in apprehending Mr. Loughty. Even Miss Price had nothing negative to say to me. I wasn't sure whether it was because I had successfully caught a murderer, or if it was because I was suddenly Lady Hadleigh, Countess to a powerful Earl.

After a few more minutes, the gentlemen joined us again, and the focus of the room was thankfully shifted off of me as Rupert and Arthur pulled out a few games and set up the card tables. I sat with Sarah and Mary, nursing my tea, as the others formed groups for whist and speculation.

"So what are you going to do now, Winifred?" Mary asked in a soft voice. "I wouldn't even know what to think if I were in your situation."

"Honestly, I have no idea. I'm going to start with enjoying the rest of the Christmas holidays here with you all and spending time with Lord Hadleigh in company. And then, after Twelfth Night, I expect I'll return home to Paris. It's going to take some time, I think, to decide if we want to resume our marriage."

"A second courtship!" Sarah looked utterly delighted at the prospect. "You could have him take you to balls and art museums, moonlit picnics by the Seine—why, I think a courtship in Paris sounds terribly romantic."

I smiled for what was probably the first time all day.

"You know what, Sarah darling? It really does. Perhaps you should take a little trip back to Paris with me and help me pick out some stunning new dresses in which to conduct this courtship."

Sarah's face lit up, and I felt a sudden pang of regret that I had not invited her to visit me in Paris sooner.

"Oh Winnie, I thought you'd never ask. I could come visit for a few weeks this spring. You know, I've always wanted to. You've always made it sound like the most beautiful place in your letters, but once Rupert and I got married and started having children, there never seemed to be time."

"I could show you around the city, and you could see the *académie* where I study and work, and meet my friends."

I began to feel truly excited at the prospect of having Sarah and Benjamin both with me in the city I called home, and we talked of our plans into the wee hours of the morning.

For the next fortnight, we passed a true quiet English country Christmas, spending our days playing cards, painting watercolors, and reading novels, and our evenings feasting and playing charades. Two days after Christmas, Lord Belvoir and Miss Loughty left for home, the roads finally passable enough for them to make the journey in safety and comfort. I would have enjoyed a continued friendship with Lord Belvoir if it hadn't been for his unfortunate cousins, but as matters stood I wasn't sure that we would ever see each other again, and I breathed a sigh of relief when Miss Loughty was out of the house.

A few days after that, Mrs. Emsworth's son arrived to bring her back to London to pack and settle her affairs there, then on to Germany to be with his wife and children. Mr. Emsworth's body had already been sent ahead to London, and they would hold a funeral there in a few days time. She bid me a tearful goodbye, then grasped Benjamin's hand and told him that she would be forever grateful for his leniency. She even invited him to come visit her every so often, just to confirm that she was indeed a reformed woman and would stay on the straight and narrow from here on out.

Finally, Miss Price and Miss Taylor departed for another house party, one that assumingly had more eligible gentlemen left in attendance. While Miss Price had ceased to disparage my character in the days since Christmas, Miss Taylor had been glaring daggers at me the entire week, heedless to anyone who saw her. The façade of a prim and proper lady had been all but abandoned, and I felt as though we were all finally getting a look at the real Miss Taylor. I was grateful, however, that she didn't try to accost me again, and I breathed an extra sigh of relief when their carriage pulled away from the house.

Soon, it was just Sarah and Rupert, Mary and Arthur, Lord Worthington, and Benjamin left at the Cunninghams, plus the children, and it finally began to feel like a holiday. The snow had mostly melted and the sun deigned to peek through the clouds in the afternoon, so Benjamin and I took to taking daily walks through the gardens, always staying far away from the woods and the gardener's shed by mutual, unspoken consent. True to his word, Benjamin made no move to press me on any kind of decision, but we spent our time together reminiscing about our happy child-hoods and filling each other in on the highlights of the last decade of our lives. He even joined me and the children in the nursery for several more watercolor sessions. Though his winter scenes looked rather more like round hedges than majestic evergreens, he kept the children entertained with tales of our antics as children and smiled so brightly when I praised his progress that my heart skipped several beats.

On Twelfth Night, none of us were in the mood for the traditional theatricals or lively dance parties, so Sarah declared it a storytelling night, and we took turns telling the most amusing stories from our lives or those of acquaintances. I had everyone howling with laughter as I told them how Benjamin had been mistaken for a new fishing recruit early one morning on our hon-eymoon, herded onto a boat despite his protests (his Italian had never been great), and forced to spend a whole morning at sea while I watched from shore and picniced on the rocks. It felt so good to be able to share the parts of my life that I'd kept carefully hidden for so long. Whatever the outcome of this second courtship,

I could finally talk freely to my closest friends, and in this I found a sort of intimacy that I'd never been aware of before—a sort of wholeness that had evaded me for so long.

As Arthur finished telling a particularly hilarious recount of a game of hide and seek gone wrong when he and Rupert were children, Jameson appeared to inform us there were carolers at the front door. Before I could join the others headed down the stairs to listen to and reward the carolers with coins and sweets, Benjamin grabbed my wrist and pulled me back into the doorway.

"Ah, I was beginning to think they'd never get here."

"What is this all about? Were you expecting the carolers?" I smiled up at him and smoothed the lapel of his evening jacket.

"I may have given a boy in the village a few pounds to round up his mates tonight and go caroling up and down this street."

"Dasterdly! And what was the purpose of this distraction?"

Benjamin pointed to a spring of mistletoe nailed above our heads in the doorway. It had certainly not been there before tonight.

"So I could steal a moment under the mistletoe before our Christmas holiday is officially over."

"You'll see me again in Paris in just a few months, you know."

"I know, but three months is a dreadfully long time. And of course, there's the problem of no mistletoe in the spring."

"You're a scapegrace, Benjamin Hadleigh. A real rogue."

"Oh yes, I'm quite aware. But I'm your rogue."

I stopped arguing and let him kiss me senseless under the mistletoe.

About the Author

Rachel Gates is a writer, entrepreneur, and life-long Francophile. She spends her time writing historical fiction set in France and England, planning trips to Europe (both real and aspirational), and curating vintage fashion. She lives in Chattanooga, Tennessee with her husband, two boys, and Murphy the big red dog. *The Perils of Poison and Former Husbands* is her second novel.

You can find her online at:
https://thefauxfrenchgirl.com